WAVE OF DECEPTION

A MURDER ON MAUI MYSTERY

ROBERT W. STEPHENS

For Felicia Dames

1

BILL

IT WAS AN IRONIC COINCIDENCE, ONE THAT I'M SURE YOU WON'T BELIEVE but is nonetheless true. Before I get to that, though, let me give you a little background on how I got to this place.

I spent most of my life living in Virginia, so I'm pretty familiar with hurricanes. We seemed to live under the threat of them every late summer and early fall. We wouldn't get hit with one each year, but there was usually one or two that we'd have to keep a close eye on. Many headed our way only to veer off at the last minute. I say all of this to explain my somewhat relaxed state of mind when I first saw the news that a hurricane was potentially going to hit my new home of Maui.

I'd moved to the island a handful of years ago after falling in love with a local cop during my vacation, which happened to be my first time to Maui. I use the word vacation, but it was anything but a relaxing event. At the time, I'd just lost my girlfriend, as well as my job as an architect. Looking back, it's easy to see just how bad both of them were for me, but it's often easy to lose perspective when you're smack in the middle of something, at least that's the excuse I tell myself whenever I reflect upon those days and groan at my decisions.

Please allow me to introduce myself before I go much further. My name is Edgar Allan Rutherford. My parents named me after the legendary mystery writer, and today people call me Poe for obvious reasons. I don't have a preference, though, so you may call me Poe or Edgar. It's purely your decision.

I had someone ask me the other day if I thought my parents had set my fate as an investigator by naming me after the man who'd basically invented the modern day murder mystery. I don't believe so. I can't recall ever wanting to do investigations. I didn't even read murder mystery books or watch those terrible television shows about the murder of the week. Instead, I had my heart set on wanting to be an architect. I dreamed of building structures that would stand the test of time, but reality crashed down on me. I spent most of my time designing schools and warehouses and other big box structures that were more about fiscal restraints and government regulations and less about beauty and wonder.

I hated my job, and the truth is I didn't really need it. My parents, God rest their souls, had left me a substantial inheritance. It would be rude of me to give you an exact number or even a ballpark figure, but I will say that I didn't have to work another day in my life if I didn't want to.

My mother came from old money, but she had a strange relationship with it. She never wanted it, so she never touched it, instead preferring to leave it all to me. My father was an orthodontist, so he did well for himself. We lived a fairly typical life, with the sole exception being our travels around the world. I believe my parents felt it necessary to have me experience various cultures and different ways of doing things. Only now that I'm an adult, do I look back on those trips and have a better appreciation for what they did for me and why.

After the loss of my architecture job, I pretty much sat around for six months and did nothing. I was lost and I had no idea what to do next. I'd saved much of my salary, which I'd used to support myself. Apparently, I also possessed my mother's reluctant feelings about her wealth, which was now my wealth, and I hadn't touched my inheritance either, except to invest it.

My best friend, Doug Foxx, knew that I was in a major funk, and he'd stepped in as friends often do. He'd moved to Maui years before after his career with the Washington Redskins ended from a nasty knee injury. He'd come to Maui for some rest and relaxation and to give himself some time to plan his next career path. He never left the island. Foxx had asked me numerous times to visit him. I kept putting him off. Why? I don't know.

During my first night on Maui, Foxx was arrested for the murder of his girlfriend, someone I'm convinced would have soon become his fiancée. It was my belief in Foxx's innocence that led me to take on the informal role of investigator. This experience changed my life in ways that I'm still now just realizing.

The biggest and most important change was that I met the half-Hawaiian, half-Japanese detective who'd arrested Foxx. Her name is Alana Hu and to say she took my breath away would be a massive understatement. I made it a point to update her on the things that I'd learned during my investigation, much to her dismay. Nevertheless, I'd sensed she wasn't completely annoyed by my presence, and I eventually asked her to join me for dinner. She said yes, something I still can't believe to this day, and now we've been married for a few years.

We currently live down the street from Foxx in a house by the water in the Kaanapali area of Maui. These last few years have been a blur, and I've spent my time on the island exploring the natural beauty the Valley Isle has to offer, as well as soaking up the sun and doing the occasional investigation. I don't mean to imply that these cases have been a small part of my life. They haven't, and they've led to the second biggest change in my life, mainly my current view of my fellow humans who inhabit this planet.

I've come to believe that we're a vicious lot. I know that's something you probably don't want to hear, especially since you've picked up this little tale for your personal amusement and possibly as an escape from the craziness of the world. I get that, but it's my mission to always be honest in these stories, and it would be a lie to attempt to pass myself off as a happy-go-lucky fellow.

I could go on and on about the small injustices I see every day, but they pale in comparison to the nasty and immoral things I've encountered in these investigations. Murder, incest, betrayal. You name it. I've seen it. It has a way of scarring your soul, and as much as I might want to go back to that naïve version of myself that first set foot on Maui, I can't. I am forever changed, for good and for bad.

Let's get back to the ironic coincidence I alluded to a little while ago. The hurricane's name was Bill, and it had been upgraded to a Category 4 storm by the time its path altered and put it on a direct course for the Big Island. That didn't mean Maui wasn't going to be impacted. The forecasters painted a rather grim picture for us, one that featured high wind, torrential rain, and catastrophic flooding.

A coincidence takes two things, though, and the second in this tale is a guy named Bill Hodges, who happened to be dating my sister-in-law, Hani. She's younger than Alana by a few years, but the two women could easily pass as twins with their long black hair, dark eyes, and physiques that would make any swimsuit model envious. I won't mention their age since a gentleman doesn't talk about such things. My wife has informed me that I can't mention my age anymore, either, since that could potentially give a massive clue as to hers.

The sisters get along rather well, which wasn't the case when I'd first met Hani. She's a bit of a self-centered individual who only tends to call you when she needs something. She's family, though, and we all have to be willing to overlook, or at least tolerate, those sorts of personality faults. I know I have my own, and most of the Hu family, well, Alana and her sister, has been willing to put up with my quirks.

I've grown much closer to Hani since the birth of her daughter, Ava. The father? That would be Foxx. He and Hani had a short fling that ended before Hani even realized she was pregnant. I had thought they might give it another go upon hearing the news, but Foxx felt the relationship would never last. He's still a big part of Ava's life, and he generously supports her, for those of you wondering about that sort of thing.

I spend a considerable amount of my time watching Ava while

Hani works as a wedding planner. That means I'm usually over at Hani's house at least a few times a week when I go to pick up Ava or drop her off after a day of exploring the island. Ava's favorite activity is to play on the beach, by the way. She's become a decent swimmer, even at such a young age. I taught her how to swim in the salt water pool behind my house.

I first met Hani's new boyfriend a few months ago when she took him to Harry's, which is a bar in Lahaina that I co-own with Foxx. Hani had brought him there to meet Alana and me. I thought it a rather transparent move on her part since she knew Foxx was working that night. I didn't know if it was her desire to make him jealous or if she just wanted him to know that she was seeing someone. Bill, as far as I knew, was the first guy she'd dated since she'd broken up with Foxx. Before, she'd spent all of her time working and taking care of Ava.

So, what did Bill look like? He could have passed as a fashion model. He had long blonde hair that he kept pulled back in a ponytail. Bill was my height, at around six-foot-two, but he probably weighed about thirty pounds more than my two-hundred frame. Although I never saw him shirtless, his arms and legs were muscular and defined, and it seemed that he'd obviously spent a good deal of time in the gym. Hani had met him while coordinating one of her weddings, which took place at one of the largest resorts in Kaanapali. Bill worked there as a pastry chef, and he'd apparently designed the cake for Hani's clients.

Foxx, for his part, was pretty nice to Bill, at least he had been on the first night we'd met him. He shook Bill's hand and made small talk with him. I didn't see one ounce of jealousy in Foxx's eyes, probably because he was dating someone new and attractive as well. That woman's name is Ashley, and I could write an entire book on her. It wouldn't be flattering, but more on that a little later.

You may be wondering what my impression of Bill was, at least in terms of him being a quality boyfriend for Hani. I'm an only child, so having a sister now, or sister-in-law, is a bit of a learning experience. I feel the need to look out for Hani. Forgive me, ladies, if you think that sounds chauvinistic. But Hani is more fragile than she lets on, and I'm not about to let my wife's sister get into trouble.

Regarding Bill, I simply didn't like him. I'm sure you may be accusing me of being jealous of Bill's good looks. I wasn't, nor was I envious of his ability to make world-class cupcakes. There was just something about him that set off warning bells. My gut said the guy was a bad dude, and I don't mean bad in the cool kind of way. I'd never heard anything disturbing about Bill from Hani, though, so I pretty much put him out of my mind. I would see him every once in a while. I would say hello or nod my head or do any of the other little things one does to acknowledge the presence of another. Bill would do the same in return, and then we would go our separate ways. Alana and I rarely spoke about him, and that was that.

The bottom line, as this story officially began, was that we had two Bills, and I was on a collision course with them both.

As I mentioned earlier, our house is on the coast, so it wasn't a safe place to ride out the storm. I made the decision to go to Hani's house since it's more inland. Hani's mother, Luana Hu, was also going to be there. Alana had to work since there were bound to be numerous emergencies once the hurricane hit. We promised to stay in touch for as long as our cell phones worked.

I did my best to stormproof our house in Kaanapali. All of the lawn furniture was brought into the garage. The windows and sliding glass doors were boarded up. I wished the house good luck and prayed that it would be in one piece when I returned.

I arrived at Hani's just as the wind and rain were really starting to pick up. The bad stuff wasn't due for another several hours, but I didn't want to take any chances. I brought my dog, Maui, with me. He's a ten-pound Morkie, which is one of those new breeds of dogs that's a mix between a Yorkshire Terrier and a Maltese. He was blissfully unaware of the coming storm and was thrilled to be taking a ride in my Lexus SUV. My main vehicle, a BMW Z3 convertible, was tucked away in the garage.

Maui gets along great with Ava, and the little girl squealed with delight when Maui rushed through the door and raced around the house as if he were seeing it for the first time. I'd gotten to the house before my mother-in-law. We have a frosty relationship, one that has improved somewhat since I helped her with a little problem she'd had regarding a new man she'd been dating. I don't want to spill the details on that case, but I'd come to the conclusion that the Hu women were incapable of picking good men. Well, if you don't count Alana being with me and Hani's brief fling with Foxx.

I constantly remind my dear wife of that, only for her to tell me that I'm really the lucky one. She's not joking. I hit the jackpot when I landed her, and if you ever saw the two of us together, I'm guessing you'd say the same thing. Don't get me wrong. I'm not a bad looking guy, but there's a noticeable difference between a solid seven and a ten-pushing-eleven-or-maybe-twelve on the beauty scale. I'm clearly punching way, way above my weight class, to use that old analogy.

Hani had sent me a text a few minutes before I arrived and told me to come into the house. She said she had a migraine and had decided to lie down in her bedroom. I spent about an hour or so playing with Ava. She'd set up a little tea party for me and her grandmother, as well as Maui and my mother-in-law's dog, Ollie.

Ms. Hu eventually showed, and the three of us (five, if you count the two dogs who spent more time chasing each other) enjoyed our pretend tea as the rain and the wind increased outside. Hani didn't participate, which didn't surprise us since we knew she was sleeping off her headache.

Ms. Hu went to check on her after our tea party ended, and she called out to me a few moments later.

"Edgar, get in here."

"What's wrong?" I asked.

"It's nothing. I'm fine," Hani said.

I felt a little awkward entering her bedroom, but I had been summoned. I found Ms. Hu standing beside Hani, who was sitting on the edge of the bed. Her long black hair concealed one side of her face.

"Show him," Ms. Hu said.

"I'm fine," Hani repeated.

"You're not fine."

Hani pulled back her hair, and I saw that her left eye was closed. It was swollen and red. I wasn't sure how many punches it would take to make someone's eye completely close. One punch? Five? More? Then I noticed the red marks on her arms that had clearly been caused by someone with strong hands grabbing her.

"Don't tell me you walked into the door," Ms. Hu said.

"What happened?" I asked.

"It was Bill, wasn't it?" Ms. Hu asked.

Hani said nothing.

"Hani, we can't let him get away with this," Ms. Hu said.

"Bill hit me," Hani whispered.

"When did this happen?" I asked.

"A few hours ago. He got angry when I told him you and Mom were coming over. He thought it was just going to be the three of us. I told him that you two had nowhere else to go, and he told me you could go to one of the shelters. He hit me when I refused to ask you not to come over."

"Has he done this before?" Ms. Hu asked.

Hani didn't reply, but she started to cry and that gave us our answer.

Ms. Hu sat beside her on the bed and wrapped her arm around Hani.

I walked over to the nightstand and grabbed Hani's phone. I pulled up Bill's listing under her contacts. I texted myself his information, which included his home address.

"I know you'll take care of her. I'll be back in a little while," I told Ms. Hu.

"Get that BLANK," Ms. Hu said.

For those of you new to these stories, I usually leave the offending words out. I've discovered that many readers are sensitive folks, and I don't want to cause anyone undue stress. I once had a man write and admonish me for using a strong word in an earlier tale. Apparently, he'd been listening to the audio version of the book since he enjoyed working in the yard while hearing the mystery unfold. He was so startled by the offending word that his heart began racing and he accidentally cut off one of the heads of his beloved begonias. I'm not sure if he just wanted me to stop using curse words, or if he was asking, in a roundabout way, to reimburse him for the flower. Either way, I thanked him for his kind message and left it at that.

Nevertheless, I know there are some readers who like to try to figure out the offending words, so I will offer a clue. It started with the letter F. I'd never heard my mother-in-law use such salty language, and I probably would have laughed if I wasn't so furious with Bill. I walked outside, only to be hit with the pounding rain. I knew I was insane to attempt to drive in this weather, and even if I made it to Bill's house, I would be going after him on his territory. The only advantage I had, and I thought it was a big one, was that Bill probably assumed no one would be crazy enough to fight him in the early throes of a hurricane.

Fortunately, Bill's house was relatively close, but it still took me about thirty minutes since I had to drive so slowly. I could barely see out of the windshield, despite the wipers being on full speed. I'd never seen rain come down so hard, and I began to fear that I wouldn't even make it back if I turned around then.

Bill lived in a relatively small neighborhood. I didn't think anyone would be able to make out the details of my vehicle since it was so difficult to see in this weather. Nevertheless, I parked around the corner from his house. I keep my lock-picking toolkit in my glove compartment, and I grabbed it after turning off the ignition. I climbed out of my vehicle. A gust of wind hit me and almost threw me across the street.

I managed to keep my balance, and I ran toward his house. I entered his backyard. The wind was so loud that I doubted he'd hear me messing with the lock on his door. I felt more than heard the lock click open, and I turned the doorknob.

The backdoor opened to a small kitchen. I suddenly realized that although the wind might have concealed my tinkering with the lock, it was going to give away my presence since the noise had just gotten much louder inside his house now that I'd opened the door. I moved quickly through the kitchen, anticipating Bill's appearance at any moment.

He turned the corner just as I reached the far end of the room. I jammed my thumb hard into his windpipe before he had a chance to react. He instinctively raised his hands to his neck as he gasped for breath. I grabbed a cast-iron pan off the counter and hit Bill across the face with it. I aimed for his left eye, the same place he'd struck Hani. Bill dropped to the tiled floor and landed on his back, as he continued to struggle to breathe.

"I never liked you, Bill, but I guess you know that by now," I said, and I stomped onto his stomach, making it even harder for him to get precious air.

I grabbed one of Bill's ankles and dragged him across the kitchen floor. I hadn't bothered to shut the door, and the wind had blown everything off the table. I kicked the plates and empty beer bottles to the side and hauled Bill into the backyard.

"Get up," I said.

Bill struggled to his knees. I could tell he was trying to talk, but the words wouldn't come out. Even if they had, I doubted I would have been able to hear him above the rain and the wind.

"You beat on the wrong woman, Bill."

I kicked him in the face, and he fell backward onto the wet grass.

I kneeled and got close to him so he could hear me.

"You stay away from Hani. You don't call her. You don't text her. You don't even glance her way should you happen to find yourself on the same part of Maui. Do I make myself clear?"

Bill didn't reply, so I hit him again in the eye.

"Do you understand?" I asked.

Bill barely nodded.

I stood and walked to the backdoor. I turned the lock on the door-knob and closed it, essentially locking Bill out of his house.

"Take care, Bill. Your namesake is bearing down on us. I'd hate to see you get blown away."

I left Bill lying on the grass. He wasn't unconscious, but he was hardly moving.

I was about halfway back to Hani's house when my phone rang. I looked at the display and saw it was Alana. A part of me thought about letting it go to voicemail, but I was worried she might need something.

"Hello," I said through the vehicle's Bluetooth system.

She hesitated a moment.

Then she asked, "Are you outside?"

"No. I'm in my SUV."

"I thought you left for Hani's hours ago."

"I did. I had to run a little errand."

"Are you crazy?"

"Maybe. Don't worry about me. I'm almost back."

"Seriously, Poe. Why would you leave the house?"

"It couldn't be helped."

"What couldn't be helped?"

I knew it was only a matter of time before Alana found out about Hani, and I didn't want her upset that I wasn't the one to tell her.

"Something happened with Hani, but she's going to be okay."

"What happened?"

I told Alana about Hani's injuries and the cause of them. Alana said nothing.

"Are you there?" I asked.

"I'm here."

"You sound awfully calm."

"I'm trying to figure out how I can get to his house to arrest him. Wait a minute. That's why you're out now."

"The problem has been resolved," I said.

"What did you do?"

"He's still breathing, although just barely if that's what you're worried about. I'm almost back to Hani's house now. She'll be okay. I promise you."

"Call me when you get there. Let me know you're all right. Also, I want to speak to Hani."

"Okay."

"Poe, thank you."

"Is that the cop speaking?"

"No. The cop didn't hear anything you just said. It was the sister talking."

I said goodbye and ended the call so I could concentrate on driving. Bill-the-boyfriend wasn't done with us yet. He had Alana to deal with, and she would be much harder on him than I'd ever been.

2

HARRY'S

BILL-THE-HURRICANE WAS MUCH WORSE THAN I COULD HAVE POSSIBLY imagined. It was unlike anything I'd experienced in Virginia. Rainfall records were smashed, and the predicted flooding covered most roads. Fallen trees and mudslides blocked and damaged other areas. These were all things I learned later since Hani, Ms. Hu, Ava, and myself were effectively stuck in the house with no information and no way to communicate with the outside world, at least for the first couple of days.

We lost electricity at almost the exact moment the worst of the hurricane arrived. We lost cell phone service shortly after that. I'd been watching the local news cover a story about a massive fire in Lahaina that had occurred when the high wind blew a power line down onto a local building. The really scary part, as if a massive fire isn't scary enough, is that I was pretty sure the building they showed was just a block away from the bar I co-own with Foxx.

Fortunately, the cell phone service was restored a day or two after Hurricane Bill finally veered away from the islands, but the signal wasn't strong enough to get the internet on my phone, and I wasn't able to check on the Lahaina-based fire.

Alana managed to call me on day three of my house lockdown and told me she hadn't slept in a few days since the police and other emergency personnel were needed all over the island. She was the one who informed me just how bad things had been. I asked her about the fire. She said she'd heard that several buildings had been lost. Despite her best efforts, she hadn't been able to discover if Harry's was one of them. She promised to call whenever she had a chance. I called her my hero, told her to be safe, and said I would see her when she eventually got home.

By the time things had calmed down enough to leave, I'd been at Hani's house for a week. It was the longest time of my life, unless you count those days I spent in jail. Want to know more on that? Check out *Sunset Dead*. Otherwise, trust me. This week was almost as bad as that one.

I wish I could say we passed the time playing board games and engaging in interesting conversation. We didn't. The trauma of Bill-the-boyfriend's attack on Hani hung over everything like a dark cloud. Her eye stayed shut for most of that week, and although she did her best to hide the injury from her daughter, there was simply no way for Ava to avoid seeing it.

She never asked her mother what the injury was from, which I found confusing at first. Then I learned that Ava had been present for the fight. I'd known that she'd been in the house, but I'd hoped that she'd been in her bedroom, either napping or playing. Hani let it slip that Ava had started crying after Bill had struck Hani.

The strange thing was that Ava had been laughing and playing when I'd first arrived. I chalked that up to some sort of psychological defense mechanism, and my anger at Bill only grew as the days passed.

Hani begged me not to tell Foxx. I believe she thought that Foxx might actually kill her ex-boyfriend, especially if he learned that the attack had also come in front of his daughter. I didn't think that Hani was completely off base, but I told her that Foxx should still be trusted to have some degree of self-control. Was I kidding myself, though? Probably. In the end, I gave in to Hani's request, mainly because I didn't want to upset her any more than she already was.

Maui and I managed to leave Hani's house on the seventh day. The floods hadn't completely receded, but I was able to navigate the roads well enough so that I never felt we were in danger of getting stuck. I'm always intrigued at how the weather is often so nice after a hurricane leaves the area. This was true during the drive. The sky seemed to blend in with the ocean, and I felt like I was enveloped in a field of deep blue. What is it about a blue sky and blue water that instantly makes your problems seem less significant? I don't know, but I don't believe I'll ever get tired of gazing out at the ocean as I drive down the coast.

My first destination was Harry's, or what I hoped was still Harry's. Foxx beat me to it. My cell phone rang just as I passed the Maui Ocean Center.

"Hey Foxx, how are you?"

"Not good, man. It's gone."

"Harry's?"

"What's left of it, which isn't much."

"So it's a total loss?" I asked.

"Total. I can't believe it."

"Are you there now? Should I stop by?"

"What's the point? There's nothing to see but the ashes."

Foxx told me he was headed home himself and that he'd probably see me soon.

Alana's car wasn't there when I got home, so I assumed she was still on duty. I couldn't imagine how tired she was. I was worried for her and prayed that she hadn't been injured.

I usually went through the garage door, but the power was still off, so I used the front door instead. The house was pitch black. I used the flashlight I kept in my SUV to navigate to the garage. I pulled the cord to disengage the automatic garage door system and manually pulled the two doors open. I let Maui in the backyard so he could explore his territory and make sure everything was the way he'd left it. I walked back to the garage and grabbed a crowbar to pry off the boards from the windows and sliding glass doors. The good news was that the boards had done a great job of protecting everything. The bad news was that two large trees on the back side of the house had fallen and created a decent-sized hole in the roof.

I removed the boards from the rear of the house first to let the light inside. Then I walked back into the house to examine the damage done to the spare bedroom. The hole in the roof was about three feet wide, and the carpet and bed were soaked from all of the rain that had gotten inside. The room would need to be gutted, but the house was still standing. I thought we'd gotten off lightly.

I went back to the garage and grabbed a tarp, a hammer and nails, and my ladder. I'd just leaned the ladder against the side of the house when I heard Foxx call out.

"Need to borrow my chainsaw?"

I turned to him.

"You have a chainsaw?"

"Yeah. I've pretty much got every tool you can think of. The chainsaw's still in the box. Hopefully, it works. I assume since you're already home that you took my advice and skipped going to Harry's."

"I didn't have the heart."

I looked at Foxx's shoes. They were covered in black ash. It looked like he'd taken a walk through the remains of the bar. Foxx pulled his phone out of his pocket and opened the photos application. He handed it to me.

"Check it out," he said.

"I'm not sure I want to."

I looked at the several photos that he'd taken. It was worse than he'd described. The place had been completely leveled by the fire.

"I've already called the insurance company. I don't know when they'll send someone out. Sounds like they've been overwhelmed with calls."

"I'm sure. What are we going to do about the employees?" I asked.

"I've been thinking about that. I think we should keep everyone on the payroll. We've got the funds to cover it, even if it takes months to get the place rebuilt."

"That's a great idea. I guess we can start calling everyone tomorrow."

"I'll do it tonight. I'm sure they've probably seen the news by now. No reason for them to start freaking out over their jobs."

Foxx was a good guy. It's one of the reasons I admired him so much.

"Harry's aside, how did you and Ashley get on at your friends' house?"

"Longest week of my life," Foxx said.

I laughed.

"That's my line."

"Oh, things didn't go so well with Hani and your dear mother-in-law?"

"You could say that. What went wrong with you and Ashley?"

"It wasn't so much us as it was those friends of hers. I wanted to strangle them both. All they did was drink. I'm pretty sure they were drunk the entire time."

"A week-long hurricane party?"

"Something like that. I'm sure their livers are about to give up the ghost."

"How did Ashley meet them?"

"They've been to Harry's a few times. I never spoke to them that much, but Ashley started playing tennis with the lady. Once word of the hurricane got out, they invited us to stay. We should have gone to the shelter."

I was about to say that Foxx and Ashley should have stayed with Hani, but that would have been a complete disaster. Although Foxx and Hani were on better terms, things between Hani and Ashley couldn't have been worse. I'd come to believe that Ashley was jealous of Hani, even though her relationship with Foxx was long over. Ashley is a good looking woman, and I don't think she's used to her guys' ex-girlfriends being better looking than she is. There was also Ava, who represented a bond between Foxx and Hani that could never be broken.

There was one other thing that could have been the cause: Hani's biting tongue. I hadn't witnessed Hani being rude to Ashley, but it wasn't like I was around her all of the time. Hani has a talent for insulting people while pretending that she's doing the opposite, but she did seem to be on her best behavior around Ashley for Foxx's sake. Still, I could have easily missed something that Ashley might still be smarting over.

Things between Ashley and I weren't great either. Foxx had met her years ago when he and I had gone to the Fort Lauderdale area on a college spring break. Yes, it's a bit of a cliché, but it's what happened. Sex with Ashley was so good, according to Foxx, that he went back to Florida a few times throughout his college career. They went their separate ways after graduation, but they reconnected several months ago when Foxx and I traveled to Miami as part of one of my investigations.

Imagine our surprise when Ashley showed up at Harry's a few weeks after we returned to Maui. She told us that she was only on the island for a couple of weeks. I knew it was a lie. Foxx had let her stay with him since she'd conveniently forgotten to book a hotel. Who does that? Would you ever get on a plane and fly several thousand miles, only to remember you didn't arrange for a place to sleep when you landed? It was such an obvious ploy, and I assumed Foxx only went along because he thought she'd soon be gone again. She wasn't, and she'd been living with Foxx for the past several months.

I don't know if he enjoys her being there or if he just doesn't know how to get rid of her. I would do it in a hot minute if he asked, but I couldn't get a good read on the situation. One second he'd be telling me how frustrated he was with Ashley, the next he'd say he'd just had the best sex of his life. I know us men are often a superficial bunch, and we're often driven by our lusts more than our minds. Foxx and I aren't teenagers anymore, though. I wanted to tell him enough was enough and he needed to escort the woman to the airport for her return flight to Miami. This was the first time in our friendship where I felt like I was walking on eggshells around him. I'd always been able to tell Foxx anything, and he wouldn't judge me. He knew I only wanted the best for him. Things were different now. There was Ashley and her antics between us.

Alana felt the same way, at least about her feelings toward Ashley. I hadn't told her how I felt my friendship with Foxx had somewhat deteriorated. She liked Ashley even less than I did, but she also loved Foxx. She wasn't about to ruin her friendship with him by telling him what she really thought about his new girlfriend. It was awkward to say the least, and there didn't seem to be an end in sight. The only thing that made me feel somewhat better was that Foxx had never been married and he didn't seem to be in a rush to change that status. I didn't know what I would do if Ashley ever showed up with a diamond on her finger. I would probably go into shock like that guy I talked about earlier who'd cut the head off his begonia.

"How does your house look?" I asked.

"The house is fine. Wish I could say the same about the yard. Every tree is down."

"Every one?"

"Yep. Lost fifteen trees total. I can't believe you kept most of yours. Mine all fell in different directions. Strangest thing I've ever seen. How's Alana?" Foxx asked.

"It's been at least a day since I've spoken with her. She told me she'd try to get home tonight."

Foxx looked at the tree leaning against my house.

"How bad is it?"

"The hole isn't that big, but the rain ruined the inside of the guest bedroom."

"It's going to be a long time before you can get someone to fix this. There are only so many contractors on the island," Foxx said.

"That thought crossed my mind."

"You know I worked construction during the summers in college. If you're able to help, we can probably do the work ourselves."

"That would be great. Just let me know when you want to start."

"How about now? I could use a break from Ashley."

"Sounds good."

See what I mean? How would you have responded to that

comment about needing a break? He'd opened the door for me to criticize her, or at least ask him exactly why he needed a break. I said nothing, though. I pretended I didn't hear it, and I climbed the ladder to my roof. With any luck, Ashley would be gone soon, but who was I kidding? I knew that wasn't going to happen.

3

SOMETHING IN THE AIR

WE SPENT THE NEXT FEW HOURS WORKING ON MY HOUSE, WHICH included putting a temporary patch on the roof and removing all of the water-damaged items from the bedroom. The carpet was torn out, too.

We ended our work by drinking room-temperature beers from my refrigerator, which hadn't had power since the storm. It definitely wasn't a fun way to spend the day, but it beat spending another hour around my mother-in-law. I was hoping the physical labor would help clear my mind, but I hadn't been able to stop thinking about Hani's abuse while I was around Foxx. I almost told him several times about it, but I ultimately didn't say anything.

While we drank our beers, we discussed the rebuilding of Harry's. Foxx suggested that we expand the square footage by adding a second floor and a deck. My immediate reaction was to be against the idea since I thought we should remake it exactly as it had been. I didn't express those feelings, however. I just listened to his pitch on how a larger bar would bring in more income. I was a little surprised by the argument. Money had never been our main motivation for buying the business, which may seem a bit odd to you. From my point of view, one of the main reasons people came to Harry's was because it was a hole in the wall. Adding more square footage might destroy that atmosphere.

Foxx eventually left to go home to Ashley. I halfway expected her to come down at some point and check on us, but she never did. Maybe she needed a break from him like he did her.

There was a nice breeze coming off the ocean, so Maui and I plopped down on the patio furniture to cool off. Actually, I was the one on the furniture. He took his usual place under one of the chairs after lapping up water from his bowl.

I looked up to the sky and was amazed to see how clear everything was. All in all, it should have been a relaxing time on the patio. Instead, I was filled with anxiety. I was worried about a number of things, including my wife's safety as she was dealing with God-knows-what on this island. I closed my eyes for a moment, and the next thing I knew Alana was touching my arm. I opened my eyes and she smiled. It was the first time I'd seen that beautiful face since the hurricane's outer bands had struck Maui.

"For a second I thought someone had shot you. You wouldn't believe how you looked when I came around the corner," she said.

I tried to sit up but painful muscle spasms raced across my lower back.

"Oh, man. I wasn't expecting that. I'd give you a hug, but I'm guessing I smell like a sewer," I said.

"I'm sure I smell like one, too."

Alana looked across the yard at the two trees Foxx and I had cut up with the chainsaw.

"What happened?"

"A couple of trees put a nice hole in the corner of our roof. Foxx and I gutted the guest room a few hours ago."

"Well, if there was a room that was going to be damaged, I'm glad it was that one. I've been thinking about redoing that room for a while now."

I finally managed to sit up straight as Maui made his way from under my chair. He stretched his own back and then rolled over for Alana to scratch his belly.

"Hello, Maui," she said. "Did you enjoy your time with Ollie?"

"I think he did for the first day or two. Then I suspect he got tired of the little fella constantly jumping on him."

"Sometimes I think Ollie is Maui's groupie."

"That's a good description. How have things been going with you?"

Alana plopped down on the chair beside me.

"You can't even begin to imagine the stuff I've been through. I think that storm did something to people's brainwaves. There must have been some crazy signal in the air that told half the people on this island to act like complete idiots."

"What do you mean?"

"What's the first thing you thought of when you heard about the hurricane?" she asked.

"Where do we take cover?"

"So it wasn't 'where do I catch the best waves?'"

"I hadn't even thought about that, but that is something people do, isn't it?"

"We had to set up road blocks in Paia to keep people from going to Ho'okipa Beach."

"Did it work?"

"They stopped some people, but they were never going to be able to keep everyone off those waves. You heard about Nicholas Jansen, didn't you?"

"Who's that?" I asked.

"I took you to see him on the North Shore last year."

"The Pipeline Masters?"

"Yeah. Remember I wanted you to see him before he retired."

"What happened?"

"Jansen's body washed ashore two days ago. I couldn't believe it."

"He lived on Maui?"

"He had homes on Oahu and Maui. I guess the call of the waves was just too much for him."

"How old was he?"

"He was close to forty. I still can't believe he died."

I thought about saying at least he went out doing something he loved, but I thought that might sound a bit heartless, especially considering how much of a fan Alana is of the islands' pro surfers. For those of you who are new to these stories, Alana is an avid surfer herself. She used to go a few times a week, but now she manages just once or twice. She tried to teach me how to surf but finally gave up when it became apparent I was a hopeless cause. I'm a good swimmer, but I've got horrible balance. I think she once said I looked like a drunk Flamingo on the board. I don't think I've ever seen a drunk Flamingo before, nor do I know how one would even become intoxicated, but I got her point. My brief surfing career came to an abrupt end after that comment.

"You said people lost their minds. Was it just the surfers?" I asked.

"Hardly. I think when these disasters strike you either see people at their best or their worst. There doesn't seem to be any middle ground. I hate the fact that I'm concentrating on the crazies, but that's who I get called to deal with."

"So what else happened?"

"It was everything from people looting, to I-can't-find-my-cat, to murder."

"Murder?"

"Yeah. This woman came home to find her husband stabbed to death in their living room."

"Did you pick up that case?" I asked.

"No. Detective Makamae Kalani."

"I don't think you've mentioned her before."

"She just came over from Oahu."

"How is she?"

"She seems fine, so far. She'd only been here a week or two when the hurricane first popped up."

"Did they figure out who killed that guy?"

"Not that I know of."

Alana hesitated a moment, and she looked out toward the ocean.

"I haven't been able to stop thinking about Hani," she finally said.

"Me neither."

She turned to me.

"I appreciate what you did for her, but promise me you won't do anything like that again."

"You sounded okay with it when we talked on the phone."

"I know, and I'm kind of ashamed by my reaction. You should have let the police deal with it. He could still press assault charges against you."

"Sure, and Hani can press charges against him. I took several photos of her injuries by the way."

"We don't know this guy, not really. It makes sense that he wouldn't go to the police, hoping Hani won't say anything to them, either. But people are nuts. I've seen many a person sacrifice themselves just so they can watch someone else burn."

It was a valid statement, and it was something I'd already considered myself many times since leaving Bill's house. It was one of the few times in my life when I'd completely let my anger get the better of me. Did that mean I'd regretted what I'd done? Not for a second.

"Have you had a chance to see Hani?" I asked.

"I swung by her house on the way back here."

"Was your mom still there?"

"Yes. I was only there for thirty minutes or so. Hani seems to be doing okay."

"She's a tough girl."

"I think we both know that's not true."

"I know, but she's handling this better than I thought she would. No one should be put in that situation."

"Especially in front of her child. You didn't tell Foxx about this, did you?"

"You guys asked me not to."

"I know, but I also know how much you hate keeping secrets from him."

"I never did, until now."

"You know what he'd do to Bill if he found out."

"He's going to find out. Things like this have a habit of coming to the light."

"I'm guessing Hani will eventually tell him, maybe after her wounds have healed."

I wanted to debate the point more with her, but I didn't think it would do any good. Her mind was made up, as were the minds of the other Hu women. I didn't agree with them, at least not entirely, even if I understood their logic.

"I also drove by Harry's. Have you been?" Alana asked.

"No, but I saw the photos Foxx took. Depressing doesn't begin to describe how I feel about it."

"At least no one was there, and you guys can always rebuild."

I told Alana about our plans to keep everyone on payroll, as well as Fox's idea to potentially add a second floor to the new bar. She wasn't in favor of the addition either, and she suggested we build it exactly as it had been before the fire.

"Your place wasn't the only one destroyed. Gray's old restaurant was trashed," Alana continued.

Alana was referencing a restaurant space located on the beach in Wailea. The place used to be called Eighty-Eight. I'd gone there on one of my cases. Later, Eighty-Eight had been sold to a man named Gray Darcy, only for it to end up owned by the bank after Gray declared bankruptcy. I was somewhat surprised no one had bought it after that. The property was gorgeous, but it wasn't exactly a large parcel of land. It was doubtful it would be big enough for a hotel, even a small one.

"No one bothered boarding up the place. Most of the windows were blown out. The interior was flooded."

"That's a real shame. It was a beautiful place," I said.

"It can be again. Who knows how long it's going to take to rebuild everything."

Mother Nature can be a deadly force, I thought, and she wasn't to ever be taken lightly. I leaned back in my chair again and looked up to the sky. Alana was safe. My friends were safe. I was safe. All things considered, we'd been lucky.

4

BATTER UP

Foxx called me the next morning and said he had the afternoon available to work on my damaged guest bedroom. He needed the morning to finish contacting our employees, as well as speak with the insurance company. He was also trying to use his contacts on the island to get us near the top of various contractors' lists. I suspected this involved paying substantially more than their normal rates. Let the fleecing begin.

I decided to take advantage of my free time by driving down the coast to check out the restaurant in Wailea. I'd always sworn that I would never invest in another restaurant. It wasn't that Harry's had been a bad experience. It hadn't. Granted, Foxx did most of the work, but I didn't want all of my time consumed with working in the restaurant business. Nevertheless, I couldn't stop thinking that the former Eighty-Eight restaurant would be a good investment, although I didn't intend to reopen it as a dining establishment. I had other ideas in mind.

Driving down the coast was like cruising through a warzone in a BMW Z3 convertible. Countless houses and buildings were damaged or destroyed. Trees were down. Roads were covered with dirt and sand. I realized I'd taken the wrong vehicle, and I hoped I wouldn't get stuck.

I made it to Wailea all right, and I swung the little silver car into the parking lot. Alana had used the appropriate word when she'd described the place as trashed. All of the windows were blown out and glass was everywhere. Fortunately, the building had been constructed of steel and concrete. This had made it an unusual looking restaurant for Maui, but its materials had saved it from complete destruction. The building was relatively intact, despite the superficial damage of the broken windows and sliding glass doors. The previous owner had removed all of the carpet in favor of a concrete floor, so all of the rainwater that had gotten into the building was already dry from the sun and the wind coming off the ocean.

The other damage was that the wooden deck on the back of the building was gone. The wind and waves had ripped it away from the main structure. I saw what looked like half of the deck on the beach below. The rest of the wood must have washed into the ocean. No one wanted to see such a large deck destroyed, but I saw it as a relatively easy fix, all things considered. I decided I needed to have a conversation with a few people and then potentially make an offer to the bank to buy the place. In the past, I'd thought the restaurant had bad karma, but perhaps that was due to the people associated with it. The land was beautiful, and it needed to be managed by someone who would treat it with the respect it deserved.

I walked back to my car, slipped a classical music CD into the disc player, something I often listen to when I'm super stressed, and drove back to Kaanapali. In case you're wondering, the CD was Wagner's *Der Ring des Nibelung*.

The next week went by in a blur. I regained power at my house sometime on the second day. Foxx and I spent most of that week repairing my roof and redoing the floor in the bedroom. Fortunately, we were able to find the exact flooring material Alana had picked out. The walls had also gotten water-damaged, so we replaced half the drywall, which necessitated repainting the entire room. The color

Alana picked? *Gazelles of the Desert.* No, I'm not kidding. That's the name of the color. It looked like light-brown to me.

Alana called me late that Friday evening and told me that she had to work late. I expected to spend the evening having a beer or two and watching a rerun of *Battlestar Galactica*, the original television version from the 70s, not the remake. Yeah, I know it's a bad rip-off of *Star Wars*, but I couldn't help myself. Cheesy television is a great way to take your mind off your problems. The Cylons had just attacked the colonies when I got a phone call from Foxx. He reminded me of that important business meeting we had. Side note, we didn't, but I was fortunately alert enough to figure something was up, and I went along with everything, especially since I'd gotten the impression he'd put me on speakerphone.

Foxx told me he'd be over in a few minutes to pick me up. I said okay and ended the call. I put my sandals back on, said goodbye to the dog, and walked out the front door. Foxx pulled into my driveway sixty seconds later.

"That was fast," I said, as I climbed into his SUV.

"Thank God you could make our meeting."

"Do you mind telling me what meeting we have?"

"A meeting with some beers."

Foxx backed out of the driveway and headed out of the neighborhood.

"Ashley set a dinner date with that couple we stayed with during the hurricane. She said it was a thank you for their hospitality," Foxx continued.

"You're blowing off the thank-you dinner for our mystery meeting?"

"You don't know these crazies, Poe. Ashley can thank them on her own."

"She's not upset that you're ditching the dinner?"

"Of course she's upset. She's furious."

"Maybe you should turn around and go out to dinner with them," I suggested.

"It's not just dinner. They'll want to go somewhere for after-dinner drinks. Then they'll suggest we go back to their place for more wine and conversation around their fire pit."

"Maybe these people are swingers. Perhaps they're setting you and Ashley up for the big suggestion that you swap partners."

"Don't say that. I don't want to even accidentally picture myself with that woman."

"Where are we headed?"

"That bar in Lahaina that's a few blocks from ours. Ashley hates that place so there's no way she'll suggest it for the dinner. I figure we just need to hang there for a few hours, and I should be fine."

"A few hours?"

"What's the problem? I thought you said earlier that Alana was going to be late?"

"She is."

"So you've got nothing going on. Don't you want to hang with your dear old buddy?" Foxx asked, and he smiled.

I was dead tired, and all I really wanted to do was go back home and lie down. Foxx had helped me repair my house, though. The least I could do was have some drinks with him.

There was a good reason Ashley didn't like the bar. I won't say the name since I don't want to get sued for libel, if that's the right word when you trash the reputation of a business. The place was a dump, to put it mildly. I don't mean dump in a good way, like a fun dive bar. The place was dirty and loud and it smelled like old laundry. Can you tell I'm getting older? Those were probably the things I would have looked for in my twenties.

Foxx and I had a seat at one end of the bar. I was about to order a Manhattan when I got a good look at the bartender. Something told me I was better off sticking to bottled beer. We both ordered Negra Modelos. Foxx sucked his first one down pretty quickly, while I lingered a bit with mine. I was worried too many beers would knock me out in my already exhausted condition, and I didn't want to fall asleep and wake up naked on the curb with all my possessions stolen.

We spoke some more about our plans for the Harry's rebuild. Foxx was now leaning toward abandoning the idea of adding a second floor. I suggested that I thought it was a good idea to stick to the original design. I kept waiting for him to bring up Ashley and his thoughts on the future of their relationship. He didn't. After a few hours of drinking and making small talk, the subject switched to one I'd hoped to avoid.

"Ava was with me this morning."

"That's good," I said.

"Something's going on."

"What do you mean?"

"I've picked up Ava from Hani's house three times this week. Hani's never there. It's always her mother."

"What's strange about that? Ms. Hu watches Ava all the time."

"True, but it was fairly early a couple of the times I got there. It doesn't make sense for her mother to be there at that time of day," Foxx said.

"Maybe Hani had early morning appointments."

"For wedding planning? Most of her appointments are on the phone, or she has a meeting with a local resort or wedding venue. No one wants to meet that early in her business."

Okay, we all know what the real issue was. Hani had been avoiding Foxx for obvious reasons, and I'd now come to a moment of truth. Do what my wife and sister-in-law asked for or come clean to my best friend.

"There's something going on with Ava, too. She's not herself. I tried talking to her about it, but good luck having an in-depth conversation with someone that young," he continued.

Foxx took a long gulp of his beer. He put it back on the bar and stared off into the distance.

"I love that little girl. It kills me thinking something might be wrong," Foxx continued.

Now it was my turn to take a long pull from my beer.

"I know what's wrong," I said.

Foxx turned to me.

"How do you know?"

"Hani cares about you. You know that, don't you?"

"Of course, she cares. I'm her kid's father."

"It's not just that. I know you guys haven't been on the best of terms for a while."

"Things have gotten a lot better between us."

"Sure they have, and she doesn't want anything bad to happen to you," I said.

"Why would it?"

"If you were to end up in jail, for example."

"Poe, you're not making any sense. What in the hell are you talking about?"

"They asked me not to say anything, but I'm going to."

"Who did?"

"The Hu women, all three of them. But it was my decision not to talk, and I regret that."

"If you don't spill the beans now, I'm going to hit you over the head with this beer bottle."

I paused a moment. Then I told Foxx everything, including Bill's attack on Hani, Ava witnessing it, and my subsequent fight with Bill in his house and backyard. I expected Foxx to say something in response. He didn't. He just stared into the distance like he had a moment before.

"How long have you known about Ava?" he finally asked without turning to me.

"Hani told me when I was staying with her."

"So it's been over a week?"

"Yes," I admitted.

Foxx turned to me.

"Damn you, Poe. How could you keep this from me?"

"You're right. I should have told you, but I also thought it was Ava's mother's place to tell you. I feel like I'm walking a very thin line when it comes to you, too. You're my best friend, but I'm also not part of your family. You and Hani and Ava are, whether you guys are married or not."

Foxx didn't respond. He finished his beer and pushed the stool back from the bar.

"Where are you going?" I asked.

"I want to get the hell away from you. I'll deal with this tomorrow."

Foxx walked away from the bar. I waited several seconds. Then I pulled out my wallet and put cash down on the counter to cover our tab. When I got to the door, I didn't see Foxx anywhere. I thought he might have gone into the bathroom, or maybe he'd already left and I would need to call for a taxi. I knew he was furious at me, and I didn't blame him.

I walked outside to look for his SUV and stopped almost immediately. There were three guys with baseball bats standing at the edge of the parking lot. It was Bill and two of his friends. I looked more closely at one of them. I was pretty sure his name was Ryan. I thought I'd seen him before at Harry's. Then I realized he'd been at the bar when Foxx and I had first entered earlier that night. He'd looked at me like he'd known me but hadn't bothered to nod or say hello. I hadn't greeted him, either. Now it was obvious why he'd left in such a hurry. He'd gone outside to call Bill to alert him to my presence.

Bill took a step toward me. Ryan and the other guy stayed a few paces behind him.

"You made a big mistake when you broke into my house," Bill said.

"I understand you're upset, but I think it would be best if you leave now. You don't want to be in this parking lot in about sixty seconds," I said, as I finally noticed that Foxx's SUV was still there.

Bill laughed.

"We're not going anywhere."

"I know you think I'm bluffing, but trust me. You need to get the hell out of here, now."

He didn't move. My warning was never going to work, and my stomach grew sick at the violence that was about to occur.

Foxx exited the bar and walked up beside me. He said nothing.

I watched as Bill eyeballed Foxx and then snapped his eyes to me. Then he looked back to Foxx.

"You take the two guys on the right. I want Bill," Foxx finally said to me.

"They have bats, Foxx."

"I'm sure a smart guy like you can figure something out," Foxx said.

Yep, he was still mad at me, even with a new target on the scene.

Foxx walked up to Bill.

"You're going to attack a member of my family? Then you're going to come here and threaten us? Do you have any idea what I'm going to do to you?" Foxx asked.

"We're not here for you. I want him," Bill said, and he pointed the bat at me.

"Your business with him has nothing to do with me, but you beat on the mother of my child. You did it in front of my child. No, Bill. Your business is with me."

Bill swung the bat at Foxx's head. Foxx caught the bat with his left hand. Bill tried to yank it back, but Foxx pulled at the bat, which brought Bill closer to him. He struck Bill across the face with his free right hand. Bill dropped to the pavement as Foxx struck him a second time. Foxx was so concentrated on Bill that he didn't notice Ryan charge him from behind.

"Foxx," I yelled, and I ran toward Foxx and dove just as Ryan swung the bat at him. Fortunately, the bat hit my right shoulder instead of my head. I fell to the parking lot and tried to gather my senses as Foxx fended off a second bat swing by Ryan.

The third friend charged Foxx. I grabbed at his legs as he passed. He tried to push me off, and I punched him where no man wants to get hit. Hey, I knew it was a low blow, but the fight hadn't exactly started with fair odds. The guy dropped the bat, and I grabbed it. I thrusted the bat at him, and the end of it struck him on the chin. I saw his eyes glaze over, and he went down.

I turned and saw that Foxx was taking on both Ryan and Bill. I swung the bat at Ryan, only for him to hold up his bat at the last second. He and I took turns swinging at each other. We were engaging in some kind of sword play with wooden bats. He took a wild swing at me, and I was able to sidestep it. Ryan's forward momentum left him wide open, and I swung the bat down hard against his upper back. He went down to one knee, and I hit him on the back three more times.

I was about to go to Foxx again when I heard a shotgun blast. I turned to see the owner of the bar standing a few feet from the front door. His rifle was pointed in the air.

"Let go of him. Right now," the owner said.

He was looking past me, so I turned again and saw Foxx on top of Bill, who was lying motionless on his back in the middle of the parking lot. Foxx's right hand was covered in blood. I looked at Bill and saw a mask of red. I didn't know if Foxx had killed him. Hani's fear had come true.

5

A HUNCH

THE POLICE ARRIVED IN LESS THAN FIFTEEN MINUTES. I TRIED TO HELP
Bill before that, but the bar owner pointed the shotgun at me and
threatened to blow my head off if I went near Bill.

The police put Foxx and me in the back of one squad car. Ryan
and the other friend went into another. An ambulance arrived for
Bill, and I watched as the emergency techs lifted him onto a stretcher.
I looked at Foxx a couple of times while we were in the car, but he
never said anything. He just stared out the windshield.

It took about two hours for them to take us back to the station,
photograph us, and print us. Foxx and I were placed in one group-
holding area. I don't know where they put the other guys. Foxx sat on
one of the benches, while I opted to sit on the floor with my back
against the concrete wall.

There were seven other guys in the cell with us. Half of them were
obviously drunk. Two guys were passed out and snoring, but I knew
they'd been drinking because of the strong smell of alcohol
emanating from their bodies. The other two drunk guys were
slumped against the wall and drooling while they mumbled about
something that I couldn't make out.

The fifth guy was also talking to himself. His voice was

clear, but he was making no sense. I heard talk about the coming apocalypse, which might have made for an interesting topic and entertaining way to pass the night. He was a lousy storyteller, though, and his take on the world ending had no inciting incident, nor did it have much more of a plot beyond the fact that we were all going to hell where we would be slaves to the devil.

The sixth guy looked fairly normal, if it was possible to be in jail and be normal. I thought Foxx and I were, but maybe my sense of self-awareness needed a tune up. Anyway, the sixth guy spent most of his time glaring at our jailhouse prophet. I kept expecting him to tell the guy to shut up, but he never said anything.

The seventh guy looked like a psychopathic killer. He had a pair of pale eyes that looked like they could bore a hole through the metal bars. I did my best to position Foxx between me and the nutcase. The guy didn't have any blood on him, and I didn't have the courage to ask him why he was in there since I was sure it had something to do with causing physical harm to someone.

There was no television in the cell, not that I expected there to be, but I could hear the guards watching a football game in the distance. It sounded boring by the way.

After about half an hour of continued silence between us, Foxx finally spoke.

"I guess I should have had that dinner with Ashley and her friends after all."

"Is that some kind of joke?" I asked.

"No, it's a statement of fact."

Foxx paused.

Then he continued, "It's better that it worked out this way. Those guys would have taken your head off."

"They tried to take both our heads off. One of those guys was in the bar earlier. That's how they knew we were there."

"I figured it was something like that," Foxx said.

"I wonder when we're going to get our phone calls."

"You don't need one. I'm here."

I turned at the sound of Alana's voice. She was standing outside our cage and glaring at me.

"I guess they called you," I said.

"You think?"

She looked over at Foxx and then turned back to me.

"I suppose you told him," she continued.

"Told me what?" Foxx asked.

"Don't try to cover for him."

"Cover? He said nothing. We walked outside and found those guys waiting for us with baseball bats. Bill's attack on Hani came out in our little pre-fight discussion," Foxx said.

"Your pre-fight discussion?" she asked.

"Yeah. When both sides sort of size each other up and talk smack."

"Is that right?" Alana asked me.

"Don't try to deflect the blame on him. You and your sister should have told me what happened," Foxx said.

"I'm sorry you found out that way, but it was a tough call. Hani asked us not to," Alana said.

"I get that, but sometimes you need to go against her wishes if you know it's a bad idea. What if Bill had gone back to her house? She needs someone looking after her."

"Don't you think I know that, but beating the hell out of three guys in a bar parking lot is not the answer. You could have killed that guy tonight. He might have brain damage."

"He deserves it," Foxx said.

"And that's exactly why Hani didn't want you to know. She knows you can't control your impulses."

"That's ridiculous."

"Is it? Then how do you explain the man in the hospital?" Alana asked.

"Sounds like you keep defending the guy who beat the hell out of your sister."

"Don't you dare say that."

Alana turned back to me.

"I'll call Mara on my way to the bar. I want to make sure that owner doesn't delete any security footage he might have."

"Thank you," I said.

"Are you all right?" she asked.

"That should have been the first question you asked him. He took a bat to the head to protect me," Foxx said.

"It's best if you stop talking now," Alana told Foxx. "Are you all right?" she asked me again.

"I have a hard head. I'll be fine."

"Good."

Alana left after giving both Foxx and me another glare. Several more seconds passed.

Then I said, "I didn't get hit in the head."

"What?" Foxx asked.

"The bat missed my head. It hit me on the shoulder."

"Either way, you jumped in front of me. I appreciate that."

"You're welcome. I'm sorry I didn't tell you about Hani."

"You were right about her being my family, but you're family, too. I don't see you as a friend. I see you as a brother."

"Thanks."

"Brothers fight. We'll get past this. Hell, we're already past this as far as I'm concerned."

"Good."

"We really beat the hell out of those dudes, didn't we?"

"They messed with the wrong guys," I said.

"You can say that again."

We spent a few more minutes inflating each other's manly egos. Then Foxx closed his eyes and tried to sleep. I didn't bother trying. I knew it wouldn't work. Besides, I had no desire to let my guard down around psycho eyes and doomsday boy. I was in for a long night.

An officer came and got Foxx early in the morning. The same cop came back an hour or so later and brought me to one of the interrogation rooms. Mara Winters, my attorney and sometimes employer, was already inside. The officer told me to have a seat, and then he locked the door behind him as he left the room.

I turned to Mara. She was dressed in her typical attire of a business suit. Her dark red hair was pulled back. She looked tired, and I assumed Alana had probably called her in the middle of the night.

"How are you doing?" she asked.

"Exhausted."

"I'm sure. We need to work on you staying out of this place."

"I'm guessing Alana filled you in on what happened, so I won't bother telling you my defense."

"You do attract trouble. Don't try to deny that."

"How much time do you think I'm going to get for this one?" I asked.

"The detective should be here soon. Do yourself a favor and let me do the talking. If you have to say something, say very little and deny everything. I'm going to play a hunch."

"What hunch?"

"Three words: deny, deny, deny."

I had no idea what hunch she was referring to, but I nodded at her deny mantra and practiced keeping my mouth shut as we waited for the detective to arrive.

Eventually, a Hawaiian woman walked into the room. I guessed her age at around twenty-eight or so. She was a touch on the curvy side, but all of those curves were placed perfectly on her body. She sat down across from Mara and me, and her dark, expressive eyes began to study me while she temporarily ignored my attorney. I was tempted to say something, like hello or good morning, but then I remembered Mara's advice and kept quiet. The more I looked at her, though, the more convinced I became that we'd met before. Nevertheless, I didn't mention that.

"Mr. Rutherford, you've gotten yourself into a bit of trouble, haven't you?" she asked.

I thought it was pretty obvious that I had, so I said nothing.

"My name's Makamae Kalani," she continued.

Detective Kalani turned to Mara.

"You're Ms. Winters?"

"That's right."

Detective Kalani had entered the room with a manila folder in her hand. She opened it and slid the contents onto the table. It was a photograph of Hani's bruised face and a DVD with a date written in black ink on the label. The date was from the previous day.

"I arrived this morning to find these two things on my desk. I assume they were placed there by your wife," Kalani told me.

"I've reviewed the bar's security footage myself. This is about as clear-cut a case of self-defense that I've ever seen," Mara said.

"Yes, I agree. But there's another incident we need to discuss. I went to see Bill Hodges in the hospital this morning. Your clients did a real number on him."

She paused, waiting for me to respond, but I said nothing.

"He told me that his attack on you was a response to you breaking into his house and assaulting him," she continued.

Mara chuckled.

"You find this funny?" Kalani asked.

"Not at all. Bill Hodges would say anything to try to deflect blame for his own actions. He assaulted his ex-girlfriend, Hani Hu. Then he convinced two of his associates to attack my client and his business partner with baseball bats as they were leaving the bar," Mara said.

"All of that is true, as evidenced by these photos and video footage, but it doesn't answer the question as to whether Mr. Rutherford attacked Mr. Hodges in his home."

"What evidence does Mr. Hodges present?" Mara asked.

"The wounds on his face," Kalani said.

"The wounds caused from last night's fight?" Mara asked.

"I saw no injuries that appeared to be more than several hours old. Of course, that could be because Mr. Hodges' face is in such bad condition, and his new wounds have concealed the older ones."

"Bill Hodges is a man who likes to beat up women, and he does so in front of toddlers. His word means nothing to me. They'll mean even less to a judge and jury," Mara said.

Detective Kalani turned to me.

"Mr. Rutherford, did you assault Bill Hodges?"

Deny, deny, deny, I repeated in my head.

"No, ma'am," I said.

She paused a long moment. Perhaps she was expecting me to get nervous (I was) and blurt out something else that might raise more questions or possibly contradict myself. I said nothing.

"There's no proof of an earlier assault, so it's essentially your word against Mr. Hodges. I'm going to let you go. The next time someone shows up in a parking lot and intends to cave your head in, go back inside and call the police," Kalani said.

"Yes, ma'am," I said.

She turned to Mara.

"Thank you, counselor. I'm sure you and I will be meeting again."

Detective Kalani removed a pair of keys from her pocket. I put my hands on the table, and she undid my handcuffs.

"I hope this doesn't become a pattern with you and me," she continued.

"I'm sure it won't," I said.

She studied me for another moment. She said nothing, though, nor did she give me any kind of facial expression that would give me a clue as to what she was thinking. I refused to break eye contact since that's one of the classic signs of guilt. The more I looked at her, the more I realized just how attractive she was. Her long black hair perfectly framed her face, and those dark eyes – the ones I mentioned before – reminded me a lot of Alana's in their ability to gaze inside of you. This lady would be a formidable opponent, if I ever ended up on the wrong side of the law again.

Finally, Detective Kalani stood and escorted us to the lobby.

Mara walked with me out of the station. We went down the building's stairs and made our way to the sidewalk. Alana was waiting for me by the curb.

"How did you know she was going to let me go?" I asked Mara.

"Thank your wife. She let me know that Detective Kalani used to work at a home for battered women before she became a cop. She was dying to let you go, especially after she saw those photos of your sister-in-law, all supplied by your wife."

"Thank you, Mara," Alana said. "I'm sorry for calling so early."

"It's not a problem. Anything for Mr. Alana Hu."

"Mr. Alana Hu?" I asked.

"I'm addressing you by your smarter half. Stay out of trouble, Edgar. I'd still like to use you from time to time for some of my cases."

"Thanks, Mara," I said.

She nodded and headed off toward her car.

I turned to Alana.

"Where's Foxx?"

"He was released an hour ago."

"Did you get a chance to talk to him?"

"Not yet. I guess everything's out in the open now."

"Does Hani know what happened?" I asked.

"She does. I called her late last night. I imagine Foxx will be speaking with her today. I hope he doesn't lay into her. It's the last thing she needs right now."

"I hope not, either. I'll try to call him today. We kind of patched things up in the jail cell."

"That's good to hear, I suppose."

"He has a right to be mad, just like you have the right to be disappointed in me."

"Why didn't you go back inside that bar and call the cops?" Alana asked.

"I should have, but the thought didn't occur to me."

"How is that possible?"

"Because I was still furious at Bill for what he did to Hani. Then he showed up with his friends, and it was obvious what his intentions were. I wasn't about to back down."

Alana didn't respond, and I couldn't tell if she was really angry with me or if she was secretly okay with me for taking out Bill and his friends (with a huge contribution by Foxx, of course) and she was mainly putting on a show for what she deemed as my best long-term interests.

"I guess I better call a taxi," I continued.

"I'll drive you home. I've been up all night, and I need to get some sleep."

"Did I tell you about the world ending?" I asked as we walked toward Alana's car.

"What are you talking about?"

"This charming man I met in jail last night. He told me all about it."

"I'm sure. You know there's a part of me that thinks you're proud of yourself."

"I'm not."

"Say something to convince me to believe you."

"I won't say anything, but I'll answer you with a question of my own. Would Mr. Alana Hu ever lie to you?"

Alana cracked the faintest of smiles.

"Is that a smile I see?" I asked.

"No. Never under these circumstances."

"Hey, do you have a copy of that security video?"

"Why do you ask?"

"I'd like to see a replay of that fight. You wouldn't believe some of my moves."

"You're digging yourself a hole again."

"Maybe so. Thanks again for helping to get me out of there."

"You're welcome," she said, and this time she smiled broadly.

6

DEVELOPMENTS

THE NEXT TWO WEEKS WENT BY WITHOUT INCIDENT, AND THE emotional rifts that had been caused by Bill's attack on Hani had been healed with a gathering of all parties involved, which included myself, Alana, Foxx, Hani, and Ms. Hu. I guess I shouldn't say all parties since Bill was decidedly not invited, not that he would have accepted an invitation anyway.

There was only one rule for the family meeting: No fingers were to be pointed and no one was to blame another person. The goal was to discuss viewpoints and feelings and come to a general understanding. We agreed, at my prompting, not to keep information regarding our physical health and safety from each other. There were a few tears shed. I won't mention who cried so as not to embarrass the person (it was Foxx) but I also found myself getting emotional at times. The world can be a crazy and unpredictable place, and sometimes it feels like we're under attack from multiple sources. In the end, if we're lucky, all we really have is our friends and family to count on.

Foxx did speak one on one with Hani the day he and I were freed from jail, and from Hani's account of the discussion to Alana, he did so in a pretty calm and reasonable manner. Hani said it was the kindest she'd ever seen Foxx. She also told Alana that Foxx spent a long time talking to Ava and explaining that sometimes people are not nice but that he would do his best to protect her and her mother. It was a noble promise to make, but I also knew it was one that he wouldn't be able to keep. He didn't live with them, and the lack of a male in the house caused me anxiety. Sorry if that sounds chauvinistic, but it's how I felt.

Hani's home didn't have an alarm system, much to my dismay. So I took it upon myself to have the security company I used for my house install cameras around the exterior of her home, as well as sensors on all of the doors and locks. I made her promise to arm the system each night. She agreed without hesitation, somewhat to my surprise. You may be wondering why I would be surprised by that. I knew my request was a reasonable one, but sometimes Hani has a habit of doing the opposite of what you'd like her to do. It's that stubborn streak in the Hu women.

I'm sure you're wondering about Bill, Ryan, and the other guy, whose name I still didn't know. Ryan and the other guy posted bail the day after I was released. I didn't know when they'd go before a judge for the assault charge, but I had a feeling they'd get off with a stiff fine and maybe probation.

I didn't know if that would be the same for Bill. He was arrested after spending a day in the hospital. He didn't have brain damage, as Alana had warned. But he did have a broken nose, three chipped teeth, and two black eyes. I know this because it was in the letter sent to Mara announcing Bill's intentions to sue Foxx and me over the physical abuse he sustained. I didn't recognize the name of his attorney, but Mara described him as an ambulance chaser who'd probably approached Bill while he was lying in the hospital bed.

She said it might be in our best interest to settle with Bill since it would be cheaper than paying her legal fees if this became a long and drawn out litigation, as it almost certainly would given the reputation of the other lawyer. Foxx and I spoke about it and decided, after all of sixty seconds of discussion, that we'd rather pay a small fortune to Mara than give Bill a penny. We asked Mara to file a countersuit in which we sought payment from Bill for the emotional distress he caused us, as well as the damage I sustained by getting hit with the bat. I didn't really have much damage, but Mara instructed me to go to my doctor to complain about the pain and at least get it on record that I'd been injured.

There was one other development during those two weeks that is worth noting. I reached an agreement with the bank that owned the vacated restaurant property in Wailea. I'd pitched Foxx on my vision for the business, and he agreed with it. We'd formed an LLC when we'd bought Harry's years ago, so that company would ultimately be the entity making the purchase of the Wailea property. Hani was a big part of the business plan. If things went the way I hoped they would, the new venture would make her quite a bit of money.

Foxx paid her a decent chunk of money each month for Ava's care. Those funds alone covered all of her bills. It's one thing to have someone give you money, but it's an entirely different feeling of pride and accomplishment when you make it yourself. I knew her wedding planning business was doing well, but I thought the new business in Wailea would take her income to a different level. I decided not to approach her yet until I had more of the pieces in place, but I was sure she would jump at it once I talked her through my plan.

I'm sure you're wondering about the aforementioned Harry's. The insurance company was going to foot the bill for the rebuild, minus the hefty deductible, of course. Construction was slated to begin later that month with the goal of having Harry's back open for business in four to five months. It was a little later than I'd hoped it would be, but all things considered, we were fortunate it wouldn't take longer than a year given how slow the overall recovery was on the island. Some places were still without power, and some of the smaller roads remained blocked by debris, dirt, and sand.

Probably the most surprising event to occur came at the end of those two weeks. I got a call in the morning from Detective Makamae Kalani. She asked if she could meet me for coffee that afternoon when she got off work. I said okay and casually mentioned it to Alana when I spoke with her later in the day. Alana's reaction surprised me.

She seemed somewhat offended by the idea. My conversation with Alana had been brief, but I got the impression that we were on the verge of an argument by the end of it. I didn't understand why that was the case, especially since I hadn't reacted in any kind of negative way while we'd been talking. I thought about cancelling the meeting with Detective Kalani after ending the call with Alana, but I decided not to since the whole thing seemed a bit silly. In retrospect, I should have realized this was another shining example of my lack of knowledge about women.

Detective Kalani suggested we meet at a café in Lahaina near the Banyan Tree Park. I'd been to the café several times before, and the park was a common place I chose when meeting with some people during my cases. It's a beautiful location that was almost always crawling with tourists. That's why I loved it so much. It was quite easy to be inconspicuous there.

I arrived to our meeting a few minutes late since I'd gotten a call from Foxx right as I was walking out the door. He told me the construction on the new Harry's was to begin a week earlier than we thought. I was happy about the news, but then he quickly transitioned into a complaint about Ashley and a comment she'd made earlier that day about his weight. I don't like talking on the cell phone while I'm driving the convertible, so I had a ten-minute conversation about "Ashley and her judgmental ways" before finally telling Foxx I had to go.

The café was fairly busy by the time I arrived. There was a long line leading up to the counter and every table was full. I scanned the café and saw Detective Kalani sitting at a table in the back corner. She nodded to me, and I made my way through the crowd.

Detective Kalani was dressed similarly to the last time I'd seen her. Detectives don't wear uniforms, which I assume you already know. Alana tended to wear business attire, as did Detective Kalani on the one occasion I'd met her. Today she was wearing a light-green silk tank top and tan pants.

I saw a tan jacket that was placed over the back of one of the other chairs. Did I think it odd that she'd removed her jacket for our meeting? I wasn't sure. If you've read these books before, you know I tend to overthink things, so that's the excuse I'll give for why I spent several seconds analyzing the tank top. It was a touch on the low side, revealing a couple of inches of cleavage, nothing that could be remotely compared to a nightclub outfit, but it was enough to draw attention. Maybe she was just warm, though. As I mentioned, the café was busy and the extra bodies seemed to have raised the temperature a bit. Another reason, perhaps Detective Kalani had simply decided to ditch the jacket because she was off work.

"Good afternoon, Detective. May I sit?"

"Of course."

I pulled out a chair and sat opposite her.

"I don't know that I've ever seen this place so busy," I said.

"I've only been here a couple of times, but they were about this crowded before."

"What did you want to see me about?"

I failed to mention this earlier, but she had an iced coffee on the table. She now took a sip of that after I asked my question. She put the cup back down and looked past me out the window. Did I find this odd? Sure.

"I've heard a lot about you at the station," she said.

I waited for her to say more. She paused a few seconds. Perhaps she was wanting me to ask what she'd heard. I didn't.

She turned back to me.

"From what I can gather, you've solved eight major crimes on the island. Well, one of those was off the island if you count the one on the yacht."

"I don't know that you can say I solved them. I had a lot of help."

"You mean from people like your wife and Detective Adcock?"

"Something like that."

"Perhaps they just benefitted by taking credit for your work," she suggested.

"It would be inaccurate for you to say Alana ever stole the credit for something I did."

"I don't think she stole it. I'm sure you gave it to her willingly."

"What's your point?" I said, my voice sounding a bit on the harsh side.

"Have I offended you?" she asked.

"No, but I feel like we're on the verge of this conversation going in a direction I don't want it to go."

"That wasn't my intention. Let's start over. I didn't mean to imply your wife is anything but an outstanding detective. I'm sure I have a lot to learn from her. My goal for this meeting is more about you. I want your help."

"My help?"

"I think you have a unique talent that is frightfully underutilized by the department. You're a valuable resource, and I have no idea why they aren't tapping into it."

"I don't know that I'd agree with that. You said you've heard a lot about me, but I'm guessing there's a lot you don't know. I don't do these investigations full time. It's not something I'm really interested in."

"Is it the money you're worried about?"

"What do you mean?" I asked.

"I'm sure the department couldn't afford to pay you. It would have to be on a voluntary basis."

"Have you spoken to your captain about this?"

"No. I wanted to feel you out first."

"Money has never been a motivation for me."

"I'm sure. You have all you could ever need, from what I hear."

"May I ask who told you that?"

"It wasn't one person. It's a small island. People talk. Wealth is one of the hot topics. I'm sure you know that."

"Then I'm guessing you also heard I own a bar in this town. That alone keeps me busy," I said, which wasn't quite true since Foxx did most of the work.

"Then what is your motivation for doing these cases?"

"Curiosity, I suppose."

"That's what I assumed. You like the thrill of the hunt. You enjoy the mystery. It's like a puzzle, just waiting to be solved piece by little piece."

I was a little freaked out because she'd not only nailed my motivation, but she'd done so in terms that I'd used myself.

"I have a case you might be interested in. A woman returned home during the early stages of the hurricane. She found her husband hacked to death in their house," she continued.

"Alana mentioned something about that, but she said he'd been stabbed, not hacked to death."

"What did she say, exactly?" Detective Kalani asked.

"Nothing more than that. I never followed up on it, and she never said another word. Do you have any suspects?"

"None, beyond the obvious, that is."

"You mean the wife?"

"Yes."

"When you said he was hacked to death, do you mean he was killed with something like an ax?"

"The medical examiner thinks it was a meat cleaver. There were several long cuts across the upper body."

"That's not a kitchen tool everyone has. Did you find something like that at the scene?" I asked.

"No. They had the standard knife set but nothing that could have caused his injuries."

"How many times was he struck?"

"At least five times. He had a large gash between the neck and shoulder. He also had three or four slashes across his chest. The killing blow was the one across his neck. His neck looked like it had been put through a meat grinder."

"Like jagged cuts?" I asked.

"Yes."

"That doesn't sound like something that could be done with a meat cleaver."

"Exactly, and I asked the medical examiner about that. He said there could have been two weapons used."

"You mentioned the wife before. What kind of alibi did she present?"

"She claimed she was out shopping when her husband was murdered. She paid cash at the store, so there are no credit records. However, she has a receipt proving what time she was there. The medical examiner places the time of death in the general time zone of when she got home. So either the killer made his or her getaway right as she was arriving at the house, or she killed her husband, went to the store to create her alibi, and then came home for the supposed discovery."

"Are there traffic cameras that show her coming and going?"

"No, not in the section of the island where they live."

"You've mentioned the wife. Anyone else? A business partner, lover, disgruntled neighbor?"

"The victim's sister has been demanding. She works for the clothing company her brother started. The business is doing well and the money is good. If she's to be believed, there were no disagreements between them, no fights about that money or how the business was to be operated."

"So it's been a few weeks now and you have no solid leads," I said.

"Not a good way to start my career on Maui."

"Have you approached Alana about any of this?"

"No."

"May I ask why?"

"You may ask..." Her words trailed off. Then she said, "I'd rather keep this conversation between the two of us by the way."

"I've already mentioned to Alana that we'd be meeting."

"I see. I guess it was a foolish assumption on my part that you could be my secret weapon."

"I don't keep secrets from my wife."

She didn't reply, and we both sat in silence for several moments.

Then I said, "I appreciate the offer to help with the case. Here's what I propose. If your captain's okay with it, then I'll consider getting involved."

"That's a fair request, but I'd prefer not to go to him until I know for sure that you'd be in."

"I understand. Can you give me a day or two to think about it?"

"Of course."

I looked over to the line at the counter. It had gotten even longer since I'd arrived.

"Well, I don't think I want to wait in that line for a drink, so I'll probably just head home now. I appreciate you asking for my help. It's flattering."

"I'm a little surprised by you."

"How's that?"

"You didn't ask me about Bill Hodges and the case against him."

"That would be inappropriate."

She laughed.

"Is that funny?" I asked.

"Not exactly, but it confirmed something else I heard about you."

"Which is?"

"I'll never tell."

She stood before I had a chance to reply.

"Thank you for your time, Mr. Rutherford, and give my best to Detective Hu."

She left while I stayed at the table. I was somewhat shocked by the end of our discussion. The truth is I found the whole conversation odd, and it wasn't something I'd have expected in a million years. Now I would have to try to explain all of this to Alana. How would she react? Something told me it wouldn't be good.

7

ACCUSATIONS

AFTER I GOT HOME, I DECIDED TO TAKE MAUI FOR A WALK. WE SAW Foxx washing his SUV in the driveway as we were passing his house. He called out to me and I walked up to greet him. I noticed a white mustang in the garage as I got closer. It was Ashley's rental car, a car that Foxx was paying for, by the way.

"That's pretty good news about the construction starting early, isn't it?" Foxx asked.

"Maybe we'll get even luckier and they'll finish ahead of schedule."

"I hope so. I plan to be up there every day."

I nodded toward Ashley's car.

"I see Ashley's home. Did you guys manage to get past your little tiff?"

"Not sure."

"You're not sure?"

"She didn't really say much when she got back from tennis. Then I came out here to wash the vehicle."

I was about to respond when I heard the interior garage door open and Ashley stepped out. She walked down the four stairs in the garage and came out to join us.

"You look okay to me," she said.

"What do you mean?" I asked.

"Foxx said you took a nasty hit with that baseball bat, but you look okay."

"I got lucky."

"Lucky? More like Foxx saved you, I'd say."

I wasn't sure how to take that. Actually, I knew exactly how to take it, but I tried to let it pass for the sake of my friendship with Foxx.

"Did Foxx tell you about our conversation this morning?" she asked.

"He doesn't want to hear about that," Foxx said.

"We're thinking of suing for full custody," she said.

"Full custody of what?" I asked before I realized she had to be talking about Ava.

"Ava, of course."

"That's enough, Ashley," Foxx said.

"Why in the world would Foxx want to do that?" I asked.

"I'm surprised you wouldn't know," she said.

"That's enough," Foxx repeated.

"Ava's mother is putting her in danger. She's invited violent men into her house. Bill Hodges could just have easily struck Ava. He could have killed her," Ashley said.

"You sound like Hani knew Bill was violent and chose to ignore it," I said.

"Of course, she knew."

"And how do you know that?" I asked.

"Stop, both of you. We're not having this conversation. Ashley, I told you that I'm not suing for full custody. Hani's a good mother," Foxx said.

Ashley didn't respond, at least not verbally, but the hostile look she shot Foxx wasn't hard to decipher.

I looked down at Maui, who was already staring at me. I like to think he was encouraging me to stop holding back my opinion when I was around Ashley. Unfortunately, she'd beaten me to the punch and unloaded on me first.

"I know it was your idea to exclude me," she said.

"From what?" I asked.

"From that little family meeting you guys had the other day. I should have been there."

"Oh, I'd love to hear why," I said.

"Foxx and I have been living together for six months. I've been around Ava for hundreds of hours."

"The conversation had little to do with her, and it was for family members only."

"We'll see about that," she said.

"There's nothing to see. The meeting already happened," I said, but I knew what she was getting at. She thought she was going to get a ring. Would she? God, I hoped not.

"I'm going to finish my dog's walk. By the way, Ashley, you said 'we're thinking of suing for full custody' a second ago. There's no 'we.' It's just Foxx and Hani."

"No it isn't, Poe. Excuse me. I meant to say Edgar. What kind of nickname is Poe anyway?"

I felt like my proverbial gasket was about to blow. I counted to ten in my head, took several deep breaths, and then looked down at my cute dog's face for a moment of Zen.

I turned back to Foxx.

"Have a good evening."

Foxx nodded, and Maui and I left the two of them. Foxx went back to washing his SUV as if there hadn't just been an exceptionally unpleasant encounter.

I was completely flabbergasted by my conversation with Ashley, both for what she'd said and for Foxx's rather weak response. He'd pushed back at first, but then he'd just stayed silent as the woman tried to run over me.

I took Maui on a much longer walk than usual. He was panting and ready to collapse by the time we got back home. I was about to call Alana and tell her about the verbal duel when I heard the garage door open. She walked in the house a moment later.

"How was your meeting with Makamae?" she asked.

I tried to decipher her tone, but she didn't really have one.

"It was fine."

"Why did she want to meet?"

"I'm more than willing to talk about that, but I need to tell you what Ashley just said to me."

"Ashley?"

I told Alana about Ashley's comments regarding Foxx suing for full custody of Ava.

"Are you serious? She really suggested that?"

"Yes. Multiple times. And she said 'we,' as if she had anything to do with it," I said.

"What was Foxx's reaction?"

"He didn't have one."

"He said nothing?"

"No, well not during that part of the conversation. Ashley called Hani a bad mother by letting Bill into her life. Foxx told her not to say that and then he said he didn't want to talk about it."

"Makes you think they'd already had that conversation before," Alana said.

"Of course, they have. He mentioned to me earlier that they'd gotten into a big fight this morning. He said it had something to do with Ashley making a comment about his weight. Maybe it was really about her telling him to get Ava away from Hani."

"It was probably both. Let me ask you something. You know Foxx better than anyone. Why do you think he's still with her? What does he see in her beyond the physical attraction?"

"I don't know."

"How can you not know?"

"Because he doesn't talk to me about it, and I feel awkward asking him. How can I possibly ask without sounding like I think she's a horrible person who needs to be kicked to the curb? Do you think Hani has any idea Ashley is saying these things?"

"How could she?"

"Are you going to tell her?" I asked.

"Do you think Foxx is even remotely considering this?"

"No. He said he thought Hani was a good mother."

"Sure, but you also said he didn't push back on Ashley's comments, except at first. Maybe she's getting to him a little. The Bill thing was a big deal."

"It was an isolated incident."

"We know that, and so does Foxx. But this is an emotional issue."

"Maybe I should talk to him."

"No. This is between Hani and him. We need to stay out of this," Alana said.

"I'm surprised to hear you say that."

"Okay. Whose side are you going to choose? Your best friend, who's also your business partner, or your sister-in-law?"

"I'm going to back whoever is in the right," I said.

"That's a dangerous game since sometimes it's hard to know who is right and who is wrong."

I knew Alana was correct, but I couldn't stand the thought of Ashley influencing Foxx to do something he shouldn't do. On the other hand, maybe I was completely overreacting to the conversation. Maybe Foxx was just as outraged by Ashley as I was, but he didn't want to make a scene in front of me. Perhaps he was inside his house at this very moment, reading her the riot act.

"Can you tell me now what Makamae wanted?" Alana asked.

"She asked me to help her with a case, the one where the lady's husband was killed when she was out shopping."

"Are you kidding?"

I'd made the decision while walking Maui that I was going to tell Alana most but not everything about my conversation with Detective Kalani. I didn't see any reason to mention her comments about Alana and Detective Adcock taking credit for my work. For one thing, it wasn't true. Well, actually, Adcock had taken credit for my work, but he did so with my blessing. I also didn't want Alana to know about Detective Kalani's accusation because it would certainly ruin her working relationship with a new co-worker. I know what you're thinking. You're thinking that I should've warned Alana there was a potential snake in her office. You're possibly right.

"She really said you are the most underutilized asset the department has?" Alana asked.

"That was basically what she said. It might not be word for word."

"What game is she playing?"

"I don't know that she is. I got the impression that she's worried she won't be able to solve this crime. She seemed kind of insecure about it."

"Why hasn't she come to me for help or asked any of the other detectives? That's why we're there."

"That's a good question."

"Did you ask her?"

"I don't remember," I said, which wasn't true since I very much did remember.

How was I going to tell Alana, though, that Detective Kalani's response had been that she'd rather not say? Again, that would lead to a confrontational relationship between the two detectives, and I still had no idea why she didn't want Alana's help anyway.

"You don't remember?" Alana asked.

"No, I don't."

"Where did you leave everything?"

"I told her I'd have to think about it, but I'm probably not going to do it."

"Did you tell her that?"

"Not yet. I told her that I'd need your captain to sign off on everything first, but she said she didn't want to go to him until I was committed to the case."

We spoke for a few more minutes about my conversation with Detective Kalani. Those minutes mostly consisted of Alana asking me questions that she'd already asked. I repeated the same answers, but I got the distinct impression that she was interrogating me. It was a common technique of looking for inconsistencies within the suspect's answers. Was I now a suspect? Apparently, but I didn't know what my crime was.

After my impromptu interview/interrogation was over, we spent the rest of the evening watching television. We chose a documentary about the hunt for escaped Nazis in Argentina. The show talked about the various atrocities these war criminals committed against their fellow man. I knew it was all real, but there was a part of me that had a hard time believing people could be so evil. That brought up a philosophical question, one that I kept to myself versus speaking it out loud to Alana. I'll share it with you, though. Is there a difference between murdering one person and killing a million? I've heard the phrase that killing one person is a tragedy but killing a million is a war statistic. I'm not sure if I'm saying that right, and I can't remember for the life of me where I heard it. I thought I might agree with it, at least in how history views events, but I thought it was a false statement when one considers the moral implications. Murder was murder.

After the show was over, I walked upstairs and went to bed. I stared at the ceiling and went over the conversation with Ashley and Foxx in my head again. I couldn't contemplate how she could think those things. Was she just saying them to try to get on Foxx's good side, meaning she was trying to paint a portrait of him being the superior parent? Could this all be chalked up to her jealousy of Foxx's previous relationship with Hani? Had Foxx and Ashley already discussed marriage, and was Ashley laying the ground work for creating a family with Foxx, one that included getting Ava away from Hani?

I heard Alana's words in my mind. "Don't get involved." It was sound advice. I just wasn't sure I was going to be able to follow it.

8

JULIANA GIORDANO

THE NEXT MORNING ALANA AND I SPOKE FOR SEVERAL MINUTES ABOUT Ashley's comments regarding Hani's mothering skills. It was nothing more than a rehash of the previous night's discussion. Alana didn't bring up my café meeting with Detective Kalani, and I wondered if she would say anything to the new detective once she got to work.

After Alana left, I decided to get back on my exercise regimen. For the first time in a few weeks, I was able to conduct my morning routine of swimming in my pool and then running a few miles around the neighborhood. I had trouble completing the run. It's amazing how quickly you can get out of shape. I usually ran with my phone so I could listen to music. For this run, I listened to Miles Davis' album, *Kind of Blue*. One word: wow. Perhaps you're asking yourself, is jazz the best type of music to run to? Jazz is good for everything, in my humble opinion.

I received a phone call from Mara as I was walking up my driveway. Seeing her name on the display sent minor waves of anxiety in my stomach since the last time I'd seen her had been during my brief stay at Chateau Jail.

"Hey, Mara. Please don't tell me the police have changed their mind and decided to arrest me after all."

"I'm sure if they had, they wouldn't bother calling me first."

"Good point. How can I help you?"

"I know you've got a lot going on with your businesses, but I was wondering if you'd be up for another investigation."

"What does this one concern? No cheating spouses, I hope."

"Nothing of the sort, at least I don't think that's an element of this one, but you never know. A man has been murdered. His sister reached out to me."

"How did she know to call you?"

"I'm not sure. I don't represent the family in any legal matters, and she didn't mention how she got my name. She did specifically ask for you, though."

"Does this have anything to do with a man getting stabbed in his home?" I asked.

"Yes. How did you know?"

I told Mara how I'd first learned of the murder from Alana, as well as my conversation with Detective Kalani.

"It had to be Detective Kalani then. I'm sure Alana would have said something to you. Is this something you're interested in or should I tell her you're going to pass?"

"I'm willing to talk to her. What time does she want to meet?"

"She said she had this morning available, around eleven, but I told her that might be too short notice."

"I can make that work. I'll see you in a couple of hours."

I ended the call with Mara and went inside the house to take a shower. If it was Detective Kalani who'd suggested the sister contact me, she must have called her shortly after our conversation at the café. She was a determined lady, and I didn't know if I was potentially making a mistake by playing into her hands. On the other hand, I could use an interesting investigation to get my mind off all the family and business drama. Foxx was handling the Harry's rebuild. It wasn't like I could accomplish much by standing beside him and watching the construction workers do their thing.

There was also Alana's feelings. She hadn't explained her suspicion of Detective Kalani's motives when we'd spoken the previous night. How would she react to me potentially taking the case, especially after I'd told her I was probably going to decline to help? Granted, I'd be working for a family member versus directly for the detective, but I didn't think that would make much difference to Alana. My curiosity had won out when I'd agreed to take the meeting at Mara's office. I decided to wait until after I'd heard what the sister had to say and then hopefully make a decision later in the evening.

The drive to Mara's office was a pleasant one. The sun was shining and there was a nice breeze that kept me cool as I traveled down the coast. I must admit to you that I felt a certain amount of excitement about the possibility of another investigation. It's strange to admit that because I'd had decidedly mixed emotions about them before. On the one hand, I'd enjoyed the thrill of the hunt and the mental battle between myself and the criminal. On the other, the close-up view of the crime is always a constant reminder of how people can be cruel to each other. The experience of seeing those things takes a little slice of you with it, and I wondered how long I could keep doing this before I would run out of pieces to give.

I arrived at Mara's and her assistant led me back to her office. Mara was about to give me some information about the potential client when the assistant returned and announced the arrival of Juliana Giordano. Mara asked her assistant to send her into the office, and Juliana entered a few seconds later. She was tall and slender, like Mara, and she had short black hair that was similar to styles I'd seen the actress Halle Berry wear. Juliana had olive skin and grey eyes, physical traits I'd seen a million times during my trips to Italy. Of course, the last name sort of gave away her ancestry.

Juliana, Mara, and I introduced ourselves and then we sat on furniture placed on the opposite side of the room from Mara's desk. Mara usually sat on the sofa with the client, while I took the matching chair off to the side. This morning was no different.

"Ms. Giordano, thank you for joining us. I understand you're looking for an investigator to look into the death of your brother, Marco," Mara said.

"That's right."

"Let me first say how sorry we are over the loss of your family member," Mara said.

"Thank you. Marco was a special person. If you're lucky, you may meet someone of his quality only once in your lifetime."

"I spoke briefly to the detective in charge of your brother's case," I said.

"She was the one who gave me your name," Juliana said, confirming what I'd already suspected.

"Did she say why she was recommending him? It seems a bit odd that she would recommend anyone outside of the department," Mara said.

"I was expressing to her how unhappy I've been regarding her performance."

Expressing? By that I assumed she meant she'd read Detective Kalani the riot act. Nevertheless, I enjoyed her use of "expressing" and decided to steal it in the future.

"It's been more than two weeks since my brother was stabbed in his own home," she continued. "It's obvious who the killer is, yet that detective won't do anything. I told her I was going to look into finding someone who could get the evidence we need."

"That's when she gave you my name?" I asked.

"Yes. She didn't hesitate. She told me your name and also gave me the name of Ms. Winters and said I could hire you through this firm. I must admit that I was a little taken aback when she threw out your name so quickly. I looked into you last night, but I didn't find much."

"Most of his work is done behind the scenes," Mara said. "It's doubtful you'd find anything, which is indicative of his discretion."

Juliana nodded.

"A moment ago you mentioned that you know who the killer is," I said.

"It's his wife, Sophia. Who else would it be?"

"Why do you think it's her?" Mara asked.

"She wants Marco's money. He told me how unhappy he'd been with her. He was going to leave her."

"Did he tell you he was leaving for certain?" I asked.

"No, not for certain, but I knew he was miserable. It was only a matter of time."

"I don't know much about your family, only that your brother owned a clothing line. Was your brother a wealthy man?" I asked.

"That depends on your version of wealthy," Juliana said.

"Did your brother have a will?" Mara asked.

"Yes, and he left everything to his wife. He even had a large life insurance policy that she'll receive."

"How do you know these things?" I asked.

"Because I asked him. Marco and I never kept anything from each other."

"Did you work for the clothing company?" I asked.

"I still do. I'm running things now, although I don't know for how long. Marco owned the majority share of the business. I suppose the company is hers now, too."

"Did your sister-in-law indicate what she intends to do with the business?" Mara asked.

"Not yet, and I've hesitated to ask her. I believe that if she were to be convicted of his murder, then that would nullify the will."

"That's correct. She also wouldn't be able to collect on the life insurance policy," Mara said.

It was a fact that I thought rather obvious, but perhaps it wasn't to some. It did raise an interesting question. Was this Juliana's main reasoning for pointing the finger at Sophia?

"What do you do for the business?" I asked.

"I'm the chief designer. Marco provided the funding for the business, and he started out as the main designer. As the company grew, he brought me into it. He got so busy with the marketing and business side of things that he slowly faded out of the design end."

"I'm just curious. Do you think the company can continue without him?" I asked.

"I'm not sure. He did so much there. I don't know the business side of things like he did. I helped some with the marketing but not much."

"I'm sure there are people you can hire who can help with those things," Mara said.

"If Sophia doesn't sell the company out from under me. Marco had a good offer a few months ago to sell the company, but he refused."

"Why?" Mara asked.

"He loved the work too much."

"Did he tell Sophia about the offer?" I asked.

"Yes, and she encouraged him to sell. She said she didn't think they'd ever get an offer like that again. She said the money would set them up for life. She was very upset when he said no."

Another motivation for murder, I thought.

"You said Marco was unhappy with Sophia. Do you know specifically what their problems were?" I asked.

"It was money, always money. She'd spend it as fast as Marco and I could make it. They'd argue about money all the time."

"Other than Sophia, is there anyone else who Marco was having issues with?" Mara asked.

"No, not that I know of."

"Was there anyone else he might have confided in?" I asked.

Juliana thought a moment.

Then she said, "Perhaps Eleanor. She worked as his marketing assistant."

"Is she still at the company?" I asked.

"Yes, and I can arrange for her to meet with you. Just let me know a time."

"Have you been in communication with Sophia since your brother's death?" I asked.

"Not much. I asked her if she needed help planning the funeral and she refused."

"Did she say why?" Mara asked.

"She just said that she could handle it."

"Is there anything else you'd like to tell me right now?" I asked.

"No. I'm sure I'll think of something as soon as I leave, though."

"Why don't we do this: I can meet you at your business tomorrow.

I can speak with Eleanor and perhaps you can provide me with a list of others I should talk to," I said.

Juliana reached into her purse and removed a business card, which she handed me.

"The address for the business is on there. Does ten o'clock work?" she asked.

"Yes. That's fine."

"Thank you for taking this case. I don't have a lot of faith in that detective, and Sophia can't be allowed to get away with this."

I didn't reply to her comment. Instead, I wished her a good day and stayed in Mara's office while Mara escorted Juliana to the door. Mara returned a moment later.

"How do you think that went?" she asked.

"About as I expected. I assumed she would blame the wife."

"It's usually the spouse, though, statistically speaking."

"Yes, but she also has a large motive for saying it's Sophia."

"The ownership of the business."

"It's clearly one of the most important things to her."

"I'm still fairly confused as to why Detective Kalani would offer up your services so quickly. She has to know it makes her look incompetent," Mara said.

"It is odd, but who would know she did that? I'm sure she's not telling her boss at work."

"What does Alana have to say about this?"

"Nothing specific. She seemed rather annoyed by Detective Kalani asking me for help, but she wouldn't say why."

"Is there tension between them in the office?"

"If there is, she didn't say."

"How's your sister-in-law doing?" Mara asked.

"Better. Thank you for asking."

"Let me know if there's anything I can do to help with Ms. Giordano's case."

"I will."

I said goodbye to Mara and walked out to my convertible. I thought about the case as I made the drive back to Kaanapali. We had a dead husband who'd been a wealthy business owner with a large insurance policy. If his sister was to be believed, we also had a wife who liked to spend all of his money and was angered by the fact he wouldn't sell his business for a huge payday. It seemed like a classic reason for murder, so why hadn't Detective Kalani been able to prove it? I also couldn't stop thinking about the fact that she'd given my name to Juliana? Why would she do that, and what kind of game was she playing?

9

TWO SIDES

"How close are you to Hani's house?" Alana asked.

"Maybe fifteen minutes."

"Can you do me a favor and head there now. I'm on my way."

"What's happened?"

"Bill came by. He tried to get into the house."

I'd been halfway back home when Alana had phoned. I'd assumed she was calling about my meeting with Mara and Juliana, but the tension in her voice from her first words told me I'd gotten that wrong. I'd assumed Bill had gotten out on bail, but I didn't know his status beyond that. I knew Foxx wasn't that far from Hani's house, either, so I phoned him and asked him to meet me over there. In hindsight, that was a huge mistake.

When I arrived at Hani's, I saw a squad car parked in front of her house. Hani was standing near the bottom of the driveway. She was speaking to two uniformed police officers. I recognized one of the officers, and he nodded to me as I approached.

Hani's mother's car was also in the driveway. Ms. Hu opened the front door of the house as I walked up the driveway.

"Edgar," she called out.

I walked over to her, and we both stood on the front porch.

"I'm glad you're here," she continued.

That was the first time I'd ever heard her say that.

"Were you here when Bill came over?"

"Yes. I was in the living room with Ava. Hani was in her office making some phone calls for an upcoming wedding."

Hani used a spare bedroom for her office. She'd often ask her mother to watch over Ava so she could shut the bedroom door and concentrate on her business.

"Did he try to break in?" I asked.

"He started banging on the door and screaming for us to let him in. I immediately called Alana, and she said she'd send a car over."

"Did he say what he wanted?" I asked.

"He blamed Hani for his arrest. He said he would get back at her. I yelled out the window and said that we'd called the police. He banged on the door for another minute and then he left."

I looked back to Hani. She was still speaking with the police.

"How is she holding up?"

"Better than what I would have expected. She was more angry than afraid."

"How is Ava?" I asked.

"She was scared. She's better now."

Both Ms. Hu and I turned when we heard a vehicle approaching. It was Foxx. He parked behind the police car and climbed out of his vehicle. He nodded to me and then walked over to Hani and the cops.

"What's he doing here?" Ms. Hu asked.

The hostility was clear in her voice.

"I called him and asked him to come over."

"Why would you do that?"

"I thought he could help."

"He's done enough," she said.

Ms. Hu turned from me and went back into the house. She shut the door behind her.

I had no idea what she was talking about, so I brushed it off and made my way down the driveway, just as the police wrapped up their report. I said hello to the two officers. We spoke for another minute and then they left while Hani, Foxx, and I stayed on the driveway.

"What are you doing here?" Hani asked Foxx, duplicating an earlier question by her mother.

"Poe called me."

"I'm fine. You can leave now," Hani said.

"What kind of greeting is that? I came by to help."

"Oh, you want to help? Is that right?" Hani asked.

"Why are you acting like this?" Foxx said, not exactly the smartest question to ask an angry woman. I know. I've made that mistake before.

"Are you going to try to deny it?"

"Deny what?"

"I know what you're doing. What I want to know is, was it your idea or that slut you're living with?"

"Hani, what the hell are you talking about?" Foxx asked.

"You're not getting custody of Ava. It's never going to happen."

Hani didn't wait for Foxx to respond. She turned from us and walked back to the house.

"Did you tell her what Ashley said?" Foxx asked.

It wasn't so much a question as it was a snarl.

"No, but I did tell someone. I really don't think she would have told Hani."

"Well, she must have."

As if on cue, Alana arrived. Neither Foxx nor I said a word as she exited her car and walked over to us.

"Is Hani okay?" Alana asked.

"Depends on what you're talking about. Thanks a lot by the way. Thanks a lot," Foxx said.

He didn't wait for Alana to reply. He walked back to his SUV, climbed inside, gunned the engine and sped off.

"What was he talking about?" Alana asked.

"Did you repeat to Hani what I told you about Ashley?"

"What about Ashley?"

"Her comments where she said that Foxx was possibly going to sue for full custody."

"Oh, no."

"So you did tell her?" I asked.

"No, but I spoke with my mother. I told her not to tell Hani."

There's something I've learned about the Hu family. Hani and her mother are the same person when it comes to gossip. If you tell them something, you may as well put it on the internet for everyone to see. The knowledge of that personality trait wasn't a big secret, and Alana was more than aware of it. So why had she told her mother about Ashley's threats? Did she intentionally tell her so that her mother would relate it to Hani, or had she said it in a moment of stress and anxiety? Once it was out, though, it was out. You may be wondering if I was upset with Alana. Of course I was, but I wasn't about to voice that, mainly because the fault really lay with me. I could have easily kept my mouth shut and not repeated Ashley's comments.

I tried to change the subject and told Alana what her mother had told me regarding Bill's arrival at Hani's house and his threat to get back at her, presumably for getting Foxx and me involved.

Alana and I went inside to check on Hani, who hadn't calmed down any, still angry from both Bill's appearance and her brief encounter with Foxx on the driveway. I won't transcribe the dialogue here, mainly because it's a repeat of things and emotions you already know.

We ended the conversation with Alana going back to work and me going home. I thought about calling Foxx and trying to broker a peace deal between him and Hani, but then I came to my senses and spent the afternoon swimming in the pool and playing with Maui. The little fella had become more than a companion for me. He was sort of a fur-covered stress relief ball who happened to like racing around the yard at top speed.

While I watched Maui play, I thought more about my conversation with Juliana and her opinions on the case of her brother's death. The same questions that I'd had as I was leaving Mara's office popped into my mind again. I decided that I still didn't have the answers and that I'd have to wait for my interviews with other people associated with the Giordano family.

I did do some research on their clothing line by bringing my laptop out to the poolside. The clothing line was called Pomaika'i. I had to look this up, but the word meant "Bliss," which I found an apt metaphor for life on the islands, although it certainly wasn't feeling that way at the moment. Their clothing line could best be described as fancy clothing for the tropics. Most of it was targeted toward women, but they did have several items for men. The colors all reminded me of things you'd see on and around Maui, whether it be the vibrant blue associated with the ocean or the magnificent greens, yellows, reds, and oranges that could be seen in the tropical landscapes.

The clothing was all modeled by women and men who looked like they were either Greek gods or had just been photoshopped that way. Everyone had a perfect body and, of course, all of the guys had more abs than I could count. How could I see that since they were modeling clothes, you might ask? Well, all the men had their shirts strategically open. I was scanning through the website while I was outside by the pool, so naturally I looked down at my own stomach and determined that I needed to add another mile to my jogging routine.

The website did have some pretty interesting quotes throughout its pages that centered on the word bliss. My favorites were, "Follow your bliss and the universe will open doors where there were only walls," by Joseph Campbell and "The philosophy of life is this: Life is not a struggle, not a tension. Life is bliss. It is eternal wisdom, eternal existence," by Maharishi Mahesh Yogi.

As I was about to close the web page, I realized they were missing probably the most famous bliss quote of all time. Know what it is? Of course. "Ignorance is bliss." It was an appropriate thought for the day as I wished I'd never been present for that conversation with Ashley.

I was about to settle in for the evening (yeah, I know, that's pretty much what I'd been doing all afternoon) when I received a phone call from Foxx. He asked if I was willing to meet him at a bar in Lahaina.

He first mentioned the bar where we'd had the fight with Bill and his two friends. Then I realized he was just joking. Instead, we agreed to rendezvous at a place down the street from there.

Alana wasn't due back for a couple of hours, so I sent her a text message when I was about to leave and told her I was going to meet with Foxx. She sent me a one word response: OK. I sort of expected more of an in-depth reply after everything that had gone on at Hani's house.

The bar had mostly tourists there, despite the fact that we were only a few weeks removed from the hurricane. I guess they already had their airline tickets purchased, as well as their vacation time set with their job, and they weren't about to miss out on some Maui time. The décor had an ocean vibe to it with a mix of water-themed items on the walls such a surf boards, fishing nets, and a faded orange life preserver. It was nothing original, and I'd seen much, much worse.

It was decidedly better than the last place we'd been which had celebrity photographs on the wall. It felt incredibly out of place and something you'd be more likely to see in a comedy club or New York deli. Besides, I'm pretty sure they were all cut out of magazines and had been faked since I couldn't imagine any celebrities actually going to a dump like that. I say all of this to explain why I was missing Harry's. Our place was much more laid back and authentic, and I definitely felt like a stranger at these bars.

Like last time, Foxx picked the stool at the end of the bar and I slid onto the seat beside him. We each ordered a beer, and the bartender placed the two bottles in front of us.

"Have you spoken to Hani since her house?" Foxx asked.

"No. I'm guessing Alana will check up on her."

"What does Alana have to say about Bill? Should Hani try to get a restraining order against him?"

"I suppose she can. It won't keep him away, but maybe it can add to his jail time if he violates it."

"I've got to do something about this guy. I can't have him scaring the hell out of my daughter like that."

I understood where Foxx was coming from, but I found it a bit odd that he didn't mention Hani in that same breath. I decided not to press the issue.

"I think I owe you an explanation," he continued.

"Regarding what?"

"This thing Ashley brought up about custody of Ava."

"You don't owe me anything, especially an explanation about that. What you guys do as parents is none of my concern."

"Nice try, but I'm not buying that. You spend a ton of time watching Ava, and I know how much you care about her."

"Sure, I do, but she's your child, not mine."

"I get that, but there's a second reason I want to talk to you about it. I'm guessing you think I'm crazy to be with Ashley."

I was tempted to make some smartass comment, like "The thought had crossed my mind," or "Now that you've mentioned it." Instead, I didn't respond.

"I know you and Alana thought I was nuts when I let her move in with me. I knew what she was doing," Foxx continued.

"So you knew it was going to be more than a two week visit?"

"She didn't say it, but I assumed as much. It wasn't like I was surprised. I invited her to come out when we were in Miami."

"This is none of my business, Foxx."

"We're friends, aren't we?"

"Why would you even ask that?"

"Because that's what friends do. They talk about this stuff."

"Are you asking for my opinion on something?"

"The whole custody thing, Ashley shouldn't have said what she said, but it wasn't like she just pulled that out of thin air."

"It was your idea?" I asked.

"Not exactly."

"Come on, Foxx. It either was or it wasn't."

"I was angry when I suggested it. Hani is a good mother, most of the time."

"Most of the time?"

"She admitted some things to me that really pissed me off."

"Like what?"

"She said she'd heard things about Bill."

"What kind of things?"

"She'd heard that he'd hit a woman before. Apparently, one of Hani's friends warned her about Bill, but she chose to ignore it. I don't know why. I asked her about it, and she couldn't, or wouldn't, give me an answer," Foxx said.

"I don't even know what to say about that."

"Look at this from my perspective. Hani's a parent now. Who she lets into her life is more important now than ever before. She let that bastard into her house with my kid present. She knew there was a possibility something like that could happen, but she still did it."

"When did she tell you this?" I asked.

"When I got out of jail. I went to her house to talk to her about what happened. We spoke for a long time, and she let it slip what her friend had told her."

"That's when you made the comment about the custody?"

"I didn't say one word to Hani about it, but I was still angry by the time I got home. Ashley assumed it was because I'd spent the night in jail. Don't get me wrong. I was still plenty pissed about that, but I told her how Hani knew about Bill's past. I told her that maybe I should get custody of Ava if Hani couldn't be trusted not to bring guys like that into our daughter's life."

"What happened after I left you and Ashley in your driveway the other day?" I asked.

"I told her not to say anything about custody. I told her I was just mad at Hani but that I didn't intend to sue for custody."

"What did she say about that?"

"She understood and she accepted it. I thought it was completely dropped until Hani confronted me about it today."

Enter my big mouth and the domino effect of me talking to Alana about it.

"Is there something I can do to help fix this?" I asked.

"No. I'll call Hani tomorrow. I'll try to reassure her that I have no intention of ending up in some kind of legal battle with her."

Foxx took a long pull from his beer and then put the empty bottle back on the bar.

"Where do you see things going with you and Ashley?" I asked.

"I don't know. We enjoy each other's company. Everything is great ninety-five percent of the time."

I didn't ask him about the remaining five percent, mainly because I thought that if he was hitting that high a statistic, then he was possibly happier than the majority of couples. It also made me realize that they were perhaps much closer to marriage than I'd originally thought. Of course, that was all just a technicality since Ashley and Foxx were already living with each other. A piece of paper wasn't really going to alter the reality of the situation.

"One more thing," Foxx said. "I'm sorry that Ashley made fun of your nickname."

"It's no big deal. I grew up with people making fun of the name Edgar. I'm kind of bulletproof when it comes to people making fun of my name."

"She was really hurt when we excluded her from that family gathering."

I tried to be objective and looked at it from her perspective. Ashley was an integral part of Foxx's life now, and I'd failed to invite her to the discussion. It wasn't just a failed invite, though. I hadn't even thought about her. That was the truth. The woman hadn't even entered my mind. That made me question whether or not I was putting out subconscious vibes that I disliked her. Perhaps Ashley was way more observant than I'd given her credit for.

The entire conversation with Foxx caused me to push the reset button on how I viewed Foxx, Ashley, and Hani and their interaction with each other. It was another example of how I just needed to stay out of it and let them do their thing.

I knew Foxx had never lied to me, at least I didn't think he had. But I had a really hard time accepting the fact that Hani would have knowingly dated a violent man and allowed him to come into her home, especially with her daughter present. She was a beautiful and successful woman. I thought she could have her pick of almost any guy she wanted, so why had she chosen a violent person like Bill? What was she thinking? Yes, it was judgmental of me to have those thoughts, but we're all that way whether we want to be or not.

I'm sure you're wondering whether or not I shared the contents of my discussion with Foxx to Alana after she got home, especially after the last conversation download had gone so badly. The answer was yes. I told Alana everything. The information was explosive, and I thought she needed to know that about her sister. I also wanted to reassure her that the whole custody thing was going nowhere, if Foxx was to be believed, and I had no reason to doubt his veracity.

Your next big question is: What was Alana's reaction? That's when things got even more interesting. I thought I was going to have heart palpitations. Forgive me if I'm sounding dramatic, but I was thinking of calling Hani and asking her if I could have some of her anti-anxiety medication. Alana accused Foxx of lying. She said he was covering for Ashley, but she didn't know why. Alana was convinced that it had been Ashley's idea to try to get custody from Hani. She believed Ashley wanted to take over Foxx's entire life, which obviously included Ava.

One of the things I've learned in life, and I'm not saying this to pander to female readers, is that women, on average, have way better instincts when it comes to people and their true motivations. I wasn't about to dismiss Alana's theories on Ashley and her potential Machiavellian schemes, even if that meant conceding that Foxx might have been less than honest with me. Sure, he might have viewed that lie as a harmless one and more of an attempt to keep the peace between his friend and his live-in girlfriend.

Alana and I went to bed without really agreeing on anything or coming up with any kind of action plan. I'd thought that we'd made a decision to stay out of it, but Alana now seemed to be leaning toward jumping into the situation with both feet. I might have been misreading her intentions, though, and her words could have been a result of her anger and less about her rational thoughts that might take over in the morning.

I fell asleep pretty quickly. It had been an exhausting day and I was beyond tired. I got up around two in the morning to use the restroom. When I came back to bed, I noticed Alana had her eyes open.

"Sorry if I woke you," I said.

"You didn't. I've been awake for at least an hour."

"What's wrong?"

Yes, it was a dumb question.

"I want you to promise me something."

"What is it?" I asked.

"If Foxx tries to take Ava, you'll help me protect Hani."

"He won't do that."

"Normally, I'd agree with you, but things have changed."

"Let's say he does want to do that, which he doesn't. His case would be relatively weak, and the courts always favor the mother."

"The courts favor the best attorney, and money gets you that. Hani's business is doing better than it ever has. She can't compete with Foxx, though, and what if he suddenly stops paying child support as a strategy against her?" Alana asked.

"I think these hypotheticals are way overboard. None of this is going to happen."

"You don't know that. And not preparing for all contingencies is a surefire way to failure."

"You make it sound like a battle plan."

"I wouldn't call it that."

"You said you wanted me to help protect Hani. What exactly are you asking me to do?"

"If this becomes a legal battle, and I acknowledge that it's a big 'if,' I'd like your promise that we can help her financially."

This was a moment I never thought I'd see. Alana was asking me to fund a legal battle between her sister and my best friend and business partner. Sure, this was all hypothetical as Alana had just mentioned, but I don't throw out promises lightly. I had to consider that this was a real possibility and then ask myself what my reaction would be. It really wasn't about Hani, though. It was about someone else. On one side there was my wife and her request of a promise. On the other was my best friend and his perceived intentions. There was really no question who would win.

"I would back Hani."

"Why?" Alana asked.

"Because you asked me to, and I know what it takes for you to do that, especially where Foxx is concerned."

"Thank you. I know you think I'm being irrational, but I've seen families tear each other apart. They never think it can happen, but it does all the time."

It was a true statement if I'd ever heard one, and I began to question whether it really could happen to us. I was about to respond to Alana when her cell phone rang on the nightstand. She turned and looked at the display.

"It's Hani," she said.

The next few hours went by in what seemed like fifteen minutes. Bill had returned to Hani's house in the middle of the night and thrown a brick through Ava's bedroom window.

Alana and I drove separately to Hani's house since Alana thought she might end up at the station afterward. Hani and Ava were pretty shaken, as I'm sure you would expect them to be. I did a quick walk around the outside of the house but didn't see anyone.

I went back into the house. Hani, Ava, and Alana were in the living room. I walked past them and went to Ava's bedroom where I saw a fist-sized rock on the carpet. I looked at the window and saw the rock had entered through one of the lower panes. Fortunately, Ava's bed was on the opposite wall and the rock hadn't land anywhere near her, not that that lessened the severity of what happened.

I walked into Hani's office, which was the room across the hall from Ava's. I'd bought a small laptop specifically for Hani's new security system. It was way overkill since the security company stored the footage on their servers, but I wanted the ability to access the footage without having to wait on them. I had the same setup at my house.

I logged onto the computer and pulled up the footage from the backyard cameras. I had two cameras placed on each back corner of the house. These were state-of-the-art cameras, and they could record equally well in the day and at night. I selected the camera closest to Ava's bedroom and clicked on a time a few minutes before Hani's phone call to Alana. I'd only been watching for ninety seconds or so before I saw Bill, or at least the person I assumed was Bill, enter the camera's field of view. He was dressed in a black hoodie that was pulled over his head so the camera couldn't see his face. He was also wearing gray board shorts. He already had the rock in his hand, and he threw it at Ava's window. The camera was only a few feet from her room, so it looked like the rock was coming straight for the lens.

Bill didn't flee immediately afterward. He stood in place and looked up toward the window. The black hoodie still obscured his face. He made an obscene gesture with his hand and then walked out of the camera's frame. I rewound the video a few seconds and then froze it on the moment Bill was raising his finger. I chose that spot because Bill had his head raised and I hoped I'd be able to make out his face if I could zoom in. I right clicked on the frame and exported a JPEG still image of the video, which I saved to the desktop. I zoomed into the image and tried to make out his face. I couldn't. Despite the camera's high resolution, the image still broke down into large pixels, further concealing his identity. I also exported the video clip as a QuickTime file. I emailed both files to myself and to Alana's personal and work email addresses.

Bill's middle finger salute raised an interesting question. Had Hani been yelling at him from the bedroom window or had he known the camera was there and he was delivering a message to her? Either way, he'd committed another crime and we'd caught him in the act. But would he go back to jail since his face had been hidden? I didn't know.

I walked back to the living room just as the police were arriving to file a report. Hani talked them through what had happened as I took over watching Ava. The little girl was still crying. I can't say I blamed her. As I tried to console her, I thought about my earlier conversation with Alana. Foxx had to be told about this, and it didn't take a rocket scientist to figure out what his response was going to be. He had every right to be furious and every right to question whether or not Ava was safe in this house. The security system would only work so far. It couldn't stop Bill from breaking down the door and shooting Hani and/or Ava. I hated even imagining that, but it would have been irresponsible not to.

I somewhat blamed myself for this. I questioned whether Bill would be taking things to such an extreme if I hadn't gone to his house to seek revenge for his attack on Hani during the hurricane. That had led to another fight outside the bar and his subsequent arrest. Maybe these things would never have happened if Hani had just broken up with the guy. Then I came to my senses and realized I was making excuses for the guy's deplorable behavior.

Bill needed to be dealt with swiftly. Hopefully, the police would handle that. They had the assault charge against him, and now they had this attack on Hani's home. I would give them a chance to make things right. If they couldn't, then I'd need to come up with a Plan B.

It was close to four in the morning before the police left. Hani took Ava to her master bedroom since the little girl was too scared to go back to her own. I told Alana I would stay at the house until later that morning when I planned on contacting a local firm that provided security personnel. I'd hired them before on previous cases and felt confident they could deal with Bill should he return to Hani's before the police found him.

Alana went home to shower and get dressed for work. Hani came to the living room after Ava had finally gone to sleep. She sat beside me on the sofa. I thought back to the first time I'd met her. I'd been dating Alana for a while and didn't even know she had a sister. The two women hadn't been getting along back then, and Hani had been living in Los Angeles for a while. She'd returned to Maui to announce her surprise engagement. I won't say more than that right now, but it was pretty weird to have come from that kind of introduction to now be sitting here in the early morning and hoping her abusive exboyfriend wouldn't come back to the house. How the hell did we even get to this point?

"Thank you for staying with me," Hani said.

"It's not a problem. I'm sorry this is happening."

"I know what you're thinking. You're wondering when I'm going to call Foxx about this."

"That's not what I was thinking," I said, but let's be honest. It was.

"I'll call him in a couple of hours."

She paused for several seconds.

Then she said, "I've tried so hard to protect her. I can't believe I let this threat in."

"Blaming yourself for Bill's actions isn't going to do any good. Besides, you're not to blame for anything. You picked the wrong guy. That's it."

"He's not going to stop until he kills me."

"That's not going to happen."

"I'm going to ask Foxx if Ava can stay with him for a while."

"Are you sure you want to do that?" I asked.

"What else am I supposed to do? She's all that matters to me. She needs to be safe, even if it means me losing her."

"Losing her? Why would that happen?"

"Because I'm afraid once he gets her, he and Ashley won't give her back."

"So stay with Alana and me. It's only a matter of time before the police get this guy anyway. I'm sure they'll have him in the next few hours."

"And then what? He goes to jail for a day or two and then he's out on bail. The police don't care. You should have seen the way they looked at me while they were writing the report. They couldn't wait to get out of here, even with Alana at my side."

"Even if you're right about those two cops, and I don't think you are, you're badly underestimating your sister. You think she's going to let Bill get away with this? She's already out looking for him."

I waited for Hani to respond, but she didn't.

"As far as Ashley is concerned, I wouldn't worry about her. She has no say in any of this, and I was just talking to Foxx last night. He doesn't want to take custody from you. He thinks you're doing a great job as Ava's mother," I continued.

"Then why did Ashley say what she said?" Hani asked.

"Because Ashley is an idiot. I'm sorry, but it's the truth. I suspect she was just sucking up to Foxx and saying what she thought he wanted to hear, but it's not. She guessed wrong."

"Are you sure about that?"

"Yes, I'm positive," I said.

I wasn't, though, not by a long shot.

10

ELEANOR HADLEY

IT TOOK WAY LESS TIME FOR THE POLICE TO FIND BILL THAN I THOUGHT it would. In retrospect, I wasn't sure what I expected him to do after leaving Hani's house. The guy had just thrown a rock through the bedroom window of a child. He had to have known it was a crime, but I didn't know if that meant he was going to try to hide somewhere, such as a friend's house. He didn't, though.

The police found him in his home. According to Alana, he wasn't wearing either the black hoodie or gray shorts when he came to the door. The police asked him if he'd gone to Hani's house that night. He denied it. They asked him if he owned a black hoodie and gray shorts. He said that he did but so did most of the guys on Maui. That was a true statement. I owned both articles of clothing myself. Ultimately, they had no solid evidence on which to arrest him, so Bill got away with it.

Hani, despite still being scared from the rock attack, asked me not to call the security team. She said she didn't want their presence to frighten Ava, and she was worried they'd make her feel like a prisoner in her own home. I disagreed but acquiesced. It wasn't my child or my home and there was really nothing more I could do.

I drove home, showered, and put on fresh clothes for my meeting at Pomaika'i. I arrived on time and saw Juliana Giordano standing outside underneath a clean, modern sign that said Pomaika'i. There was nothing below the company name to indicate they were a fashion line or any other kind of business for that matter. The space that housed the Giordano clothing company was much larger than I expected it to be. They didn't have a retail storefront. Rather, Pomaika'i was located in an industrial section of Kahului.

Juliana was smoking a cigarette. She didn't wave or nod to me as I climbed out of my convertible. Instead, she dropped the cigarette on the sidewalk and ground it out with her high-heeled shoe. I tried to judge her mood as I approached her. She had a serious expression that could have been interpreted any number of ways.

She nodded toward my BMW.

"How many of those are on the island?"

"I have no idea. So far I've only seen mine."

"It's beautiful. A little old, though. Don't you think?"

I found it beyond strange that she would both compliment and insult my vehicle as a way of greeting me to her company. If there's one thing I've learned about these investigations, it's that people are far odder than you could ever imagine.

"I don't see it as old. It's approaching classic status in my mind."

She didn't respond except to offer a half smile. I wasn't sure if she found my comment somewhat amusing or if it was more of a pity smile.

I followed Juliana inside where I saw a small reception area. A woman with short blond hair and blue eyes was sitting behind a desk and entering some sort of data into a large Mac computer. She looked up at me but didn't smile. Then she turned back to her computer screen and started typing again. Another strange greeting, I thought. Had these people never heard of manners?

Juliana didn't bother introducing me to the young woman. Instead, we walked past her and headed down a hallway that led to four offices, two on the left and two on the right. I glanced in the rooms as we passed. They all had small desks and Mac computers in the same model as the one I'd seen in the front lobby.

We eventually entered a warehouse space that was located in the back of the building. It looked like an odd combination of a designer shop and a storage facility. There were several tables with clothing materials and design patterns scattered on top of them, but it also had dozens of boxes of what I assumed was inventory stacked on tall industrial metal shelves.

There was only one person in the warehouse space. She was a woman of average height and maybe thirty-five years old. She had long brown hair that was pulled to one side. She stood in front of one of the designer tables and looked over several of the fabric samples.

"These are beautiful, Juliana," she said.

"Eleanor, this is the gentleman I was talking to you about."

Juliana turned to me.

"This is Eleanor Hadley. She worked side by side with my brother for the last few years," Juliana continued.

"It's a pleasure to meet you," I said.

Eleanor gave me a half smile but said nothing.

"I'll leave you two so you can speak in private," Juliana said.

"Thank you," I said.

I walked closer to the table and looked at the fabrics. They were beautiful, as Eleanor had said.

"Are these for some of the new designs?" I asked.

"Yes. Juliana just got them in."

"How often do you release new clothing designs?"

"At least three to four times a year. Juliana is very good about putting out fresh designs. Customers get bored so quickly. They're always looking for the next thing. It's tough to keep up, though. We have a small staff here. It's almost too much for us."

"I've heard your hard work has paid off. Sounds like the company's designs are very much in demand. Just curious, where do most of your sales come from? Retail or online?"

"We have a few retail locations on the island, but they represent just a small fraction of our sales. Most of it is online. The online profit margins are higher, too."

"Why have the retail stores then?"

"That's how a lot of people discover us. They come to Hawaii, and they eventually get bored with the beach. They go out shopping, and they see some dress they like or a shirt for their husbands. Our clothing is of very high quality. They get home to the mainland and then decide they want to order more items."

"So it's the repeat business."

"I guess you could say that. What exactly do you want to speak with me about?" she asked.

"Juliana said you helped Marco with the marketing of Pomaika'i. Is that correct?"

"Yes. He brought me on as his personal assistant. After a while, I started helping him more and more with the marketing. Now I do that full time."

"I'm sure you get to know someone pretty fast when you're their assistant."

"You have to if you want to keep your job."

"What kind of person was Marco?" I asked.

"Very driven. Very focused. He knew exactly what he wanted and what he didn't."

"When was the last time you saw Marco?"

"The day before he was killed. I helped him get the office ready for the storm."

"How did he seem?"

"He was more annoyed than anything else."

"Annoyed?"

"Marco was obsessed with his work. We were prepping a fashion show to introduce the new line. All of that came to a halt with the hurricane."

"Do you know if Marco was having fights with anyone?" I asked.

Eleanor looked away.

"I'm not sure I want to talk about that," she said.

Was she serious? What did she think we were going to talk about?

"I'll take that as a yes."

She turned back to me.

"All couples fight."

"I assume you're talking about Marco and Sophia."

Eleanor nodded.

"What were they arguing about?" I asked.

"I never heard them, but Marco was always complaining about how much money Sophia spent. It's not easy making this company work. Fashion is an extremely competitive marketplace, and the margins aren't as big as people think. It's hard to make money when you're up against massive online stores. That's why we have to be the best. Our designs have to inspire people. We have to give them a reason to spend more money with us. Sophia didn't care about any of that. She just wanted the proceeds. Marco said he was going to cut her off."

"So he wasn't just upset about the money. You think he was upset about her lack of appreciation for your efforts?"

"That's right. She had no interest in any of this. Just what it could get her."

"What about Juliana?"

"What about her?"

"What kind of relationship did she have with Sophia?"

"It was fine, I guess."

"You guess?"

"I never heard them arguing, if that's what you're asking."

"That's surprising."

"Why?"

"With Juliana being the head designer, I would think that she'd be very invested in this place. I'm sure she was deeply upset over Sophia's spending habits. They could have sunk this company."

"If she said anything, then it must have been to Marco."

"What did Juliana say about me?" I asked.

"What do you mean?"

"When she told you that she wanted you to speak with me, what did she say?"

"She said she'd hired an investigator to find out who killed Marco. She asked me to help you in any way that I could."

"In addition to his wife, was there anyone else Marco was having trouble with? An employee, a competitor?" I asked.

"No. There was no one."

"Is there anything else that you can think of that might help me?"

"Nothing. Do you think you're going to be able to find the killer? The police haven't been able to do anything."

"I'll do my best. That's all I can promise."

I thanked Eleanor for her time and walked back to the office area where I found Juliana behind a computer in one of the four offices. I thought the office was strangely decorated. Actually, that's probably not the best way to describe it. There were simply no decorations at all. No paintings or photographs. No color on the wall. Not even any fabric samples similar to what I'd seen in the warehouse. It was a stark white office with uncomfortable looking furniture. I found it odd that someone who could design such attractive clothing could do so in such a dull environment.

"How did everything go?" she asked.

"It went fine. She was very helpful."

"Eleanor has worked more closely with him than anyone but me."

"Is there anyone else here I should meet? Maybe the woman in the lobby?"

"No. She mainly just answers the phones. She knew Marco, of course, but she has no idea what's really going on with the business. There are other employees, of course, but they mainly deal with order fulfillment, shipping, that sort of thing. They didn't really know Marco well, and I don't see how they could be involved in his death."

"Does Sophia know about my investigation?" I asked.

"Not yet, and I don't intend to tell her."

"Do you think Eleanor will?"

"No. She's very discreet."

I asked Juliana if I could have a look at Marco's office. She took me directly across the hall. His office had the same white walls and the same uncomfortable-looking furniture. However, there were several photographs hanging on the walls. They were shots similar to the ones I'd seen on the Pomaika'i website where various models show-cased the clothing.

"It's beautiful photography," I remarked.

"Thank you. You wouldn't believe what the models and the photographers cost, but it sells the product, much better than just showing the clothing against a white background."

"Eleanor mentioned something about a fashion show. Is that still going to happen?"

"Probably not. It just seems wrong to put on some glitzy show now that Marco's gone."

"Perhaps that would be a good way to celebrate his life and what was obviously a passion for him."

Juliana didn't respond, but I thought she'd absorbed my words and was thinking about them. She led me back to the lobby. I looked at the receptionist as I was leaving. She made brief eye contact with me and smiled. I smiled back, but neither of us said anything.

I thanked Juliana again for arranging the interview. I exited the building and walked back to my convertible. I climbed inside, started the car, and drove away.

I hadn't really accomplished much during the interview. Yes, Eleanor had confirmed what Juliana had told me about Sophia's spending habits, but I wasn't sure how much I could trust that second opinion. Juliana was presumably Eleanor's boss, at least by family connections. It wasn't like Eleanor was going to contradict her, and I had a feeling Juliana had told her what she wanted me to know. Why did I think that?

It was the dramatic look away Eleanor did when I asked her if Marco had been fighting with anyone. Yes, that's a common physical tell that people often do, but it hadn't come off as natural to me. She had looked like a bad soap opera actor reacting to her character being told her husband was having an affair with another woman. The only thing that was missing to make it more staged was if she'd placed the back of her hand against her forehead and proclaimed that she might faint.

Need more proof? Her hesitation had only lasted a few seconds before she'd gone into a long monologue about how hard they had to work and Sophia never appreciated it. That could have been all true, but it seemed rehearsed to me, like Juliana had written a script and put it on a teleprompter for Eleanor to repeat word for word. I wouldn't have been surprised to find out that Juliana had installed a microphone in the warehouse and had been monitoring the entire conversation.

Furthermore, where were the other employees Juliana had mentioned? This was supposed to be a decent-sized fashion line yet there were only three employees in the building. Did everyone else work different hours, or had Juliana given them the time off so I couldn't interact with them and discover a conflicting opinion on Marco?

I wasn't sure what my next move should be outside of speaking with Sophia, but I wasn't ready to do that just yet. I was about to call Alana and ask for an update on Bill when I noticed a folded piece of paper stuck in the cup holder of my car. I waited until I got to a stop light and then opened the paper. It had just two things written on it: a phone number and a time, five o'clock.

11

THE NOTE

THERE WERE THREE OPTIONS. THE FIRST WAS THAT JULIANA HAD LEFT the note in my car. That didn't really make a lot of sense since she could have easily spoken to me in her office. Option two was also far-fetched. Eleanor had left it. The third and only sensible option was that the Pomaika'i receptionist had left it. Perhaps that had been the reason she hadn't said anything. Maybe she didn't want to draw attention to a potential interaction with me, especially in front of Juliana.

In my experience, receptionists are often the ones who really know what's going on, despite Juliana's claims that her receptionist knew nothing. Offices tend to get really busy and the employees stop noticing that the receptionist is always there in the background, listening to every word that's being said and often taking notes. Her desk was relatively close to the offices. It probably wasn't that hard to eavesdrop without anyone noticing.

I made a detour on my way home and swung by Harry's to see where things were at with the construction. Foxx wasn't there, but the construction crew was. They were busy framing the new walls. We were a long way from reopening, but it was good to see things moving in that direction.

I got back home and took Maui for a long walk. I went in the direction opposite to Foxx's house since I didn't want to get into another discussion about Hani or Ashley or any other topic that somehow connected to child custody, abusive boyfriends, or manipulative girlfriends.

As I returned home I saw a person at my front door. I was a little slow on guessing who it was, which I'm more than happy to blame on my lack of sleep, but I finally recognized Ashley as she turned around and headed toward the sidewalk. I was tempted to grab the dog and dive behind a nearby tree. Unfortunately, there wasn't one. I intentionally slowed, hoping that she'd somehow not look in my direction as she walked down my driveway. It didn't work.

"Poe," she called out.

She stopped when she got to the bottom of my driveway and waited for me to get there. Did you notice that she called me Poe? I did.

"Good afternoon, Ashley."

"I'm so glad I caught you."

Caught was an appropriate word, I thought.

"How can I help you?"

"I just want to apologize for my attitude the other day."

"Oh, what attitude is that?" I asked, and I'd like to pat myself on the back and possibly give myself an acting award for not having an ounce of sarcasm in my voice when I asked that little question.

"I was upset for not having been invited to the family gathering. I was out of line speaking to you the way I did. I also feel really bad for making fun of your name."

"It's not a big deal."

"It is. I know how much you've done for Foxx over the years. You guys are such good friends, and I don't want there to be any tension between us."

"So why are you acting like such a bitch?" Okay, I didn't really say that out loud, but I did ask the question in my mind.

"That's very thoughtful of you," I said.

"This thing with Hani is very stressful. The last thing you guys need is me making things worse. Foxx is very concerned about Ava. I hear about it all the time. I'm not complaining. That's what partners do. I was just upset after a long conversation he and I had. I let my emotions get the better of me."

"That happens to me all the time. I completely understand. I appreciate your willingness to come down here and let me know how you feel. It means a lot."

I was about to make some sort of wrap up comment to end the conversation when I noticed a car driving down the street. Again, I'll blame my general fatigue on my brain's slow reaction. It wasn't until the vehicle slowed down that I realized it was Hani behind the wheel. This wasn't going to be good.

Hani slowed to a stop. I stepped back since I assumed she wanted to turn onto my driveway. Ashley, who was currently standing in the middle of the driveway, didn't move. She just looked at the car for three or four seconds. Hani put her turn signal on. Ashley still didn't move. I held my breath and waited for Hani to blast the horn. She didn't, thank God.

"I think she's trying to turn onto my driveway," I said.

"Is she?" Ashley asked.

"Yes. Perhaps you should step to the side."

Ashley finally moved and walked over to me.

"Anyway, thank you for accepting my apology. Maybe you and Alana can come over one night soon and have dinner with us. I'd love for us all to spend more time together."

"That would be nice. I'll mention it to Alana."

"Great. Talk to you soon."

Ashley turned away from me without looking at Hani, and with that little gesture, completely nullified all of the goodwill she tried to spread with her fake apology. I assumed Foxx had asked her to be nicer to me, and I appreciated his efforts. Despite my earlier second-guessing of my actions and attitudes toward Ashley, I came to the conclusion (for the seventy-ninth time, but who's counting) that I didn't like the lady and probably never would.

I turned to Hani and saw her getting Ava out of the backseat of her car.

"Did Alana call you?" she asked.

"Not for a while. What's up?"

"She invited us to stay with you guys until things with Bill calm down."

I'd made the same invitation while at Hani's house, but she'd rejected it. Apparently, Alana had been able to convince her.

"Ava's very excited. I told her we're going to have a sleepover with Maui. She can't wait," Hani continued.

Yes, I know. I rate lower than the dog, but Maui is a tough act to beat.

"I appreciate you being open to this. Maybe I can actually get some sleep tonight," she continued.

"Of course. Can I help you carry anything in?" I asked.

"I have our bags in the back."

"Let me take the dog inside and then I'll get your bags."

I walked Maui back into the house where he proceeded to chase Ava around the living room, much to her delight. He ended their game by doing a dramatic roll onto his back so she could scratch his chest. She laughed with delight, and I was glad the little dog could help ease Ava's drama from that morning.

I went back outside to get Hani's bags and was somewhat surprised to see that she'd managed to cram six suitcases into the trunk of her car and the backseat. How long did she intend on staying?

I carried everything into the house - it took multiple trips - and I brought all of her luggage into one of the spare bedrooms.

Hani asked me if I could watch Ava for a few hours as she had multiple calls to make for an upcoming wedding. I'd suddenly become her innkeeper as well as her babysitter. I felt a little bad about complaining, mainly because I knew how much she'd been through, and I had made the offer to help her in any way I could.

The three of us - Ava, Maui and myself - spent the afternoon in and around the swimming pool. It ended up being a relaxing event, and it managed to calm my mind somewhat. Before I knew it, the time was approaching five o'clock. Hani was still busy with her phone calls. She'd been in my office for close to five hours and not the aforementioned three, so I decided to make my own call under the patio umbrella.

I called the number on the note and was surprised to hear Eleanor answer.

"Is this Eleanor?" I asked.

"Yes."

"You had the receptionist put the note in my car. That's why you were in the warehouse when I arrived and not in your office. It would have been too easy for Juliana to have spotted the receptionist walking out the door and over to my car," I guessed.

"That's right."

"What do you want to talk to me about?"

"I want to amend my comments from our earlier interview. Sophia isn't anything like I described her."

"Okay. How is the situation different?"

"It's true that she likes to spend money, but Marco was okay with all of it. In fact, he encouraged it. He was always showering her with gifts."

"I take it that means they had a strong relationship."

"Sophia could do no wrong in Marco's eyes. He really loved her. I worked with him every day, and I never once heard him say anything bad about her."

"Did Juliana tell you what to say to me? Did she threaten you in any way?"

"There was nothing direct, but the message was clear."

"Which was?" I asked.

"She thinks Sophia killed Marco. She's also convinced Sophia is going to sell the company and we'll all be out of a job."

"Do you agree with that?"

"I don't think Sophia murdered Marco. I just can't see that happening. But if you ask me about her selling the company, then yes, she may very well do that. Marco got an offer to sell the company, and he almost did. Sophia was disappointed when he didn't. Even then they weren't really fighting. She made her opinion known, but Marco wasn't interested in selling."

"Why do you think Sophia wanted him to sell?"

"Because the job was so stressful for Marco. He was always working. We both averaged close to seventy hours a week. I still do. Marco and Sophia didn't see each other nearly as much as she wanted. She thought it was the best thing for him, at least that's what he told me she said."

"Do you think Juliana knew how Marco felt about Sophia's spending?"

"Of course she did, but she wanted to take that money and hire more people to help with the company. She thought we could get a lot bigger if we just had help. I think she resented Marco spending it on expensive gifts for Sophia."

"Juliana told me that Marco owned the majority share of the company. Did you know that?"

"Everyone did. It was common knowledge with the employees."

"Did Juliana ever mention anything about that to you?"

"In what way?" she asked.

"I'm wondering if she ever expressed dissatisfaction with her lack of company shares."

"I knew she didn't think it was fair."

"She said that specifically?"

"No, but Marco did. We were having lunch one day after meeting with a supplier. Marco seemed bothered by something, so I asked him what was wrong. I must have caught him at a weak moment because he told me Juliana was pressing him to give her a larger share of the company. She wanted to be equal partners."

"What did he think about that?"

"He was completely against it. I don't think it had anything to do with the money. He just didn't want to be in a situation where he had to answer to anyone else."

"You said you caught him in a weak moment. What did you mean by that?"

"Marco rarely spoke about Juliana, at least not in the way family talks about one another. We would speak about what she was doing for the business, but he never expressed an opinion about her as a sibling, either good or bad."

"Did they seem to work well together?" I asked.

"Yes, and that was the only time I saw him upset. I wouldn't even say he was mad. He didn't seem to hold it against her. He was just stressed that he wasn't going to be able to give her what she wanted."

"So who do you think killed Marco?" I asked.

"I have no idea. He got along with everyone. The man had a magnetic personality. He was larger than life. People just flocked to him."

"I appreciate you telling me this. I won't mention any of it to Juliana."

"Thank you."

I ended the call just as Hani opened the sliding glass door and called out to Ava. The little girl went back into the house. Maui opted to stay outside with me.

The phone call with Eleanor had been an interesting one, and it confirmed my theory that she hadn't been truthful with me during our initial interview. It had the possibility of shifting the number one suspect from Sophia to Juliana, but I didn't really see what Juliana would have gained if she'd killed Marco. She'd clearly known that Marco's shares would go to his wife upon his passing. She'd also known that Sophia was in favor of selling the company, so everything would have been in jeopardy if Marco was out of the picture.

On the other hand, a murderer can't inherit property from the victim, as we'd discussed earlier, so there was a good reason Juliana might have killed her brother and then pointed the finger squarely in Sophia's direction. If Juliana had killed her brother, or hired someone to do it for her, then they'd done a fairly lousy job of framing the wife.

I'd spent several hours in the sun, and I was thirsty. I stood and turned to Maui before I walked into the house to grab a bottle of water.

"Come on, Maui. Let's go inside."

I started to walk toward the door when I realized the dog wasn't following me like he normally did. I turned back to him and saw he was still sitting by my chair. He seemed to have no intention of going back inside. Was he predicting a crazy evening with the Hu women, and so decided to stay in the backyard for as long as possible? Probably. I debated whether I should grab a sleeping bag and spend the night outside with him.

12

THE APOLOGY – SORT OF

THE NEXT FOUR OR FIVE DAYS WENT BY WITH ME MAKING LITTLE progress on the Marco Giordano murder. I still hadn't interviewed Sophia yet, mainly because I wanted to get more information before speaking with the chief suspect. Most of my investigative activities consisted of online research, which didn't yield many results in terms of the individual players. I felt like I had a pretty good handle on the history of the Pomaika'i clothing company, but that was about it.

So, how had I spent the bulk of my time since my entire online sleuthing had probably taken up just a few hours? I was on babysitting duty. Hani predominantly spent her days either in my home office making phone calls or running around the island for meetings at various hotels and other wedding venues. I guessed she assumed I was always available to watch Ava since she usually wouldn't ask me if I was okay with it until she was literally about to walk out my door. There was a part of me that was put off by her presumptuousness. There was another part that thought I was overreacting since it wasn't like I was ever going to say no to taking care of the little girl.

I didn't see or speak much to Foxx during the day. He was preoccupied with the rebuilding of Harry's. He did come by each night to spend time with Ava, as well as to show me photographs of the construction progress. Hani had told him about the rock thrown through Ava's bedroom before she'd left her house to stay with Alana and me. I'd asked her what his reaction was, and she said he was trying to remain calm since he had no desire to end up in jail again. Foxx and I didn't speak about it on his nightly visits, and I wasn't sure if that's because he didn't want to have the conversation with Ava around or if he was trying to be patient and wait to see if the judge was going to sentence Bill to any jail time for his attack on us.

It was kind of an odd thing for Foxx to see his daughter in my house versus his, but he seemed okay with her staying in the same place her mother was. Ashley didn't come by for the visits, and neither Foxx nor I brought up her little trip to see me and apologize. We all seemed to be in denial mode, or at least don't-talk-about-it mode, and I thought that might actually be a good thing for the time being.

I'd ordered a replacement window pane for Hani's house, and it arrived late in the week. I'm not nearly as handy as Foxx is, but it seemed like a fairly simple process to snap one window section out and put the new one in.

There was no one available to watch Ava since Hani was out on another round of meetings. I hadn't mentioned to Hani that I was planning to repair her window that morning. I'd barely seen her before she'd left the house. After a morning of playing and relaxing by the pool, I walked with Ava out to my SUV for the drive to Hani's. I'd bought a car seat for Ava, and it was almost always strapped into the backseat, even when I'd go weeks without babysitting her. I brought Maui along for the ride.

Here was an interesting thing that I forgot to mention earlier. Ms. Hu's car had broken down and was in the shop. Ms. Hu didn't want to pay for a rental car so Hani had lent her mother a car, figuring that she could borrow one of my vehicles. I told Hani she was welcome to, and imagine my surprise when I walked into my garage the next day and found my convertible gone. I'd assumed, falsely, that Hani would have known the BMW was my main ride. I had to admit, though, that she probably looked better driving it around the island than I did.

As we approached her house, Ava asked me when she and her mother would be returning home. I made up some story about them staying with Alana and me as part of a big game. It was a lame excuse, but what else was I going to say? I also had no idea how to truthfully answer Ava. We hadn't spoken much to Hani in regards to how long she wanted to stay. There was still no guarantee Bill would spend significant time in prison. I thought it likely, but I also wouldn't have been surprised if he got off with a slap on the wrist. Justice always seemed to be unpredictable at best.

I parked in Hani's driveway and took Ava and Maui into the house. Then I returned to the SUV to fetch the replacement window part. I'd just finished the repair in Ava's bedroom when I heard the doorbell ring. Maui immediately went into crazy mode and rushed to the front door. I walked to the foyer and squeezed myself between the dog and the door. I looked through the peephole and was surprised to see Ryan Campbell, Bill's friend, standing on the porch. The last time I'd seen him, I was smashing a baseball bat across his back multiple times. This was going to be good.

I pulled open the door and kept Maui back with one of my legs. I didn't say anything to Ryan, though. I was more interested in seeing the reaction on his face. He didn't disappoint me. His eyes went wide and he took a step backward. Neither of us said anything for a few seconds, and I thought he might just turn and leave.

Then he said, "I'm looking for Hani."

"She's not here."

"Do you know when she'll be back?"

"No, I don't."

"Can you deliver a message for me?"

"That depends on what it is."

"Please tell her I'm sorry."

"Sorry for what?" I asked.

"I was the one who introduced her to Bill."

"I thought they met at one of her weddings."

"They did, but Hani and I have known each other a while. I was sort of the one who played matchmaker."

"I thought he was your friend. Now you're sorry?"

"He was my friend. Not anymore."

"You don't appreciate getting arrested with him?"

"I'm sorry I was there that night. I never should have called him when I saw you guys at that bar."

"You didn't just call him, Ryan. You came at us with baseball bats."

"It wasn't my idea. He showed up with those things."

"That's your excuse? He handed it to you? You could have said no. You could have walked away. Instead, you tried to kill me."

"And I'm probably going to serve time because of it."

Was that supposed to make me feel bad for him? I asked myself.

"What did Bill tell you? What would make you want to crush my head in?"

"He said you kicked the hell out of him because he wouldn't break-up with Hani."

"What?" I asked, since I was sure I couldn't have possibly heard him correctly.

"He said you and Hani have a thing going, and you were jealous of him."

"That's crazy. You idiots actually thought I'd fight with Bill because I was having an affair with my sister-in-law?"

"I didn't know he'd hit her."

"How did you find out?" I asked.

"That cop told us. She wanted to know why we'd defend a guy who liked to beat on women. She showed me the photos of Hani. I had no idea."

"Well, now you know."

"Will you tell Hani I'm sorry?" he asked.

"I'll pass the message on. Don't come back."

I didn't wait for Ryan to respond. Instead, I stepped back and shut the door in his face. Did you notice how he apologized for setting Hani up with Bill but he never technically said he was sorry for trying to kill me? Yes, he said he was sorry he was at the bar that night, but that didn't mean he was sorry for swinging a weapon at me.

I went back into the living room and told Ava it was time to leave.

She said she wanted to stay and play in her room. It was heartbreaking, and my insistence that we leave quickly triggered a crying fit - Ava, not me, although the truth was, I was ready to wail myself by the time we were halfway back to my house. Her crying didn't stop until we pulled into the driveway. Who knew kids had such powerful lungs. I'm pretty sure the dog was even annoyed for he ran up the stairs after we went into the house.

Thankfully, Hani returned about twenty minutes after we'd gotten back. I told her that I'd repaired her window. I even told her about Ryan's visit and his apology for encouraging her to date Bill. She didn't have a response. She just changed the subject and started talking about the meeting she'd had that morning. She said that she'd been at the Four Seasons in Wailea and that the new wedding she was coordinating promised to be one of the largest she'd ever done. I congratulated her on her upcoming commission and then informed her that I had a meeting of my own to attend.

I retrieved my BMW car keys from her and promptly walked out of the house. Did I have a meeting? Of course not, but I did have a bag in my trunk that I kept handy should I ever feel like taking a swim. Does that sound crazy? Maybe, but I love swimming and I often have the desire to jump in the ocean when I'm out on a photography expedition.

I drove to Baldwin Beach, which is located on the other side of the island. I used one of the public restrooms to change into my swimsuit. The beach wasn't that crowded, thankfully, so I didn't find myself having to dodge people as I swam my laps. It was a relaxing swim despite the physical exertion. It's hard to think about anything else as you're focused on keeping your body moving through the waves. It usually clears my mind and eases my stress.

I walked out of the ocean and plopped down on a beach blanket. The sun was blaring, and I closed my eyes as I lay on my back. It was still early in the afternoon. Alana wouldn't be home for hours. I didn't feel like staying on the beach all of that time, so I decided to change back into my shorts and t-shirt and find someplace to grab a sandwich and maybe a beer.

I'd locked my phone in my glove compartment, so I retrieved it before starting the car and heading toward Paia for lunch. I saw that I'd missed two calls from Alana. She hadn't left a voicemail. I dialed her number and she answered after just a couple of rings.

"Where are you? I've been trying to reach you," she said.

"I'm at Baldwin Beach. I thought I'd take a little swim."

"Can you go back to the house? Hani needs you."

"What's going on? I didn't get a call from her."

"Bill's dead."

"Dead?"

"His body was found in some brush just off North Kihei Road, near the Kealia Coastal Boardwalk."

"Was he killed this morning?"

"His body has probably been there a few days, from what I've heard. A local spotted him after his dog kept trying to walk over to the brush. The guy went to check it out and then saw Bill's body."

"Do you know how he was killed?" I asked.

"Gunshot to the chest."

"I assume Hani knows."

"I just spoke to her. Do me a favor and call Mara. Hani's going to be a suspect, so are you and Foxx. We all are."

"Who has the case?"

"Makamae Kalani. She's at the crime scene now. I wouldn't be surprised if she tries to interview Hani today. Don't let her speak to anyone without Mara being there."

"You don't think Hani did this, do you?"

"No, not for a second, but I don't want her saying anything that might arouse suspicion, even if it's completely innocent."

"I understand. I'll call Mara on the way back to the house."

I ended the call with Alana and dialed Mara. It was all about to get even crazier.

13

THE INTERROGATION

DETECTIVE KALANI MOVED MUCH FASTER THAN I WOULD HAVE expected her to. Hani and Foxx were questioned in the early evening. I hadn't gotten a chance to speak to them after their interviews before I was summoned to meet with the detective. I drove to the station and found Mara waiting for me in the lobby. A police officer escorted us into the interrogation room. Mara and I only waited a minute or two before Detective Kalani joined us.

"Good evening, Mr. Rutherford, Ms. Winters," Kalani said.

Mara nodded. I said nothing.

"I'm sure you know why you're here," she continued.

"I am."

"I just have a few questions for you. First, when was the last time you saw Mr. Hodges?"

"The night he assaulted me in the bar parking lot," I said.

"You've had no communication with him since then?"

"None."

"I was informed by your sister-in-law that Mr. Hodges' friend came to see you this morning."

"He didn't come to see me. He came by Hani's house to apologize to her. I happened to be there since I was repairing her window."

"Why wasn't Ms. Hu in the house?"

"She's been staying with Alana and me."

"So you can attest to her whereabouts this week?"

"Mostly. I've been home almost the entire week watching her daughter. There were a few times here and there when she had to leave for a work meeting."

"Did you accompany her on those meetings?" Kalani asked.

"No. I stayed home."

"The medical examiner estimates that Mr. Hodges was murdered near the beginning of this week, either Monday or Tuesday. Can you account for your whereabouts on those days?"

"Yes. I was home all day on Monday and Tuesday. The video cameras on my home security system can confirm that."

"I'd like to get a copy of that video so I can determine when your sister-in-law came and went."

"Of course, but she didn't do it."

"Excuse me?"

"Murder is not in everyone's nature. She's incapable of it," I said, although I didn't really believe that. Let me clarify that comment. I think anyone is capable of committing murder, given the appropriate circumstances, but I didn't think Hani had murdered Bill.

"Do you own a gun?" Kalani asked.

"No. I have no need for one. Alana has a weapon."

"Does your sister-in-law have a gun?"

"Not that I'm aware of."

"Does your business partner, Douglas Foxx?"

Mara did something then that surprised me. We'd worked out a system of signals before an earlier interrogation. If she wanted me to say yes to a question, she would do nothing. If she wanted me to say no, however, she'd either cross her arms, put her hands on the table, or rotate her pen with two of her fingers.

So what did she do now? She put her hands on the table.

"He doesn't have a gun," I said.

"He doesn't or you're not aware of it?"

"What do you mean?"

"With Ms. Hu, you claimed you weren't aware of her having a gun, but with Mr. Foxx, you said he didn't have one, as if you were certain."

"I'm certain. I lived with him for my first few years on the island. I would have known if there was a gun in the house. Also, I know you've seen Foxx. People don't mess with him. He has no need for a gun."

"I'm surprised you don't have one at the bar. People get drunk. They mouth off. Maybe even a few crazies pull a weapon now and then."

Mara gently rolled her pen in her fingers.

"No. Foxx has never had any issues keeping people in line."

Detective Kalani studied me for several seconds.

Then she asked, "Do you have any idea who might have had motive to kill Mr. Hodges?"

"I imagine any number of people. I doubt Bill's attack on Hani was the first time he'd hit a woman. It might not have even been in retaliation for that, though. It could have been a road rage incident or a robbery."

Detective Kalani asked me a few more questions, which weren't much more than subtly reworded versions of her earlier ones. As far as interrogations went, at least the ones that I've been a part of, it was fairly easy, which sort of made me nervous. Either she didn't really consider me a suspect and she was just going through the motions, or she had something up her sleeve that she was waiting to unload on us. I didn't know why I was even anxious since I knew I hadn't murdered Bill and I found it highly unlikely that Hani or Foxx would've kill him.

Mara and I left the station. As we walked to our cars, she informed me that she'd asked Foxx and Hani to meet us at her office.

I checked my phone after climbing into my convertible. I saw a text from Alana that read "Inappropriate to talk now. Will fill you in when I get home." So what big news did Alana know?

Mara's office was pretty close to the station, so we were there in no time. Foxx's SUV was already in Mara's parking lot. I assumed he and Hani had driven to the station together.

Mara and I went inside, and her assistant informed us that Foxx and Hani were inside her office. Mara and I walked in and saw them sitting on the sofa. Mara took one chair to the side and I took the other on the opposite side.

"Thank you for waiting," Mara said.

"No problem," Foxx said.

Mara turned to me.

"I don't think Detective Kalani considers you a suspect, for whatever reason. Your interview was a fraction of the time as theirs."

"Not that I'm complaining , but why do you suppose that was?" I asked.

"I'm not sure, but consider yourself fortunate."

Mara turned to Foxx.

"Were you lying about owning a gun?"

"I wasn't lying," he said.

"I'm sure you're aware of attorney-client privilege. I won't repeat anything you tell me. If Detective Kalani catches you in a lie, that won't look good for you, especially after you already beat that man half to death."

I didn't know specifically why Mara suspected Foxx of lying. She'd been in way more interviews than I had, so she could easily be better than me at detecting falsehoods. One thing I did know, she was right to think Foxx had lied about the gun because he had. I had, too.

"I had a gun. It's gone now," Foxx said.

"Where and when did it go?" Mara asked.

"It was damaged in the fire at Harry's. I had it there for security. I forgot to get it when the hurricane hit. The fire melted parts of the grip and the sight on the gun. It wasn't worth paying to get it repaired. It's in a landfill somewhere, along with the rest of Harry's."

"Fortunately, Edgar caught my signal and backed up your claim."

"What signal?" Hani asked.

Mara ignored her question.

"You should have told Detective Kalani that," Mara said.

"Why? She would have thought I was lying."

"You did lie, and she'll find out when she learns you had a gun registered to your name," Mara said.

"It wasn't registered. I bought it off a guy."

"Off a guy?" Mara asked.

"Yeah, I met him in the K-Mart parking lot. It was a cash transaction. No record. I don't see why any of this matters. I didn't murder Bill, and the gun's been in a trash heap for weeks."

"Since we now know you were less than truthful during the interview, I feel the need to ask this again. The last time you saw Bill was when you and Edgar were together in that bar parking lot?" Mara asked.

"Yeah, that's the last time. I wasn't about to get myself arrested again."

She turned to Hani.

"And the last time you saw Bill was when he allegedly threw the rock through your daughter's window?"

"That's right," Hani said.

"No surprises. You were being truthful when you said you didn't own a gun?" Mara asked.

"I've never even held a gun, let alone fired one," Hani said.

"Okay. Don't be surprised if Detective Kalani keeps snooping. Do not talk to her without me present. You all have my phone number. Call me. I'm here to help."

Mara turned to me.

"May I have a word?"

"Sure."

Foxx and Hani took that as their cue to leave, which I supposed it was. They both thanked Mara and left the office while I stayed behind.

"I'm glad you remembered our little signals."

"That's not something one forgets," I said.

"Keep an eye on Douglas. He's his own worst enemy."

"What do you mean?"

"Detective Kalani knows he lied about the gun."

"What makes you say that?"

"He's a lousy liar. It was written all over his face, not to mention his body language. A rookie right out of the academy would have picked it up."

"He didn't murder Bill."

"Does that matter?" Mara asked.

It was a heartless question, but I understood what she was saying. Innocent people went to jail all the time, and Foxx was a lousy liar as she'd stated. I was a pretty good one, though, when I needed to be. What did that say about me? I'm sure it's nothing good.

"How long have you known Detective Kalani?" Mara asked.

"I met her the first time when she questioned me after the parking lot brawl."

"That's really the first time?"

"Yes. Alana mentioned her briefly once before, but that was it. Why do you ask?"

"I'm not sure. Something just seemed different about your interviews."

I had no idea what Mara was talking about, so I decided to let it go. We spoke for a few more minutes, this time talking about the Marco Giordano investigation. I told her about the interviews I'd conducted, including Eleanor originally backing up Juliana's claims and then calling me in secret to let me know the real story, at least the real story according to her. What is truth anyway? We all seem to have our unique version of it. Sorry for getting all philosophical.

I left Mara's office and expected to see Foxx and Hani in the parking lot. They'd left already. I drove home to Kaanapali. Foxx's SUV, Hani's car, and Alana's sedan were in my driveway. It looked like we were about to have another family gathering. No surprise there.

I walked inside and found Alana, Foxx, Hani, and Ashley sitting in the living room. They weren't talking, so either they'd stopped their conversation as I entered or they were waiting for me. It felt awkward and tense, sort of like a group of people sitting in a hospital waiting room, expecting the doctor to arrive at any moment and deliver bad news.

I turned to Hani.

"I saw your car in the driveway. Did your mom get hers fixed?"

"No. She's upstairs with Ava."

"They told me how everything went," Alana said.

"Does Detective Kalani have any leads, other than the people in this room?" I asked.

"If she does, she's not telling me. It would be inappropriate for her to."

"Is there anything we do know?" I asked.

"The gun that killed Bill was a .38. That's all I heard, other than the approximate time of death that Makamae already told you," Alana said.

"They're not looking at you, are they?" Hani asked.

"She asked me a few questions, but I've been working long days this week. I had a lot of cops around me most of the time."

"This is your fault," Ashley said.

I turned to her since I wasn't sure who she was talking about.

"My fault?" Hani asked.

Yeah, I should have known.

"Look what you've done to this family. The cops think someone in this room killed your boyfriend."

"No one here killed him. They'll figure that out sooner or later," Hani said.

"That's my point, Hani. They shouldn't have to figure it out. Nobody here should have to deal with any of this, but they are, all because you couldn't keep your legs closed to that asshole," Ashley said.

It was a shocking and vulgar thing to hear, and I apologize for having to repeat it in this tale. I thought you had to know what was said, though, for you to truly understand what came next. Hani jumped out of her chair and practically flew the seven or eight feet to Ashley. She grabbed two handfuls of hair on the top of Ashley's head and yanked her to the floor before anyone realized what was happening.

Hani landed two blows on Ashley's face before I could pull her off. Ashley, in return, lunged at Hani and was about to strike her back when Foxx grabbed her. Hani is a small woman, but it was like trying to hold a rattlesnake. She was twisting and turning and doing everything she could to get out of my grip. It wasn't one of those cases where the person pretends to try to break loose. Hani truly wanted to get at Ashley. I picked her up and carried her to the other side of the room.

"You're not going to get away with this," Ashley screamed.

"Get out of this house before I kill you," Hani yelled.

Yes, I know it wasn't the most appropriate thing to say considering where we'd all just come from earlier that night.

"This is all your fault," Ashley said.

"Come on. We're going," Foxx said.

I looked up and saw Ms. Hu at the top of the staircase. She was looking down at us in horror. I couldn't say I blamed her.

Foxx and Ashley were out of the house within a minute or so of the attack, but it still took Hani almost thirty minutes to calm down. Alana and her mother tried to console her as Hani switched between yelling, crying, and yelling again. I'd never seen her like that before.

What did I do? I did what I normally do when I get stressed. I took Maui outside to the backyard. I tried to play catch with him, but he was more interested in barking at the waves. Since the little fella was basically ignoring me, I decided to sit on the patio chair and go over everything that had happened that night. You may suspect that the fight between the two women was the most upsetting thing. It wasn't. More on that in a minute.

I went back inside around eight o'clock. Ms. Hu had already left, but Hani and Alana were still discussing Ashley and the comment she'd made. Alana was still in full-on sister mode versus the cop who'd witnessed an assault. Speaking of that, I was expecting the police to arrive at any moment to arrest Hani for her attack on Ashley. They didn't, though.

After listening to about ninety seconds of them rehashing the event, I declared that I was going for a run. Both women looked at me like I was crazy. The dog looked at me as if he were pleading with me to take him with me. Unfortunately, there was no way his little legs would keep up with me.

I decided to go for my full three-mile routine. As I approached Foxx's house on the return, I spotted him leaning against his SUV and drinking a beer. He walked toward me after seeing me, so I slowed down and was at a walking pace by the time he reached the end of his driveway.

"That was something, wasn't it?" he asked.

"I never thought I'd see that."

"Usually I'm pretty good at recognizing when something like that is about to go down, but Hani took it to a ten without any warning."

"I'm pretty sure it was that comment that elevated things so quickly. Is Ashley going to call the police?"

"She wants to, but I asked her not to. I told her Alana would get it squashed in a second, so it wasn't worth the trouble."

"I don't think she'd do that," I said.

"I don't either, but I was trying to come up with a reason to talk her off the cliff. She's furious."

"I'm sure."

"I had to get out here since I was tired of her asking me for the ten millionth time if I could believe Hani would attack her like that."

"Why do you think I'm on this run?"

"Alana and Hani doing the same thing?"

"Yeah."

"I don't know how to put an end to this feud."

"I don't know that you can. They have to work it out. The main thing right now is to concentrate on Bill's murder. I don't think Detective Kalani is done with us, especially you and Hani."

"I don't either. It will be all right. We didn't do anything."

I thought Foxx was being naive, especially since he'd spent time behind bars for a crime he didn't commit. That false arrest had led to the start of my private investigator career, such as it was. Then a thought occurred to me. Maybe he wasn't in denial mode as much as he was trying to convince me he didn't have anything to do with Bill's murder. There were many questions I could have asked him, but I didn't. Why? I'm not one hundred percent sure.

I said goodnight to Foxx and walked back to my house. Maui was waiting for me by the front door, so I hooked his leash up to his harness and took him on a long walk. It was a nice cooldown for me, and it gave me more time to contemplate the night's events.

It was close to ten o'clock by the time I got home and took a shower. I found Alana reading a book in bed as I exited the master bathroom.

"You've done a pretty good job of avoiding Hani tonight," she said.

"Is it that obvious?"

"To me. I suspect Hani's too upset to notice."

"I saw Foxx at the end of my run."

"What did he have to say?"

I filled Alana in on my brief conversation with Foxx.

"You think he'll be able to convince Ashley not to file charges?" Alana asked.

"No, I don't."

"Me, neither."

I walked over to the bed and sat on the edge.

"There's something I need to talk to you about."

"What is it?"

"Can I talk to the wife now and not the cop?"

"I'm not sure how to take that?"

"It's not meant as an insult."

"I didn't think that, but I guess you're going to tell me something you don't want the department to know."

"Maybe."

She hesitated a moment.

Then she said, "Okay, I'm putting my wife hat on now."

"The gun Foxx had was a .38."

"Does Makamae know that?"

"No. He told her he didn't have a gun. He told me the gun had been destroyed in the fire at Harry's."

"Is that true?"

"I assume so. I knew he had a gun there, but it wasn't something I even thought about when the fire happened. I was more worried about how and when we were going to get the bar rebuilt."

"When did Foxx tell you the gun had been destroyed?" Alana asked.

"Tonight, when we talked to Mara after our interview with Detective Kalani."

I told Alana about Mara's hand signal to me, and I admitted that I'd lied about Foxx owning a gun.

"That's obstruction of justice. You know that, don't you?"

"I do, and I feel horrible about it."

"Is this your way of also telling me you have doubts about Foxx's innocence?"

"No. I don't think he had anything to do with Bill's death."

"Only Mara thought it was obvious he was lying about the gun?"

"Yes, and that means Detective Kalani will probably suspect the same thing."

"What would you like me to do?" she asked.

"There's nothing to do. We just have to see how this plays out."

"Well, maybe she'll ask you to look into Bill's murder for her."

"Are you serious?"

"No, that was sarcasm."

"You don't like her. Why?"

"I don't appreciate the things she said to you."

"What things?"

"That the department refuses to use you. That we're somehow not using this valuable asset. She doesn't know your motivations. She doesn't know anything about the cases you've done or how you and I have interacted on them. I don't appreciate her showing up and thinking she knows how everything ought to be run."

"That makes sense."

"I got a bad feeling about her the moment I met her."

"How so?"

"She's ambitious."

"There's nothing wrong with that. I think you and I are both that way."

"There's a difference between being driven and having goals and being someone who is willing to run over other people to get what they want."

"How do you know she's like that?" I asked.

"I just do. She wants to use you, and the moment you have no value to her, she'll cast you aside. I don't want her taking advantage of you."

There were other questions I could have asked her regarding her opinion of Detective Kalani, but I decided not to since it seemed obvious her feelings were based more on woman's intuition and less on actual events she'd witnessed. I don't mean to imply that her intuition is not to be trusted. It is, but it's also best if I don't question it since that inevitably got Alana frustrated. That evening had already been an exhausting one, and I could tell our little discussion about Detective Kalani had riled her up again.

"I know what you're going to do, but don't," she said.

"What am I going to do?"

"You're going to try to solve Bill's murder. Stay away. Let the police handle it. Don't give them any reason to accuse you of messing with the investigation. You've already obstructed justice when you lied to Makamae about the gun. I can't believe you did that."

"Who do you think murdered him?" I asked, ignoring her previous statement. But inside, I was shaken by what I'd done.

"I have no idea. Bill was a violent man, and I'm sure there are any number of people who were upset with him, most of whom we have no idea about. Besides, it might not have been someone he knew. It could have been random."

"The section of North Kihei Road where his body was found, that's not heavily populated, is it?" I asked.

"No. It's away from the hotels and shops in Kihei."

"Do you think it's more likely he was shot there or killed somewhere else and then transported there?"

"He was definitely murdered there."

"Why?"

"Because his car wasn't that far away. It was parked off the side of the road in a dirt clearing."

"And it was just left there? No one noticed?"

"Sometimes people sleep on the beaches there. He had an old car, too. Nothing special. It wouldn't draw much attention if you were driving by."

"So they shot him and then dragged his body into the brush?"

"Probably. He was a big guy. It would have been hard to move his body, especially in the sand."

"So he was either killed close to that brush..."

"Or another strong man killed him and had no problem carrying his body across that soft surface," Alana finished my sentence.

I knew the implication of her words, as I'm sure you do, too. We spoke for a few more minutes and then decided to go to sleep. Alana turned off the light and was out within seconds. She must have been even more exhausted than I'd realized.

I was tired, too, but I didn't think I'd be able to go to sleep for a while. There were too many thoughts racing through my mind. I thought back to Alana's comments that I stay out of the investigation. She was correct, of course, but that didn't mean I was going to follow her advice. Despite knowing I should stay away, I was also well aware of my own tendencies. I would go crazy if I tried to limit myself to the sidelines, but I needed to be discreet.

Besides, I knew Detective Kalani wasn't finished with my family, and I didn't trust her, or anyone else for that matter, to get things right.

14

THE SIDEKICK

ALANA LEFT EARLY FOR WORK THE NEXT MORNING, AND I SUSPECTED SHE did so to avoid getting drawn into another lengthy discussion with her sister. I had a similar mission that morning, so I did my usual exercise routine despite my legs being sore from the previous night's run. I started by swimming laps in the pool and then went for another three-mile jog around the neighborhood. It was a difficult run, but it gave me time to think about whether or not I actually wanted to get involved in the Bill Hodges murder investigation.

I know what you're asking yourself. Didn't I make that decision last night? Well, yes and no. I did decide to get involved, but then I had second thoughts in the morning after Alana told me again to stay out of it. It wasn't until I was halfway through my jog that I decided for good to try to figure out who had murdered Bill and why. Nevertheless, I didn't want the Marco Giordano investigation to suffer. I couldn't be in two places at once, so I decided that I needed help.

Foxx has helped me with some of my investigations from time to time, but I didn't want to ask him again since he was busy with Harry's. In my last case, the one I called *The Tequila Killings*, I met a woman named Nancy Kegley who lived next door to one of the suspects, a man named Gray Darcy. Nancy could best be described as a world-class busybody. She knew what everyone in the neighborhood was doing, which both appalled and delighted me. The appalled side was upset because I knew every neighborhood has a Nancy. I just wasn't sure which neighbor of mine fit into that category. The delighted side appeared when Nancy provided me with a few pieces of information that turned out to be very valuable.

After I finished my run, I phoned Nancy and was happy to find that she remembered me. I asked if she would be willing to meet for lunch, and I told her that it involved her potentially helping me with a murder investigation. I feared she might be put off by my request. I needn't have been worried. She jumped at the opportunity and even recommended a restaurant in Kihei where we could meet.

I took a long, hot shower, changed into fresh clothes, and then walked downstairs to get a drink in the kitchen. I saw Hani's bags packed by the door that led to the garage.

"There you are."

I turned at the sound of Hani's voice.

"I've been looking for you all morning," Hani continued.

"I went for a run."

"Ava and I are returning home. I want to thank you and Alana for all the hospitality you've shown us."

"It wasn't a problem."

"There is something else you could do for me. My mother's car is still in the shop. Is there any way I can keep borrowing yours?"

"Sure, but please take the SUV, especially since you need to drive Ava home. I'm leaving shortly for a meeting, and I'd like to take the convertible."

"Thanks. Mom said she should get her car back in a day or two, so I won't have the SUV long. She did ask me to thank you for letting me use yours since it allows her to keep my car for a while longer."

I tried to say goodbye to Ava, but she was more interested in tearfully telling Maui it wouldn't be too long before they'd be seeing each other again. As much as I thought Maui liked her, I suspected he was secretly glad to see her go so he could resume his normal morning ritual of sleeping in various places of the house. He did this weird thing where he'd sleep hard as if he hadn't slept in days. After thirty minutes or so, he'd dramatically jump up, walk somewhere else in the room, and then plop down, only to fall asleep again within seconds. Ava had disrupted all of that, and she had a habit of pouncing on him just as he'd gone down for one of those morning sleep sessions.

After Hani and Ava left, I climbed into my BMW for the drive to my lunch meeting with Nancy. If you've been to Maui before, then you know the drive down the coast from Kaanapali to Kihei is a beautiful one. I must admit that I didn't enjoy it nearly as much on this day as I usually did since my mind was preoccupied with the murders of Bill and Marco. I was also worried I was making a huge mistake by asking Nancy Kegley to get involved.

The restaurant she'd recommended had sounded familiar to me. She'd given me the address, and I'd meant to look it up after my run. Instead, I'd gotten distracted by the discussion with Hani.

As I pulled into the parking lot, I realized that I'd been to this place before for interviews with various people. The restaurant had changed names and themes a few times, and now it served Thai food. If you read my last tale, then you'll also know it shared a parking lot with a shop that sold lingerie and sex toys like whips and chains, plus other devices I'm too prudish to mention here.

I swung my convertible into a parking space that was halfway between the restaurant and the aforementioned shop. Imagine my surprise when I saw Nancy Kegley exiting the sex shop with a bag in her hand. She immediately spotted me staring at her, and I could only hope my mouth wasn't hanging to the ground.

"Hi there," she said without the slightest bit of embarrassment.

She walked toward me, and I feared she was going to insist on showing me what she'd just purchased. Fortunately, that didn't happen. Instead, she stopped at the rear of a white Volkswagen Passat and popped the trunk. She placed the bag inside and then shut the trunk.

Nancy continued her walk over to me.

"I was so excited when you called," she said.

The last time I'd seen Nancy, she was dressed in a white tank top that showcased just how thin she was. I'd been able to make out the bones of her clavicles, and I'd been worried that the poor woman was malnourished. I'd guessed her age to be somewhere in the seventies, although I wasn't bold enough to confirm that. She had dark brown hair that was the obvious result of a dye job. Her most revealing feature, one that I'd hoped had been addressed, was her yellowed teeth. One of them, unfortunately, had turned brown and looked like it was about to fall out of her mouth at any point. She smiled at me now, and I saw that the little brown tooth was still hanging on for dear life.

Nancy had gotten dressed up for our little lunch meeting. She wore a matching top and long pants that were lime green with tiny watermelons all over them. I wasn't sure what style this could be described as, and I did my best not to laugh at the fact that she looked like a giant bowl of fruit. Sorry if that sounds judgmental, and I guess it is, but this lady was a sight to behold.

"I wasn't sure if you were going to bring Ross or not," I said, referring to her husband, a rather large man who was about the most opposite-looking a person as you could find to Nancy.

"He wanted to come, but he's been feeling under the weather. Shall we go inside and find a table?" she asked.

"Of course."

We turned and headed toward the restaurant door.

"By the way, have you tried the shop across the parking lot? There are some wonderful things in there. I'm sure your wife would love it," she said.

"I'll have to stop by on our way out."

"Ask for Julie. She really knows her stuff."

"I'll remember that," I said, and I held open the door for her.

The hostess seated us at a table that thankfully didn't have a view of the sex shop. Both Nancy and I ordered the Tom Yum Goong, which is a spicy shrimp soup. I brought Nancy up to speed on the Marco Giordano murder while we waited for our lunch to be served.

"He was really hacked to death?" she asked.

"I'm not sure hacked is the right word. The detective described the wounds as log cuts versus a relatively narrow but deep cut that would be made by a knife thrusting into the body. Still, I haven't seen any autopsy photos."

"This is so exciting."

"I don't know that I would describe it as that."

"I hope you don't think I'm taking this man's murder lightly. It's a tragedy. Thankfully, we can do something about it."

I guessed she saw the look of confusion on my face for she followed that up with, "By catching the man who committed this horrible crime."

"What makes you think a man did this?"

"Well, if I were going to kill someone, especially a man, I'd either do it by poisoning them or shooting them. I certainly wouldn't risk the man being able to fend off a knife attack, especially if I was going to take wild swings at him with something like a meat cleaver."

"That's something I considered, but I'm not willing to write off a woman."

"Especially since it sounds like your best suspects are both women."

"I don't think we have two, just one."

"Yes, but it seems like Juliana has a good motive for framing Sophia."

"True. Yet Juliana is now in a worse position than she was before. Marco seemed to have no interest in selling the company, which is how Juliana felt as well."

"But he also wasn't willing to give her any more company stock, so maybe she murdered her brother and is now trying to frame the sister-in-law. If that happens, then she gets one hundred percent of the company and pays nothing for it, except for her guilty conscience, which many people don't have," Nancy said.

"There are way more sociopaths out there than I ever thought possible."

"What a wonderful job you have, matching your intellect against the killer. So, is this a one-time thing for us or are you suggesting a more permanent partnership? When do we discuss payment?"

I hadn't expected Nancy to help with my case for free, but I also hadn't spent more than two seconds thinking about what payment would be appropriate. I didn't get paid for many of my investigations, and I certainly had no idea what the going rate was for a sidekick.

"Is there an amount you had in mind?" I asked.

"Twenty-five dollars an hour plus expenses."

She'd said it so quickly that it was obvious it was a number she'd already come up with on the drive over.

"I think I can swing that."

"I'd like to be paid in cash by the way. I assume that won't be an issue."

I wasn't sure if I admired this lady's directness or not.

"How would you like me to get started?" she asked, without waiting for my answer on whether or not cash would be an agreeable form of payment.

"I'd like you to follow Sophia Giordano. Get whatever dirt you can on her before I meet with her."

"You're wondering if she's having an affair," Nancy said.

"It would be a strong motive to murder Marco. She might have wanted to leave him for some other man, but she also didn't want to lose his money."

"Does Juliana suspect Sophia was having an affair?"

"Not in so many words, but it's a classic case for killing someone. Love, greed, and power, the big three."

"I think there's a fourth."

"Which is?"

"Some people murder for the thrill of it. I've seen many episodes on the Discovery Channel. They get off on the ecstasy of seeing someone's life drain from their bodies," Nancy said.

God, this woman was freaking me out. What had I gotten myself into?

"It's very important that you don't get caught following her. I like the fact that you have a white Passat. That should blend in nicely."

"I also have a pair of binoculars in the house. I'll bring those with me."

"Do you have a camera, something with a long-range lens?" I asked.

"No. I just use my phone to take photos. I can buy one, though, and include it on my expense report."

"Okay, but don't buy any pro-level gear. These don't have to be award-winning shots. Just capture their faces and make sure everything is in focus."

"Don't worry. She'll never see me coming."

I didn't doubt that for a second, unless she was wearing her watermelon outfit, which was hard to miss.

15

YUTO TAKAHASHI

I MANAGED TO GET OUT OF THE PARKING LOT WITHOUT NANCY INSISTING that I visit the sex shop. She did tell me that she couldn't wait to get home and handcuff Ross to the bed. Just kidding, she didn't say that. She told me again how excited she was to be working on her first real case. Her use of the word "real" made me wonder if she'd already conducted some sort of amateur investigation on her own, perhaps a snooping mission on one of her neighbors that went further than just looking out of the window.

I hopped into my convertible for the drive back to Kaanapali. Now that I had Nancy on the Marco Giordano case, I decided to put my mental energy toward the Bill Hodges murder investigation. The problem was, I had no idea where to begin. Fortunately, fate intervened and I received a phone call around the time I was approaching Lahaina. I pulled off the road so I could better hear the caller. I didn't recognize the number, but I decided to answer it anyway.

"Mr. Rutherford, this is Makamae Kalani."

She hadn't used the title of detective. Did that mean something?

"What can I do for you, Detective?"

"I thought I'd check in on your investigation into the Marco Giordano murder. Perhaps we can get together and compare notes."

"I'm afraid I would be wasting your time. I've made very little progress. You were right when you said this was a difficult case. There doesn't seem to be any good suspects."

Detective Kalani laughed.

"Is that funny?" I asked.

"No, but your attempt to keep me in the dark is. I normally get upset when someone insults my intelligence, but I'll give you a pass this time since I'm not entirely sure of your motivations."

"Okay, I'll cop to that one, no pun intended. But it certainly isn't an attempt to keep things hidden from you. I just don't have anything earth-shattering to report. I'm still very much in the discovery phase, and I'm nowhere close to my theory phase."

"Apology accepted," she said.

Had I apologized? I didn't think so.

"Dare I ask if you've made any progress on the Bill Hodges murder?"

"I don't think that's something I can talk to you about, but don't worry. I don't consider you a suspect, although you certainly qualify as one," she said.

"I'm glad to hear that, the part about not being a suspect, that is."

"You have to admit you should be near the top of my list."

"Why is that?" I asked, even though I knew I was walking right into whatever she wanted me to.

"You'd already assaulted him before."

"Only in self-defense," I said.

"Oh, I'm not talking about outside that bar in Lahaina. Besides, I saw the security video. You didn't lay a hand on Bill Hodges then. That was more your friend. No, I'm talking about the time you went to his house during the hurricane and assaulted him."

"I'm pretty sure I denied that at your station, and I certainly deny it now."

"What did I tell you about insulting my intelligence?"

I ignored her question.

"Let's speak in hypothetical terms," I suggested.

"Okay."

"Let's say I did break into his home and I somehow managed to get the best of him. Why are you now discounting me in his murder? Is it purely on the evidence of my home security footage? It proves beyond a doubt that I didn't leave the house on the day he was murdered."

"There is that, but I didn't need to see that footage to know you didn't kill him. There's only one reason that I think you might kill, and this isn't it."

"We barely know each other, Detective. What makes you think that about me?" I asked.

"As I mentioned the other day in the café, this is a small island. People talk."

"Not about something like why I'd ever kill someone, not that I would."

Which wasn't really true. I would kill, but only to protect Alana. Was that what Kalani was referring to?

"Very well. I've spoken to Detective Adcock about you."

Now it was my time to laugh.

"Detective Adcock? He hates everything about me. I can't imagine him being any kind of character witness for me."

"He's as predictable as the sun coming up in the morning," she said.

"What do you find predictable about him?"

"He's jealous of you. It's quite obvious, although he'd never admit it. I'll make a deal with you. You tell me one interesting piece of information about the Giordano case, and I'll share a detail about Bill Hodges," she suggested.

I thought about it for a moment.

Then I said, "Juliana Giordano very much wanted me to believe that Sophia spent her husband's money like crazy and that it caused a huge rift between the two of them."

"That's your detail? I heard that within the first couple of days of the investigation."

"Yes, but it's not a true statement. Marco was very much in favor of her buying herself lavish gifts. He'd do anything for her."

"How do you know this?" she asked.

"That wasn't part of our agreement. You asked for a detail. I gave you one, and I believe it's reliable."

"How sure are you?"

"Can anyone ever be one hundred percent sure of anything someone tells them?"

"No. But how close are you to that?"

"Somewhere around eighty percent, close enough to think it's true. Now, what's your detail?"

"Bill Hodges was fired from his job a few days before he was murdered."

"Do you know why?" I asked.

"That wasn't part of our agreement. I gave you the detail, and I'm one hundred percent sure it's true."

"How do you think that's connected to his death?"

"Again, not part of our agreement."

"Fair enough."

"It was nice talking to you, Mr. Rutherford, but I need to go. I have to find your wife and give her a cop-to-cop courtesy."

"A courtesy?"

"Your sister-in-law is about to be arrested for assault. We got the complaint this morning. Apparently, she attacked a woman named Ashley Coyle, but I'm guessing you already knew that since you were there. Goodbye, Mr. Rutherford."

She ended the call before I could respond. So much for Foxx having convinced Ashley not to press charges. The question was: What kind of impact, if any, would this arrest have on the Bill Hodges investigation? Did this make Detective Kalani even more suspicious of Hani? Probably. I didn't see how it couldn't.

There were other questions that popped into my mind. Did Foxx know that Ashley had filed a police report? If so, would he try to warn the mother of his child? If not, what kind of reaction would he have? Would this end his relationship with Ashley or would he find a way to rationalize her behavior?

I did three things before pulling back onto the road. I called Ms.

Hu and told her what I'd learned. I asked her to get to Hani's house as soon as possible so she could take care of Ava and offer emotional support to Hani. Secondly, I called Mara and informed her that her services were needed. That call lasted a little longer than I wanted it to since Mara insisted on knowing every detail of how last night had unfolded. The third thing I did was call Hani. She already knew why I was calling since Alana had beaten me to the punch.

I was about to drive away when my phone vibrated. It was Alana.

"Can you believe that bitch?" she asked, after informing me of Hani's imminent arrest.

"Yes, I can. We knew it was a longshot that Ashley wouldn't file charges. She hates Hani."

"I really thought Foxx would be able to convince her not to. You know, you didn't sound surprised at all when I just told you about Hani."

"That's because Detective Kalani already told me. She didn't mention that to you?"

"What are you talking about?" she asked.

I told Alana about my call from Detective Kalani and how she'd dropped that little nugget of information and then quickly ended the call.

"What the hell kind of game is she playing?" Alana asked.

"I have no idea."

"Have you called Mara?"

"Yes. I got off the phone with her a few minutes before you called. I told her everything about last night."

"Hani's going to need bail, and I'm sure my mother is going to be with Ava."

"I can take care of it," I said.

"Thank you. This is getting too much, Poe. I'm not sure how much more of this I can take."

"It will be okay. We're in rough waters right now, but I can see clear weather on the horizon," I said, and then I immediately felt ridiculous for using such a lame analogy.

"Do you really believe that?" Alana asked.

"I do. I wouldn't have said it otherwise."

We ended the call after a few more minutes of me reassuring Alana that things would be okay. You may be wondering if I believed what I said. Not for one second, but it wouldn't do any good for both of us to be going down a river of despair. Sorry for all the nature clichés.

I knew it would be a while before I could bail Hani out of jail, so I decided to take advantage of the time, and I headed over to the hotel where Bill had worked. Detective Kalani had given me that piece of information about Bill's termination for a reason. Why had she? I needed to find out.

I did a quick online search with my phone after arriving at the hotel and discovered the general manager's name was Yuto Takahashi. There was a brief biography of him that said he'd started in the hotel industry as a bellhop and had worked at various hotels all over the world, culminating as the general manager at one of the most successful resort properties on the Hawaiian Islands. I closed the web browser and climbed out of my convertible.

I entered the lobby and was immediately impressed by how opulent everything was. It gave visitors a distinct taste of Hawaii with an abundance of tropical flowers in a variety of oranges, yellows, purples, and whites. The front desk was constructed of Koa wood, and it was topped with a long, thick slab of black marble. Behind the desk was a large photograph of Hawaiian cliff divers holding torches as the sun set over the ocean. I'd been to one of the cliff-diving ceremonies myself and found it impressive.

I'd arrived at the hotel at an off-time, and there was only one person working behind the desk. I asked the woman if I could speak with Mr. Takahashi. She asked me if I had an appointment and I told her I didn't. She then asked if I was a guest at the hotel. I thought about telling her I was since that would probably get their attention. Instead, I told her I was a friend of Hani's, and I assumed he'd be willing to meet with me for that reason.

I could tell she didn't recognize Hani's name from the look of confusion on her face. Nevertheless, she picked up the phone behind the desk and called Mr. Takahashi. She paused a moment while she listened to him on the other end. Then she placed the phone back in its cradle, turned to me, and informed me that he would be with me in a few minutes.

I thanked her for her assistance and took a slow walk around the lobby to pass the time. I was in the process of admiring a gorgeous pink plumeria when I heard someone behind me.

"I'm Yuto Takahashi. You wanted to speak with me?"

I turned and saw Takahashi smiling. His height was around the same as my wife's. He had a thick head of black hair and was probably somewhere between forty and forty-five years old. I wasn't sure what the average age was for someone to reach the general manager status of a resort of this size, but I assumed he'd done well for himself.

"Beautiful, aren't they?" he continued.

"They are lovely flowers. I've been thinking about planting some behind my house, but I can never decide between the plumeria, the hibiscus, or the bird of paradise."

"Why not all three?" he suggested.

"Problem solved."

"The front desk clerk said you wanted to speak with me in regards to Ms. Hu."

"That's right," I said.

"May I ask how you know her?"

"She's my sister-in-law."

He paused a moment.

Then he said, "Perhaps we should talk in my office."

"If you wish."

I followed Takahashi back to his office. It was much smaller than I would have imagined for the general manager, but I assumed space on a Maui resort was at a premium.

He sat behind his desk while I took one of the two leather chairs in the front.

"Hani has mentioned you before," he said.

"Really?"

"Yes. Your exploits on the yacht. I believe it was called The Epiphany. I read about it in the paper. I asked Hani about it, and she mentioned that you and your wife solved the murders."

Of all the cases I'd been a part of, the one on that super yacht seemed to have gotten the most media attention. Perhaps it was the mix of wealth, marriage, and a pair of murders on the high seas that proved irresistible to reporters. There was also Hani's ceaseless social media posts about it that kept it fresh in people's minds. As much as I've grown to like Hani, I was a little surprised to hear she'd even mentioned Alana and me to the hotel's manager. I'd assumed she'd taken credit for solving everything herself, all the while continuing to plan a first-rate wedding, despite the absence of a bride.

"Are you investigating Bill Hodges' death?" he continued.

"I'm helping the police with it, yes."

That wasn't exactly true, but I always felt a bit awkward during these interviews since I usually showed up unannounced and basically asked people to spill the beans when they don't really know me. Still, I've found that people are always anxious to gossip, even when they say they aren't. It usually just takes a little non-threatening encouragement on my part.

"Were you aware that Hani had a relationship with Bill?" I asked.

"Not at first, but our on-site event planner eventually told me."

"I'm not sure I follow you."

"Hani has planned several weddings here, so it's not unusual for her to be on the property. I started seeing her around much more often, though. I was a bit curious, so I asked."

"What did this planner say, exactly?"

"Not much. Just that she knew Hani and Bill had been dating."

"Was she surprised by that?"

"If she was, she didn't mention it."

"How well did you know Bill?" I asked.

"More than most of the employees here."

"Why is that?"

He paused.

Then he asked, "Are you recording this conversation?"

"No, I'm not."

He paused again, this time even longer. I expected him to ask me to show him my phone and prove I wasn't recording anything, but he didn't.

Finally, he asked, "How is Hani doing?"

"Not well. Not well."

I'm not sure why I said it, especially twice. The Hu family is very private and would never want anything negative out there, not that any family does. Then I realized that my subconscious mind had picked up on something that my conscious mind had not. I hadn't given the front desk clerk a specific reason, beyond a vague mentioning of Hani, that I wanted to speak to Takahashi. Still, he'd shown up in less than two minutes. I now knew from following him back to his office that it took around that length of time to get to the lobby. He must have immediately gotten up from his desk and headed to the lobby after getting the call. Either Hani meant way more to him than he was letting on, or he was probably the only general manager of a large resort on Maui who had nothing else to do.

I didn't know whether Takahashi's feelings or thoughts for Hani were romantic or not. I glanced at his left hand and noticed the absence of a ring. Still, some married guys don't like wearing rings. I often go days without wearing mine, much to Alana's annoyance. It's not that I'm trying to fool anyone, but I'm just not a big jewelry guy.

"I saw the photographs of Hani," he said, snapping me out of my mental investigation as to whether or not he was carrying a torch for my sister-in-law.

"Do you know who sent them?" I asked.

"Someone left them for me at the front desk. They were placed in a large envelope with my name on the outside."

"Did the front desk clerk offer a description of who dropped them off?"

"No. He said the lobby was crowded since he was checking in a few different families at once. When he finally got a break, he noticed someone had left the envelope on the corner of the desk. I checked the video surveillance and saw it was a Hawaiian woman."

"A Hawaiian woman? Could you estimate her age?"

"Maybe late twenties to early thirties."

"How was she dressed?"

"In business attire. I believe she wore navy-blue pants with a red blouse underneath a matching jacket."

"What did you first think when you saw the photographs?" I asked.

"I assumed Bill had been the one to hurt her."

"Why is that?"

"Bill had a couple of episodes here at the hotel."

"What do you mean by episodes? Had he struck someone?"

"No. He would have been terminated immediately if he'd done that. He used profanity at a few co-workers in the kitchen."

"I certainly have no interests in defending Bill, but I've worked at restaurants myself. A kitchen staff is known for its use of profanity. Every other word out of their mouths usually starts with the letter F."

"That's true, and it's no different here, despite my best efforts. Bill's incidents were...more extreme."

"Why didn't you fire him?"

"There were channels I needed to go through. It was determined that Bill's actions had not reached the threshold for termination."

"Channels?" I asked.

"We're a large corporation, but I'm sure you already know that from the name of the hotel. Every decision to fire someone must be signed off by the human resources department. Bill had not received any official counseling sessions."

"What do you mean by counseling sessions? You make them see a therapist?"

"Not at all. A counseling session would consist of him sitting down with his supervisor. That person would then explain how his behavior did not meant the standards of the company. He'd either receive a verbal or written warning with future actions clearly laid out should he repeat the offending behavior."

"So the company was worried about him suing for wrongful termination?"

"It's a constant hassle. You would be surprised by the number of employees who sue for any reason. There are no shortage of lawyers out there who encourage it since they assume a large company with very deep pockets would more likely settle than go to court. It's usually easy money for them."

"Did you witness these outbursts Bill had?"

"No, I didn't. The head chef did, and she came to me."

"Was she surprised by them or do you know if she'd seen them coming?"

"She was shocked. She said that Bill had been a model employee up until then. He'd been very friendly and outgoing."

"Did she know what specifically caused these outbursts?" I asked.

"That was another reason that it was so surprising. The arguments were over ridiculous issues. These were things that could have easily been resolved with a short conversation. Instead, Bill flew into a rage."

"What was it that ultimately led to you firing Bill?"

"The photographs of Hani. I couldn't have anyone like that working here."

"You confronted him and he admitted it?"

"No. He denied it, but I knew he'd done it. I fired him on the spot."

"Did Bill ever come back to the hotel to cause problems after you let him go?"

Takahashi shook his head.

"No. I never saw him again."

"How did you find out about his death?"

"The head chef told me. She'd heard about it from a colleague. I'm not sure how that other person found out. Perhaps from a news report."

"I appreciate your time, Mr. Takahashi."

I stood.

"Please tell Hani that I hope she is doing better," he said.

"I will, but you should call her yourself. I'm sure she'd love to hear from you. Do you have her phone number?"

"No."

I leaned over his desk and picked up a pen. I then wrote Hani's number on a post-it note.

"I'd wait a few weeks if I were you. Things are a bit hectic right now."

"Of course. Thank you."

Takahashi walked from behind his desk and then escorted me back to the lobby. I said goodbye and headed out to the parking lot.

In hindsight, I realized what a longshot this visit had been and how incredibly lucky I'd gotten that I'd learned anything. Employee information is confidential and no one would know that more than the general manager. Granted, Bill was dead, and it wasn't like he could sue them now. It was also highly unlikely that I would have the motivation to call the hotel corporate headquarters and inform them that Takahashi had told me private details about their former pastry chef. Still, he'd been concerned enough about it to ask me if I was recording the conversation.

So, what had I learned? Two things, at least by my account. Maybe you picked up on more. The first, and perhaps most interesting, was the physical description of the woman that dropped off the photographs of Hani's bruised face to the hotel. That had to have been Detective Kalani. Alana also owned a navy-blue pant suit, but I think she would have told me if she'd delivered the photos herself. I also think Takahashi would have noticed the physical resemblance between Hani and Alana. The women could be twins, as I've mentioned before.

What did I make of the detective essentially getting Bill fired? I found it intriguing. She was clearly willing to bend - and even break - the rules when it came to her investigations. I still didn't know if she gave me the hint about the hotel so I would learn what she'd done to Bill or if there was some other hidden purpose behind her actions. Perhaps she thought she would gain favor with me for pushing back against the abuser of my sister-in-law.

The second thing I learned was that Bill seemed to have a split personality. He could be charming and nice one moment and the next he could turn into a raving lunatic, one that liked to beat on women and attack men with baseball bats. Maybe the guy had been bipolar. Maybe not. I'm certainly not qualified to render any kind of psychological profile, but I couldn't come up with another explanation for his wild mood swings. Yes, he might have abused drugs or alcohol, but Hani hadn't mentioned anything like that before. Perhaps he'd been on some kind of prescription medication, and the outbursts were the result of him going off those meds.

As I started my car, I realized there was a third thing that I'd learned from the interview. My subconscious observation that Takahashi had a thing for Hani was definitely on the money. He'd fired Bill after seeing those photos. True, you may suspect that any decent human being would dismiss an abusive person, but Bill hadn't beaten on a co-worker. He hadn't attacked Hani while they were on the hotel property. Everything had happened while he was away from work, and Bill hadn't been convicted in a court of law. Takahashi mentioned that Bill had denied the allegations, so it had been the classic he-said-she-said scenario. Still, Takahashi had fired Bill anyway, and I guessed he had done so without the official sign-off from human resources. You heard how by-the-book the company was, yet he'd chosen the wrath of the H.R. department anyway. If you've ever tangled with that department, take my advice and don't. They're the judge, jury, and executioner.

I'm sure some of you are chastising me right about now for handing out Hani's phone number. Yeah, that's fair, but Takahashi seemed like a nice guy. Hani could use one of those in her life.

16

DONE

I'm guessing most, if not all of you who are reading this tale have never been to jail. I had never been before coming to Maui. The worst sin I'd committed, at least in terms of the law, was a handful of traffic violations, most for speeding. Architects tend not to be an adventurous bunch. Sorry if you're an architect and I've just insulted you. When one makes the transition to private investigator, however, your likelihood of running afoul of the police greatly increases by a factor of one thousand.

I say all of this to make the point that I knew exactly how Hani was feeling as she walked out of jail. Granted, this wasn't her first time doing that. If you've read *Wedding Day Dead*, then you already know about her previous incarceration. If you haven't, well, I wouldn't dream of ruining the details of the story. Suffice it to say, a simple case of assault by pulling a woman's hair was nothing in comparison to what she'd been charged with before.

I expected Hani to go off about Ashley once we got into the car. She didn't. She just thanked me for bailing her out and stayed silent during the entire ride back to her house. She didn't make any phone calls or even texts to her mother or Alana. She just looked out her side window as we drove across the island.

When we arrived at her house, I saw her mother's car in the driveway. I parked on the street and escorted Hani into the house. Her mother came around the corner and met us in the foyer. Hani's eyes filled with tears when she saw her. She was about to walk to her when Ava appeared. She said one word, "Mommy," and Hani's expression of sorrow turned to one of resolve. She wiped the tears away and ran over to her daughter. Hani picked Ava up and told her how happy she was to see her. The little girl laughed as Hani tickled her side. She carried Ava into the living room as Ms. Hu walked over to me.

"Thank you for bailing Hani out."

"It's not a problem. Have you spoken to Alana? Do you know if she's coming over here?" I asked.

"I haven't heard from her in a while. I don't know what her plans are."

"Do you think there's anything I can do for Hani before I head out?"

"No. I suspect she just needs time to calm down. I'm sure being around Ava will help."

"Is there anything you need?"

Ms. Hu looked like she was about to say something but then stopped. I didn't bother to press her for an answer.

"I guess I'll be going," I continued.

"Thank you again," she said.

I nodded and headed out the door. It had been one of the most civil exchanges we'd had, but it was obvious why it had happened. People tend to put their differences aside during stressful situations, and this certainly counted as one.

I'd intended to drive straight home after leaving Hani's, but I made a last-second decision and turned into Lahaina to swing by Harry's. I realized my subconscious had taken over again as I thought it might be a neutral place to talk to Foxx. I had mixed feelings when I arrived. The construction process was further along than I'd anticipated, and my hopes rose that we'd be able to reopen on schedule. The downside was that Foxx was nowhere to be seen.

I got out of my convertible and walked around the building. It was finally starting to look like an actual structure. I could almost see my photographs of Maui adorning the walls again. When I say Maui, I'm referring to the island, not the dog, although maybe I should put some of his portraits up there, too. People seem to get into a great mood whenever they see the little guy. He has one of those cute faces that makes people want to pet him. I'd caution against that, though, if you ever come across us on a walk. He still doesn't have an appreciation for strangers, and you might find yourself on the receiving end of a dog bite.

I pulled the BMW Z3 out of the Harry's parking lot and made the short drive back home. I saw Alana's car in the garage when I arrived. The garage door was left open, which wasn't something she normally did. I parked beside her car, turned off the ignition, and went inside the house. I found Alana and Foxx standing in the kitchen. Alana was on the side of the counter where the refrigerator and oven were. Foxx was on the opposite side. Neither of them were talking, and they both gave me that look people do when you inadvertently walk in on a discussion about you.

"Is Hani home?" Alana asked.

"I just dropped her off."

"How is she?"

"Fine, I think. She didn't say much, so it was hard to tell."

I turned to Foxx.

"I just came from Harry's. The construction is really coming along."

"Yeah, it's looking good," he said.

A few seconds of uncomfortable silence passed.

"Is everything okay?" I asked, which was a ridiculous question in hindsight. Still, it had been aimed more at the apparent tension between Alana and Foxx and not an overall inquiry about the state of things.

"I came over to let you guys know how sorry I am that Hani got arrested," Foxx said.

I waited for Alana to respond. She didn't.

"I asked Ashley not to press charges. She told me she wouldn't. Obviously, she changed her mind," he continued.

Again, I waited for Alana to comment, but she stayed silent.

"I assume she knows Hani was arrested," I said.

"She does. I told her," Foxx said.

"How did you find out?" I asked.

"Luana called me. She read me the riot act."

That seemed like another opportune moment for Alana to chime in. I expected her to make a comment such as "Good, you deserve it," or "You're lucky that's all my mother did." She didn't, though. She continued her silent treatment.

"Anyway. I'm sorry. Can you please tell Hani that, too?" Foxx asked.

"Maybe you could call her and tell her that yourself," I suggested.

"I don't want to upset her any more than I already have."

"I'll let her know," I said.

"Thanks."

Foxx turned to Alana.

"I'm sorry, Alana. I'm really sorry."

He waited a moment for her to respond. She didn't.

Foxx turned back to me.

"See ya" he said, and then he walked past me and headed out the door that led to the garage.

Now that Foxx was gone, I expected Alana to say something to me. Instead, she walked past me and headed for the stairs. I was about to call out to her but decided against it.

By the way, I forgot to mention this earlier, but the dog had not greeted me when I came into the house. I'd assumed that he was in the backyard. He wasn't. He just seemed to have some sort of instinctual knowledge that he should stay the hell out of the kitchen. Sometimes, often really, I suspect that animals are way smarter than humans.

Alana made it up one stair before she stopped and turned back to me.

"I'm done with Foxx," she said.

"What does that mean?"

"Exactly what you think it means. I'm done seeing him. I'm done talking to him. I'm done thinking about him. I realize he's your best friend and your business partner. I'm not going to put you in a bad position and ask you not to see him. I will ask that you not talk to me about him. I wish him the best, but he's out of my life."

There were all sorts of statements I could have made after her declaration of finality. Although I'm often naïve and foolish when it comes to women, I don't believe my degree of idiocy reaches the level of world-class idiot. I knew the option of staying silent wasn't viable, though. She was expecting me to say something, but I also knew I had to choose my next words carefully.

"I get it. I do, and I respect your decision. I won't press you to change your mind."

"Thank you, and thank you for bailing out Hani. I can pay you back."

"I hope you know that's not necessary."

"I know, but I want to."

Alana turned and walked up another two steps. Then she stopped again and turned back to me.

"That woman is going to destroy his life. I hope he realizes what a fool he is to be with her."

I knew Alana was talking about Ashley and Foxx. I also knew it was somewhat ironic that she couldn't even make it to the top of the stairs before bringing up Foxx when she'd just declared all of ten seconds ago that she was never going to speak of him again. Nevertheless, I kept those thoughts to myself and stuck with my plan to say as little as possible in return. If I had to talk, then I would agree with whatever my wife declared.

"I'm not sure what he's thinking right now, but I know you're right. She isn't good for him," I said.

"No, she isn't."

Alana headed up the stairs and disappeared into our bedroom.

I know what you're thinking right now. You're saying to yourself that I'm a bit of a wimp to just agree with whatever my wife said.

Maybe you're right, but I'd rather be a wimp than have that rage aimed at me. Alana has three levels of anger. The first is annoyance, and it usually comes out in the form of a sarcastic comment or a harsh glance your way. The second level is when she raises her voice or even yells at you, which is a rare occurrence. The third level, the one she was on right now, was when she is so angry that she actually becomes extremely calm and her comments come out as ice daggers aimed at your heart. This level is an even rarer one, and the previous times I'd seen it were directed at yours truly. It's not a place you want to be.

17

BANANAS

THE REST OF THE EVENING WENT BY PAINFULLY SLOW. I SPENT VERY little time speaking to Alana for obvious reasons. What did she do? She was wrapped up in some reality show. I couldn't tell you which one it was, but I recognized that it was reality-based from the shrill voices of the women screaming at each other. Alana tended to watch those shows when she was stressed and just wanted mindless entertainment, which I suppose is the appeal of those programs.

I spent the bulk of my time giving her the space she clearly needed. I decided to go for a night swim in the pool. Apparently, Maui also wanted to give Alana some room to breathe, and he dashed outside after I opened the sliding glass door. I swam laps for about half an hour, and then I spent another thirty minutes sitting on one of my patio chairs and staring out at the ocean. There was a full moon, and it cast a thick beam of white light on the rippling waves. You may be wondering how I can always spend such a long time staring at the ocean. Well, if you've been to Maui, or any of the other Hawaiian Islands, then you probably don't wonder that. There is something hypnotic about the sea. Maybe it's an instinctual link we all have to the water. It has a calming effect on my mind, better than anything else I've ever tried.

I somewhat expected that Alana might come outside at some point and talk about what had happened earlier, but she never did. While I was outside, I received a text message from Nancy stating that she had important things to report regarding the Marco Giordano case. I asked her what they were, and she texted back that she'd prefer to tell me in person. We set a time in the mid-morning to meet at the café in Lahaina where I'd met with Detective Kalani.

Alana's mood hadn't improved the next day. She told me right before she left for work that she intended to stop by Hani's house on the way home. I told her I'd call Hani after my meeting with Nancy to check on her. Alana thanked me again for bailing out Hani. There was no more mention of her repaying me for the bail, not that I expected or even wanted it.

So why did I just bring it up to you then? I'm not sure. I just did. Perhaps I was hoping that because she'd apparently changed her mind on the bail that she might decide to withdraw her declaration that she was done with my best friend, but Alana didn't mention Foxx or Ashley. I certainly wasn't going to bring them up, either.

I went for another swim in the backyard pool, jogged three miles around the neighborhood, and concluded my morning workout by taking a long walk with Maui. The sun was shining and the temperature wasn't too hot, so we had a pleasant stroll. Both of us seemed to be getting over the tension of the previous evening. After I returned home, I took a shower and then threw on a polo shirt and a pair of khaki shorts. I drove the short distance to Lahaina and found Nancy waiting for me outside the café. She was a sight to behold in her blue outfit that was adorned with dozens of bananas on her top and pants. As I got closer to her, I could have sworn I detected the subtle smell of bananas. Maybe she'd managed to purchase a perfume with that fragrance or perhaps my imagination was in overdrive again.

"Good morning, Nancy. Don't you look nice," I said without the slightest bit of sarcasm, at least I think I managed to keep a straight face and a pleasant tone.

"Thank you."

I looked down at her hands. She was holding a manila folder.

"I assume you have something important to show me. Shall we head inside?" I asked.

"Maybe we should find a more private location. The café is awfully crowded. I'd hate for someone to listen in on our conversation."

I was tempted to remark that I didn't think anyone cared about our investigation, anyone beside the Giordano family members, that is. I realized, though, that this was her first case, and she was apparently taking her action cues from television spy shows, where I assumed she'd seen people always going into a soundproof room for their top secret conversations. Since we didn't have one of those nearby, I suggested that we walk over to one of the empty benches across from the banyan trees.

We crossed the street to the park and sat down on one of the aforementioned benches. I looked at the folder in her hands again.

"What is it you have?" I asked.

Nancy looked around the park for a few seconds as if she were anticipating a member of the Giordano family (or perhaps Russian spies) to appear at any moment. She turned back to me and opened the folder.

"I took these yesterday. I think you'll find them quite interesting," she whispered.

I scanned through the eight-by-ten-inch inch photographs inside the folder. They were all shots of Sophia speaking with a man around her age in someone's driveway. The unknown man was several inches taller than her, and he had long blond hair that was pulled back in a ponytail. It was a bleached color that looked more like a dye job than a natural hue. He was wearing a pair of dark sunglasses, black pants, and a royal blue shirt with several buttons undone. The only thing that was missing was the gold chain. One of the photographs showed Sophia hugging our mystery stud.

"Where did you take these?" I asked.

"I assume it's that man's home. I followed Sophia all over the island. She eventually went there in the late afternoon."

"Did you write down the address?"

"Of course. It's on the back of the first photograph. I realized once I got home that I should have tried to go through his mail after they went inside," she continued.

"I'm glad you didn't. I'd hate for you to get caught by them or a neighbor."

"I can go back there tonight after it gets dark. Maybe he won't have checked the mail yet."

"Don't bother. There are other ways to find out his name."

"They're lovers. I know they are."

"Why do you say that?" I asked.

"Look at the photos again. Don't you see them hugging?"

"It could be just an innocent hug. People hug all the time when they greet their friends."

"True, but they seemed to stand a bit too close to each other afterward. I got the distinct impression that Sophia wanted to kiss him."

"Why? Did she lean in close or something?"

"No. It was just a feeling I got. I also saw Sophia looking around the yard, almost like she was trying to see if someone was watching them."

"Do you think she noticed you following her?"

"I don't see how. I was too far away."

"How did you get such close-up shots of them?"

"I bought a Canon L series three-hundred-millimeter lens for my camera. I also got an extender for it."

"That's a heck of a lens."

"I know, but it's worth it. I'll include it on my invoice."

She was charging me for the cost of the lens? Didn't I explicitly tell her not to buy pro gear?

"In the future, please run these purchases by me first," I said.

"Don't you want me to get good images?"

"I do, but a fifteen-hundred-dollar lens is an expensive purchase."

Nancy got this weird look on her face, and I got the distinct impression I'd been way off on the price of the lens.

"Did you buy the two-point-eight lens?" I asked.

For those of you not following this conversation about photographic lenses, there are two different three-hundred-millimeter lenses Canon offers in their L series line. L series, by the way, refers to their line of pro lenses versus their consumer brand. One of the lenses has an aperture of F/4 to F/32. This is the less expensive one. The other lens at the three-hundred-millimeter focal length is an F/2.8 to F/32 aperture range. This basically gives you the ability to shoot in much lower light. However, it increases the price tag from fifteen hundred to around six thousand bucks. Of course, these prices don't include the extender she also mentioned. Add another four to five hundred dollars for that piece of gear.

"I assumed you'd want me to go with the faster lens, especially if I have to follow her at night," she said.

Yep, she'd bought the six-thousand-dollar lens.

"Are you upset?" she asked.

I was tempted to say "Hell, yes," but how do you yell at an older woman wearing a banana pant suit who is helping you on a murder investigation?

"It's a challenging cost to absorb, but I'll eventually get past it."

"I'm sorry. I should have asked you."

"This is our first case together." And probably last, I thought. "We have to figure out our workflow and communication process."

"I understand."

"Where did she go before she went to this guy's house?"

"Just routine stops. I followed her to the nail salon, the grocery store, the post office. I thought she might go by the Pomaika'i warehouse, but she never did."

"What happened after this conversation in the driveway?"

"They walked to the back of the house, and I lost sight of them. I observed the place from my car for two hours before I had to leave."

"Could you see them through a window?" I asked.

"No. He had all the window shades pulled down. That's another reason I suspect they were fooling around. I would have staked out the house longer, but I had to go to the restroom. Her car was gone by the time I got back. I can follow her again today if you'd like."

"Sure. That sounds like a good idea. Meanwhile, I'll work on discovering who this guy is."

Nancy and I spoke for a few more minutes, and then we went our separate ways. When I got back to my car, I took a photograph of one of Nancy's photos with my phone and texted the image to Juliana along with the question, "Do you know this guy?" My phone vibrated a moment later. I looked at the display and saw I was getting a call from Juliana.

"Where did that picture come from?" she asked.

"My assistant took it. I'm not sure of the exact location. Do you recognize that man?"

"Yes. He's the make-up artist and hair stylist who Marco always used on our photo shoots. His name is Phoenix."

"I'm sorry, but did you say 'Phoenix'?"

"That's right."

"I assume that's not his real name."

"As far as I know, it is."

"What's his last name?" I asked.

"I'm not sure. I never heard Marco or anyone on the photo shoots call him by his last name. It was always just Phoenix."

"Did Sophia interact with him much on the shoots?"

"No. She was rarely even there. She had no interest in them, but she might have met him at some social function like one of the fashion shows. Marco would often invite the models to his parties. It would make sense that he'd invite Phoenix, too. They were always elaborate events. People loved to come to them."

"My assistant thought there might be a romantic thing going on between Sophia and Phoenix."

"Did she see them kiss?"

"No. Her impression was based more on body language. Still, she might have guessed wrong."

"You already know my suspicions about Sophia. I can't believe she'd cheat on Marco with a man like Phoenix."

"We don't know that's what was happening, and it's a long way from committing adultery to murdering your spouse."

"What are you going to do now?" she asked.

"I'm going to look into Phoenix more and see what I can find out."

"Do you think he might have killed Marco?"

"There's no reason to think that, but he might know something that could lead to some other discovery. That's how these cases work. There's rarely one person who knows all the pieces."

I thanked Juliana for her time and ended the call after promising to keep her informed of even the smallest of discoveries. I was about to start the ignition on my car when an image of Nancy in her banana suit holding a pair of binoculars up to her eyes as she spied on Sophia and Phoenix popped into my head. I laughed out loud for several seconds. I don't know if you've ever done that, especially when you're alone. Then I spotted a family of four walking through the parking lot. They stared at me like I was crazy. I probably was. I tried to suppress my laughter, but the effort just made me laugh even harder.

Then I felt guilty for making fun of the woman's attire. She obviously thought it was stylish, and who am I to question someone's fashion sense when I usually wear t-shirts, shorts, and sandals?

My phone vibrated again. I assumed it was Juliana, but I saw Alana's name on the display. I answered the call, and she immediately went into a long rant, the subject of which terrified me.

18

THE BIG LIE

"I got a tip that Makamae is going to bring Hani back in for more questioning," Alana said.

"That's normal, isn't it? Maybe she just has some follow-up questions."

"No, it's not normal, not unless she's zeroed in on her."

I knew it wasn't normal, but I didn't think adding to Alana's nervousness would do any good.

"They're not going to bring you in a second time unless they've gotten new information and it's pretty damning. Makamae received an anonymous phone call. The person told her that Hani stole Foxx's gun from Harry's," Alana continued.

"The one Foxx said was supposedly destroyed in the fire?"

"Yes, unless you guys had more than one gun at the bar."

"There was only one that I knew about. You said it was an anonymous phone call. It had to be Ashley."

"Of course, it was. Who else would it be?"

What does Hani have to say about all of this?" I asked.

"I called her right before I called you. She denies it, but she's lying."

"How do you know?"

"She's my little sister, Poe. I always know when she's lying."

"Did you tell her you thought she was lying?"

"No. I pretended to buy it."

"Who gave you this tip about Hani's interview? Was it Detective Kalani?"

"No. I haven't seen her this morning."

"So who told you?"

"Let's just say she hasn't made a lot of friends at the station."

"Is there anything I can do to help?"

"Yes. Call Foxx. Find out what's really going on with that gun."

"Well, there's only two possibilities. Either Foxx gave Hani the gun and was dumb enough to tell Ashley, or else Ashley is making this whole thing up. If the gun's really buried in that landfill, we can't prove Hani didn't have it."

"No, but if it was destroyed by the fire, it also couldn't have been used to shoot Bill on that beach."

"I'll call Foxx right now," I said.

"Thank you. Call me back as soon as you learn something."

I ended the call with Alana and was debating whether to immediately call Foxx or drive straight to his house. Before I could make up my mind, my phone vibrated again. It was Foxx.

"Hello."

"We need to talk, now if possible," he said.

"I assume Hani called you."

"No, but I'm sure I'll hear from her soon. Ashley's done something, and everything is about to go to hell."

"It already has," I said.

"Can we meet somewhere in person?"

"Sure. Where?"

"Let's meet up at Harry's. We can talk in my SUV."

"I'm all of thirty seconds from the bar."

"I'll see you there shortly."

I ended the call and made the short drive to Harry's. The construction crew was working as I pulled up. I parked under a tree that had survived the fire.

There were a million thoughts racing through my head all at once and they wouldn't slow down despite my best efforts to remain calm. I knew Foxx well, just as much as Alana knew her sister. What he had to tell me was bad, very bad. I'd heard the deep sense of regret and apprehension in his voice. It took a lot to shake Foxx, but something, presumably the destroyed gun that was apparently not destroyed, had clearly gotten to him.

Foxx arrived and parked beside me. I climbed out of my car and walked over to his. He kept the motor running, and I opened the passenger door to his SUV.

"Hey, there," he said.

I didn't reply. I just climbed inside and shut the door behind me.

"You said everything had already gone to hell. What do you know?" Foxx asked.

"Detective Kalani apparently got an anonymous tip last night that Hani stole your gun from Harry's."

"Hani didn't steal it. I gave it to her."

"You gave it to her?" I repeated, since I wasn't sure I'd heard him correctly.

"I gave her the gun after I found out that Bill had beaten her."

"Why didn't you mention this before?"

"How can you ask me that? You know it was a .38 that shot Bill. It's the same as my gun."

"Once you learned that, what did you say to Hani?" I asked.

"I didn't have to say anything. She came to me and asked me to get rid of the gun."

"She asked you to get rid of the gun."

Why was I suddenly repeating everything he said?

"Yeah."

"Did you?" I asked.

"Hell yes, I did. I tossed it in the ocean. They'll never find it."

"What else did Hani say when she gave you the gun?"

"Nothing. She handed it to me and said she didn't need it anymore."

"Wait a minute. There's a big difference between 'I don't need this anymore' and 'Please get rid of this for me.' Which did she say?"

"I don't remember her exact words, but it was clear that I needed to get rid of it."

"And you didn't ask anything about whether or not she used it on Bill?"

"No. I didn't want to know, either. This is a huge problem, Poe."

"I think that goes without saying."

"Then Ashley had to go and open her BLANKING mouth. I can't believe she did that."

I don't think I need to offer any clues as to what Foxx really said instead of BLANKING.

"What does she know, exactly?" I asked.

"She knows I gave the gun to Hani. I know what you're going to say, so save your breath. I was upset. Hani had been hit and Ava had witnessed the whole thing. I needed someone to talk to."

"Does she know Hani gave the gun back to you?"

"No. I didn't tell her that part, and I don't intend to ever tell her. You're the only one who knows, other than Hani and myself. And don't go telling everything to Alana."

"Give her some credit, Foxx. She's not out to get you. She certainly isn't out to get her sister."

"She's a cop, Poe. I know exactly how much that job means to her. She's never going to cover up a crime."

I had to agree with Foxx that Alana would never obstruct the law, even for a family member. Would she do so for me? That was an interesting question, but it was also one I didn't have the time to ponder during that conversation with Foxx.

"You weren't there for the first part of our conversation last night. I've never seen her like that. I thought she might leap over the kitchen counter and try to strangle me," Foxx continued.

"What did you expect would happen? Your girlfriend got Hani arrested."

"Hey, it was Hani who assaulted Ashley, but I still told Ashley to drop it. I told her it would only make things worse if she reported it. I had no idea she was going to file that assault charge. I was furious when I found out."

"How did you find out? Did Hani call you?"

"No. Ashley told me after she got back from the police station. I've never seen her so giddy. She had this smug look on her face," Foxx said.

"Where are things with you two now?"

"Where do you think they are? I'm mad as hell at her."

"But does she know that?" I asked.

He paused, which made me realize he hadn't told her how he really felt.

"You didn't say anything to her, did you?" I continued.

"I've got to be careful, Poe. She could do a lot of damage. If she found out that I threw that gun in the ocean, things could get real nasty for Hani and me."

"How is she going to know?"

"Maybe she doesn't even need to figure that out. She knows I gave the gun to Hani, and she told the cops that."

"No, that's not what she told them. She told them Hani stole the gun."

"She's not going to implicate me, not now. But she sure as hell is showing her cards. She's letting me know how far she's willing to take things."

"I'm not trying to make light of this, but there's no way the cops can prove you gave it to Hani, and there's no way they can prove she stole it from Harry's. This so-called anonymous tip ultimately means nothing."

"You're missing the point. I can't break up with Ashley, not without her telling the cops that I helped murder Hani's ex-boyfriend."

"I get it. I'm just saying there's a big difference between saying something and proving it. It's her word against yours and Hani's."

"Yeah, but who the hell knows what else she'd say if I were to give her the boot. She could say I held the guy down while Hani shot him.

Sometimes juries don't need concrete proof to convict someone. They just have to think you did it."

"Remove Ashley's potential accusations from the equation for a second. What do you want to do with her? Do you want to tell Ashley to get lost or do you want to try to repair things with her?"

"She's not worth the drama she brings, and I could never love a woman who'd be more than happy to send Ava's mother to jail for the rest of her life."

"Then tell her to leave," I suggested.

"Haven't you been listening to a word I've said?"

"Yeah, I have, but what are you going to do? Let her keep living there and pretending everything is okay? How long is that going to last with you resenting her every time you look at her? A week? A month? Let's say Hani doesn't get arrested because the cops can't prove anything, and maybe everything calms down for a year or so. What happens if you break things off? There's nothing to stop Ashley from going to the cops then."

"I don't know. I just don't know."

Foxx paused a moment.

Then he asked, "Do you think she did it?"

"Who and what?"

"Hani. Do you think she killed that guy?"

"What do you think?"

"She looked scared, Poe, when she handed me that gun. Her hands were shaking."

"Do you remember what day she gave it to you?"

"Yeah, it was around the same time of the week that Mara said Bill had been killed."

I didn't respond.

"You didn't answer my question. Do you think Hani killed him?" Foxx asked.

"If I had to guess, I would say no."

"What are you basing that on?"

"Her personality. She's not a violent person."

"This is the same woman who attacked Ashley."

"I think pulling someone's hair is a far cry from shooting someone in the chest," I said.

"You keep saying she just pulled Ashley's hair. She yanked her to the floor and started hitting her in the face. Yeah, I was just as shocked as you were, maybe even more. I didn't think Hani had that in her, but maybe she attacked Ashley because her emotions were all over the place since she'd just killed a guy days before. Remember, we were having a meeting about what to do about Bill's murder. Maybe Hani's guilt got the better of her."

"I still don't think she did it. I'm not excusing her behavior. She was wrong to attack Ashley, but I think it was entirely a reaction to Ashley's comment. Again, I'm not making excuses. I just don't think she murdered Bill. I can't see that."

"Okay, let's say she didn't shoot him. It doesn't change the fact that I gave Hani that gun, she gave it back, and I tossed it in the ocean. So what do we do?"

"I know this is going to sound like an unsatisfactory answer, but we call Mara. You need a lawyer. Hani needs one, too. You both need to keep your mouths shut until we can figure something out."

Foxx nodded. I told him I'd check in with him later in the day. I climbed out of his SUV and walked back over to my car. I started the ignition and drove out of the parking lot. Where was I headed? Home. I needed time to think.

I'm sure you're wondering if I was telling Foxx the truth when I said that I believed Hani hadn't murdered Bill. I would have thought that a while ago, but I'd seen what Bill did to her face. I knew he'd thrown a rock through her daughter's window, and I'd seen Hani attack Ashley. Hani wasn't the same person anymore, although I doubted anyone would be after what she'd gone through.

19

WASHING MY HANDS

I WAS FEELING GUILTY. FOR SEVERAL TALES NOW I'VE REMARKED HOW I always strive to tell the truth. Now I'd just advised my best friend to lie and cover up his involvement in giving my sister-in-law his gun. That was only the beginning of the lies to come. I knew what Mara's advice would be to Hani. It would be the same thing I'd tell her. Put your hand on that Bible and swear you'd never even seen Foxx's .38.

I was beyond disappointed in myself, and I wondered if I was not any better than the guilty people I'd spent the last few years chasing around Maui. You may think I'm exaggerating my emotions, and that wouldn't be the first time someone has accused me of doing so. It's how I felt, though, and I had no idea how I was going to pull myself out of this situation.

I had an even bigger problem, and it was something I couldn't put off. Alana had explicitly asked me to call her back after speaking with Foxx. He'd been right when he'd said Alana would never be part of a cover-up, but I wasn't about to lie to my wife. So how did I handle the phone call?

I did one of the things I normally do when I get stressed out. I grabbed Maui's leash and took him for a long walk. The pooch seldom gave me any feedback. Okay, he never gave me feedback, but he was a good listener, perhaps the best one I'd ever come across. I'm sure you think I'm kidding when I say I talk my problems out to my dog. I'm not. I actually spoke to him while we did our walk, and I'm certain any neighbors who happened to gaze out their windows as we passed by their houses thoroughly assumed I was bonkers, or on drugs, or both.

A question popped into my mind when I was about halfway through my walk. How did I know Foxx was telling me the truth? I didn't think he'd lied to me, but maybe he hadn't told me everything there was to know. I knew him better than most, maybe better than anyone, but he'd thoroughly convinced me when he'd told me earlier that the gun had been destroyed by the Harry's fire. Foxx is normally an open book, yet he'd fooled me anyway. I didn't know if he'd suddenly gotten better at lying or if my subconscious just allowed myself to believe him because that's what I wanted.

I did my best to push those questions away and instead concentrated on calming myself with the walk. Alana called just as Maui and I turned onto our driveway to go back into the house.

"Hello."

"Did you speak with Foxx?" she asked.

"Yes. We met up at Harry's a little while ago."

"How long ago?"

"Maybe forty-five minutes or so."

She paused.

Then she said, "I need you to do something for me."

"What is it?"

"I can't be involved. I can't hear about any of this."

"I understand."

"I know you probably think I'm trying to keep my hands clean, and maybe I am, but things would be so much worse if I were to jump into this."

I knew what Alana was saying, and I also knew why she'd come to that decision. There had been a good reason for her to ask me how much time had expired between my meeting with Foxx and her phone call. She was a perceptive person, and she'd assumed our talk had gone badly since I hadn't immediately called her back.

"There's something I want you to do for me," she continued.

"What is it?"

"Protect my sister. Do what you have to do."

"I will."

"Thank you."

I ended the call with Alana and continued into the house with Maui. I felt like my head was spinning. Alana and I had never had that kind of conversation before where I felt she'd given me permission, at least that's what I'd thought she'd done, to skirt the law. Perhaps I'd misinterpreted things, but you heard what she said. She'd explicitly used the phrase "Do what you have to do." How would you have interpreted that?

Here was a problem, though. Where did I start?

My phone vibrated again before I had too much time to ponder that question. It was Nancy. She told me she intended to spend the day following Sophia and she wanted to know if I'd be willing to ride along with her to teach her the finer points of tailing someone. I didn't have the heart to tell her that I'm probably the worst person in the world to talk to about that task. I don't think I've ever successfully followed someone and gotten away with it. That's a pretty embarrassing thing for a private investigator to admit, but it's the God's honest truth.

Nevertheless, I accepted her invitation for a couple of reasons. I thought I was too close to the Bill Hodges murder investigation. I'd gotten emotionally involved, and I thought my brain needed some distance from the case for me to start seeing things a bit more clearly. I also felt bad for neglecting the Marco Giordano case. I was being paid to discover who'd murdered him, and so far I'd gained very little information. The biggest revelation had come from my fruit-wearing sidekick.

Speaking of Nancy's wardrobe, I'm sure you're wondering what she wore when I met her for our day of following Sophia. She didn't let us down. She was dressed in a forest green suit with little apples on it. I finally broke down and asked her where she bought all of these magnificent ensembles, and she informed me, with tremendous enthusiasm in her voice, that she'd found a company online that sold them. She said she also had a collection of suits with little animals that ranged from puppies to kittens to panda bears. I'm certain you'll be disappointed in my having fun with Nancy, but I asked her to send me the link to the website so I could order a Puffin pant suit for Alana for Christmas. Not only did Nancy do so, but she texted me the link while we sat in her car.

I was deeply impressed with Nancy's ability to tail Sophia. She kept several car lengths behind Sophia's car, and despite us hitting a few red lights when Sophia had managed to get through them while they were still green, Nancy always seemed to manage to easily figure out which way our subject had gone. We never lost sight of Sophia for more than a couple of minutes. The bottom line was that I was in awe, as well as envious, of Nancy's talents.

She did ask me a few times to let her know when I thought she'd made a mistake, which made me feel like an inadequate moron because I was doing my best not to break out my little Moleskine note book and start taking notes on what I was seeing Nancy do. Instead, I spoke to her in very general terms about the nature of investigations and the importance of paying close attention during the interview process. She nodded at my supposed brilliance and kept telling me how grateful she was that I'd decided to take her on as my full-time assistant. I didn't think I had done that, at least not in the full-time terms she'd mentioned, but I decided not to correct her so we wouldn't have an uncomfortable day in her car.

Sophia ran a couple of mundane errands, including a stop at a small grocery mart and another stop at an even smaller florist. We hit the proverbial pay dirt on her third stop. She pulled into the parking lot of a medical center. Nancy parked in the back and pulled out her binoculars, which she handed to me. She then grabbed her Canon camera and that insanely expensive zoom lens that she expected me to reimburse her for. She held the camera to her eye and snapped several shots of Sophia as she walked from her car to the front door of one of the medical suites. The large DSLR camera with the even larger telephoto lens looked somewhat ridiculous pressed against Nancy's small head.

"She's not going inside," Nancy observed.

"Maybe she needs to make a phone call first."

Sophia reached into her purse and removed her phone. She didn't make a call, however. She either sent a brief text or just checked the time.

I panned the binoculars to the name on the door of the medical suite. It listed the name of the doctor along with the word "Obstetrician" underneath.

"That's interesting," I continued.

"Are you looking at what I'm looking at?"

"I think so."

"Sophia's pregnant," she said.

"Maybe she's here supporting a friend. Maybe that's why she hasn't gone in yet."

"I'm going to say you're wrong about that, not unless men can suddenly get pregnant?"

"What are you..."

My words trailed off as Phoenix, our long-haired make-up artist and stylist, walked into my line of view.

"I knew they were having an affair. I just knew it," Nancy said, as she fired off dozens of shots of Sophia greeting Phoenix with a long hug, the two of them chatting for a second, and then both of them walking into the obstetrician's office.

"Sophia cheats on Marco with Phoenix. He gets her pregnant. Then she offs her husband so she can get his money and marry her lover. It's a classic reason for murder if I've ever seen one," she continued.

"You may be right," I said.

Nancy put down the heavy camera and turned to me.

"What else could it be?"

"I'm sure that's what it is, but I always tend to overcomplicate things. This doesn't prove she killed Marco. It doesn't prove Phoenix killed him."

"No, but at least we know where to concentrate our attention."

Nancy and I spent the next hour discussing possible ways we could get the proof we needed that either Sophia or Phoenix murdered Marco. Perhaps I shouldn't have said "Nancy and I" when it was mostly Nancy talking and me listening. I had difficulty even doing that because my mind kept drifting back to earlier in the day when Foxx dropped those bombs on me. I was also worried about how Hani's interview with Detective Kalani had gone, if it had even happened yet. I trusted Mara, but I didn't trust Hani's ability to get through the interview without causing more problems for herself and Foxx. Sometimes, well, often, she has a hard time controlling her emotions, and I could see her saying the wrong thing while Detective Kalani was just waiting to pounce.

Sophia and Phoenix eventually emerged from the doctor's office, spoke for a minute or so by the door, and then walked in opposite directions to their cars. We followed Sophia out of the parking lot and tailed her another twenty minutes until it became apparent she was heading back to her house. I advised Nancy that we should call it a day, and she drove me back to Lahaina where I'd met her earlier.

I thanked Nancy for her time, asked her to send me digital copies of the photos she'd taken, and then walked back to my convertible. I opened the door but then immediately shut it without climbing into the car. Instead, I walked a few blocks to the nearest bar and ordered a Negra Modelo. I had plenty of those beers at home, and they were infinitely cheaper than at the bar, but I just wanted a place that was a bit foreign to me. I sat by myself at the end of the bar and took a long pull of the cold liquid. I knew what I needed to do. I needed to have a face-to-face conversation with Hani and ask her some difficult questions.

20

OPEN

Just before I left the bar, I took a calculated risk and texted Detective Kalani a website link to the obstetrician's office where I saw Sophia enter. She immediately texted me back and asked me the significance. I told her that Sophia was pregnant. I didn't mention anything about Phoenix, nor did I tell her how I came about this information. Detective Kalani thanked me and that was that.

Later that night, I had a brief conversation with Alana regarding her visit with Hani. She told me Hani was doing okay, all things considered. I didn't press her for more information, nor did Alana ask me anything about the rest of my day. She spent the evening glued to the television again, and I repeated my night swim and jog around the neighborhood. I often worked out whenever I got stressed or needed a distraction. The way things were going with the Bill Hodges case, it looked like I might end up in the best shape of my life.

The next morning, I called Hani and invited her to meet me at the damaged restaurant location in Wailea. It was another sunny day on Maui, so I left the top down on the convertible for the long drive down the coast. I played Frank Sinatra's *Greatest Hits* album along the way. I have a confession to make. I never understood the appeal of

Sinatra when I was younger. Now I get it. I could easily listen to the guy all day.

I arrived at the site before Hani did, so I parked next to the building and walked down to the beach. The wind was a bit stronger than usual, and the waves were much higher. I stood at the edge of the ocean and closed my eyes so I could concentrate on the sound of the waves. It was a peaceful moment in what was otherwise a turbulent time in my life.

I turned away from the water and walked back up the hill to the parking lot just as Hani arrived. She parked beside my convertible and climbed out of her car. She took a quick look at the damaged building and then turned back to me.

"Why did you want to meet here?" she asked.

"I think this place has one of the best views on the island, maybe the best."

"Looks like the hurricane did a number on this building."

"It's not as bad as it looks. The windows and doors need to be replaced and the deck in the back is completely gone. All simple stuff compared to Harry's."

"How is Harry's coming along?"

"Fine. We'll be open again before you know it."

"So why are we here? I'm assuming you didn't want to just show me the view."

"I'm the new owner of this place. So is Foxx. Our company bought it, and we'd like you to be a part of it."

Hani paused a moment.

Then she asked, "What kind of part? I don't have the money to buy into something this big."

"You don't need any money."

"I also don't have restaurant experience."

I laughed.

"You seem to be trying really hard to talk me out of this when you don't even know what I'm about to offer."

"What is it then?"

"I don't want to open another restaurant. I want to turn this into an event space. Art shows, group events, wedding receptions. That's where you come in. This is a gorgeous place to get married. Your clients could do the ceremony out there on the beach, then everyone moves into this indoor space for the reception."

"It would be perfect. There's plenty of parking. It's by several high-end hotel properties."

"There's a full kitchen and bar inside, so it would be easy to serve whatever the customer might want for their reception."

"How exactly do I fit it?" she asked.

"I want you to push this place with your customers. For every wedding and reception that comes here, you get a healthy commission, a huge commission."

"Why are you doing this for me?"

"Because I believe in you, and I've been impressed with how fast you've grown your company. I also want good things to happen in this location. It's a special place, but the previous two owners have brought it bad karma. I want to turn things around."

I didn't mention the money I was also going to make from the business. I have plenty of it, and I don't really need any more. I'm also not going to say "no" to it, however.

"There's only one problem."

"What's that?" I asked.

"I don't know if I'm going to be around by the time you get this place open."

"You're talking about Detective Kalani."

Hani nodded.

"I had a conversation with Foxx," I continued.

"What did he tell you?"

"He told me he gave you his gun. He also told me you gave it back and asked him to get rid of it."

"I didn't kill anyone."

"I'm not saying you did, but why not admit that you had the gun? Why ask Foxx to get rid of it?"

"Because I knew how things would look to that detective. It doesn't matter if I did anything or not. She'll still assume I did."

"What did you tell her yesterday when you met with her?"

"I told her the gun was destroyed by the fire. It's what Foxx told me to say."

"When you were staying at my house, did you have the gun?" I asked.

"Yes. I kept it locked in the glove compartment of your car."

She waited for me to respond, but I said nothing.

"I'm sorry. I should have told you I had it. Does Alana know everything?" she asked.

"No, and it's better that we not involve her. When was the last time you saw Bill?"

"When he threw a rock through my window."

"He never confronted you after that? You never caught him following you?"

"No."

"What about his job?"

"What about it?" she asked.

"Did you know he'd been fired after photographs of you were delivered to the manager, Yuto Takahashi?"

"God, no. I didn't hear that. Who would have sent them?"

"You didn't have anything to do with that?" I asked.

"Are you serious? I didn't want anyone to see me like that. It's humiliating."

"Do you have any idea who murdered Bill?"

"No, but I've heard things."

"What things?"

"About Ryan."

"His friend?"

"Yes. Bill used to date one of Ryan's friends. I think they broke up about six months before I started seeing him. I heard Bill beat on her, too."

"When did you hear that?"

"After I broke up with him. I spoke to a few people and I heard about Ryan's friend."

"Did you speak to this ex-girlfriend directly?" I asked.

"No, but I believe it's true."

"Do you think Ryan knows about this?"

"Yes. I think that's one of the reasons he came by my house to apologize. That was the day you were there fixing my window."

"Did you say anything to Detective Kalani about this?"

"No, but I mentioned it to Mara. She told me there was no proof of anything, and she told me to say as little as possible to the detective. I didn't do it, Poe. I swear to you."

We spoke for a few more minutes about the investigation into Bill's murder, and then we switched back to talking about the new business. Hani thanked me for thinking of her and told me that she had a few different weddings on the horizon that she thought would be perfect for this location.

Hani left the site before I did since I told her that I wanted to walk around a bit more and think about the changes I wanted to make to the building. That was true. Well, it was mostly true. I also wanted to concentrate on what I'd just heard from Hani. She came across as believable to me, but I didn't have a gut instinct about her like Alana did. Hani had fooled me before in the past. Sure, those were usually over small things and nothing as serious as Bill's death.

I walked down to the beach a second time. I looked back to the building and remembered the way the deck had looked before it had been destroyed by the storm. It had showcased a breathtaking view of the beach and the ocean. I thought the new deck would also offer a fantastic spot for a photographer to take shots of potential weddings on the sand.

I was about to head back to my car and drive home when I received a phone call from Detective Kalani.

"Good morning, Detective."

"Mr. Rutherford, how are you today? It sounds like you're on the beach."

"Yes. I'm visiting a piece of property I just bought."

"A second home?"

"Not quite. A second business."

"Impressive. Makes me wonder why your lovely wife has to work at all."

"I think you know the answer to that, and that's a bit beneath you, don't you think?"

"My apologies. Let me get to the reason I called. I had a conversation with Sophia Giordano last night."

"Last night? You didn't waste any time, did you?" I asked.

"She was surprised I knew about the pregnancy."

"She didn't try to deny it?"

"No."

"And the father?"

"She wouldn't say. What I did find interesting was her statement that she and Marco had an open marriage. Apparently, he had no issue with her seeing other men."

"If that's true, then she might not know who the father is," I said.

"Maybe not. If it's true, that is."

"You question whether or not they had an open marriage?"

"I believe open marriages are more common than one thinks, but you have to admit, it's a convenient excuse."

"Do we know if Marco knew of her pregnancy?"

"She swears he did. She said he was happy with the news, even if he might not have been the father. Who do you think is the father by the way?"

"I have no idea."

"Something tells me you're holding back."

"That's not true. If I was holding back, I never would have sent you the news of the pregnancy to begin with."

"Maybe not, but I suspect you're feeding me little morsels so I'll owe you."

"Why would I need to do that?"

"Now who's being insulting?"

"Let's get back to the original reason you called. An affair is always a potential reason for murder, but an affair with the father of your unborn child certainly raises the stakes."

"So Sophia is back on your list of top suspects?" she asked.

"She never left it, but neither did anyone else."

"Everyone's a suspect in your book?"

"Never trust anyone, Detective. That's something I've learned over the years, but I assume that's already your policy."

"And what about you?"

"What do you mean?"

"Should I trust you?" she asked.

"If I were to stick with my theory, then I'd have to answer in the negative."

"Which brings me back to my earlier statement. I don't owe you for this, and I certainly won't look the other way with your sister-in-law."

"Do you really think she did it?"

"That's not something I'm willing to answer right now."

"I don't blame you. Hani's not the murderer, though, if you're wondering what my opinion is."

"And you know this how? I suppose you asked her and she said no."

"I didn't have to ask her. You're forgetting that she lived with me the week Bill Hodges was murdered. She was at the house."

"Not all of the time, at least according to your testimony and hers."

"True, but one doesn't murder someone and then come home as if nothing had happened. Only a psychopath could do that, and Hani could never be classified as one of those."

"Then who did it? Your friend, Doug Foxx? You? Should I turn my attention back to you?"

"You can look at me all you want, Detective. I have nothing to hide."

"Oh, I disagree. We all have things to hide, don't you think?"

She ended the call before I had a chance to respond.

I slipped the phone back in my pocket and looked out to the ocean once again as I thought about her question. "We all have things to hide, don't you think?" All things considered, I would have to say yes.

I called Eleanor, Marco's marketing assistant, right as I was about to leave the parking lot and asked her if we could meet on her lunch break. I said I'd had a potential break in Marco's murder investigation but that I needed to run some things by her. She agreed to my request after a few moments of hesitation.

We arranged to meet at a small grocery mart a few miles from the Pomaika'i headquarters. She said they had an organic lunch bar that she liked to frequent once or twice a week. I was starving myself, so I thought it made sense to grab something to eat as well.

Eleanor was already there by the time I arrived. We went inside and we each made ourselves a salad. I was in the mood for an early beer since everything was so crazy, but I opted for an Evian since we were in one of those stores that considered anything more than water and green tea toxic. I'm all for being healthy but sometimes these New Age places, if that's even an accurate way to describe them, can be a bit too much. Not everything we eat has to be kale or spinach, and some of us prefer to wear clothes that are made from something other than hemp. Sorry, I'm not trying to bash those things, but can you tell I was really in the mood for a Negra Modelo?

After paying for our salads and waters, Eleanor led me to a small cluster of picnic benches and chairs on the backside of the store. We sat under the shade of a tree with small purple flowers, which I believe is called a Jacaranda tree. I added that to my mental list of things to eventually plant in my backyard.

"You said you had a breakthrough. What did you learn?" Eleanor asked.

"Before I get to that, I wanted to ask you if there's been any fallout from our discussion the other day. Do you think Juliana suspects that you spoke to me a second time?"

"She hasn't acted strangely to me. She has been a lot tenser, but it doesn't seem to be directed towards anyone in particular."

"Do you know why she's been tense? Is it over Sophia selling the business?"

Eleanor nodded.

"Sophia's made it very clear that the business is being sold. None of us know what's going to happen or when. If we do get a new owner, they may elect to get rid of some of us."

I found that unlikely, especially since they had such a small staff already.

"Has Juliana spoken to you about it?" I asked.

"Nothing at length. She's made a comment here or there about how frustrated she is with Sophia. I even heard that she's trying to find a buyer to help her purchase the company herself."

"She told you that?"

"No, but the office walls aren't very thick. I think she thought everyone had already left for the evening, or maybe she thought I was in the back, but I heard her speaking with someone on the phone. It was clear she wanted to make an offer to Sophia."

"Where would Juliana get that kind of money?" I asked.

"I don't know. It was after normal business hours so I can't imagine she was speaking with someone at a bank. It must be a private investor."

"Even if Juliana came up with the money, do you think Sophia would sell to her?"

"I think Sophia already has someone specific in mind to buy Pomaika'i, so I doubt it, not unless Juliana could somehow offer a lot more money."

"I want to ask you a sensitive question about Marco and Sophia, and I'm sorry if some of this is a bit uncomfortable. Do you know if Marco and Sophia had an open relationship? Did you see either of them flirting with another person or maybe speaking about someone they admired?"

"Marco could be very flirty with lots of people. He was with me, too, but I knew it never meant anything. That's just how he was."

"It was never to the point that you were uncomfortable?" I asked.

"No. It never even reached near that point. He was just a very outgoing person."

"What about Sophia? Did Marco ever mention anything about her seeing another person?"

"No. Never."

"Did you ever see him act jealous around another man?"

"No."

"Do you know a man named Phoenix?"

"Of course."

"How well do you know him?"

"We're not friends, but I've worked with him dozens of times. He's done all the photoshoots for Pomaika'i. Do you think Sophia might be having an affair with Phoenix? Is that the break you were talking about?"

"I think she had or is having an affair with someone. Phoenix is at the top of my list."

"Why do you think that?"

"I've seen them together. Nothing explicit, but it's clear they have a close friendship, if that's all it is."

A thought then occurred to me. Perhaps I was looking at this from the wrong direction. I didn't think I could ask Eleanor about my new line of thinking since I had the distinct feeling she was beyond loyal to Marco and would never say anything to disparage him, even if it eventually led to finding his killer.

I thanked Eleanor for her time, and we finished our salads. It was probably the most boring salad in the history of salads, for what is a salad without croutons, bacon bits, and some form of fattening dressing like ranch? We spent our remaining minutes talking about that beautiful Jacaranda tree.

As we were leaving, Eleanor asked me if I thought we'd ever learn who murdered Marco. I told her I hoped for the best. Yeah, I know that's kind of a lame answer, but I didn't want to make a promise when I wasn't one hundred percent confident I could keep it.

I climbed into my convertible and headed back toward Kaanapali. I made a mental note to drink at least two beers on my arrival at home to make up for that ridiculously healthy lunch. I decided to take advantage of the drive time and phoned Hani. For those of you new to this series, Hani used to be a model on both Maui and during her stint in Los Angeles.

I asked her how many modeling agencies there were on the island since I couldn't imagine there were that many. She told me there were a few agencies, but there was apparently only one place to go to if you were serious about getting steady work. I asked Hani if she was still on friendly terms with the owner. She said she was since she had been one of her busiest models. I know that may sound boastful of Hani, but I didn't think she was exaggerating.

I asked Hani to call the owner and find out if her agency represented the models that did the Pomaika'i fashion shows and photoshoots. If they did, could she follow that question up with an inquiry into whether or not Marco liked to get friendly with the ladies? The models might not have been receptive to the navel-bearing make-up artist with the absurd name, but one or more of them might have been open to the idea of a fling with the wealthy and charismatic owner of the fashion company they were representing.

Alluding to my earlier epiphany which I kept from Eleanor, I thought Sophia might not have killed Marco because she wanted to be rid of him since she was having an affair. Perhaps it was in revenge for his affair with one or more of the lovely models. Did that mean I'd rejected the notion of them having an open marriage? Not necessarily, but I also didn't think they were as common as Detective Kalani thought they were.

You may be wondering why I think Sophia would be okay with having an affair of her own but wouldn't be okay with Marco doing the same in return. That's a fair question, but human beings are frequently hypocrites. We often criticize others when they do the exact same thing we're doing. Would she have been angry with him enough to hack him to death? Maybe not just over the affair, but add the baby from another man, her desire for the company to be sold so she could cash in, and things were definitely pointing toward Sophia as the guilty party.

It goes back to my often repeated saying, one that I'll readily admit I didn't create, that the simplest explanation tends to be the correct one. Perhaps Juliana nailed it from the beginning when she declared that Marco's wife had committed the crime.

I decided to give my brain a brief respite from this craziness, and I spent most of the afternoon swimming in the pool. I know what you're saying. "Poe, you always spend the day in the pool." That's true, but you have to admit this investigative snooping can be mentally exhausting, and it's not like I spent the entire time in the pool. I said "most," not all.

The rest of my time was spent on a trip to the local grocery mart. Normally I would have suggested to Alana a night out at Harry's, but that wasn't a possibility now. Soon, but not tonight. I bought two tuna steaks, asparagus, garlic, and a nice bottle of Moscato. Okay, I bought two bottles, but I don't want to come across as an alcoholic with all this talk of Mexican beers and wine.

Alana needed a nice distraction. I did, too. Hell, even Maui did after the chaos of Hani and her daughter living with us for a while. My plan was to spend a quiet and relaxing evening with my wife, and with any luck, that would lead to some other relaxing activities.

I sent Alana a text and asked her when she'd be getting home. She didn't respond, which wasn't necessarily a bad sign since I knew how busy she could get at work. She arrived back at the house a couple of hours later.

"You're just in time," I said as she walked through the door.

"Just in time for what?"

Her question hadn't come out as hostile, but I thought I'd detected a slightly aggressive tone in her voice that was indicative of someone who'd had a really bad day.

"Is everything all right?"

"No, it's not all right. I don't know how long I can work with that woman."

"What woman?"

"Makamae Kalani. She's a snake."

For clarification, she added a word that ended in the letters "ing" before the word "snake."

So much for my relaxing dinner and night of seduction.

"Are you making dinner?" she asked, after taking a look at the ingredients spread across the counter.

My phone rang before I could answer. It was Nancy. Were things about to spin in another direction again?

21

WELCOME DISTRACTIONS

"Take the call. I'm going upstairs to change," Alana said.

I pressed the talk button on the phone as Alana walked past me toward the staircase.

"Hey, Nancy. What do you have to report?"

"I followed Sophia again like you asked. I think we've been looking at the wrong lover."

"What do you mean?"

"She spent the entire morning at her home. Then around two-thirty, she left and drove straight for Kahului where she went to a motel."

"I'm assuming someone joined her."

"Yes. I had a great view of the lobby entrance from the shopping center parking lot across the street. Sophia was outside for maybe ten minutes or so before a man showed up. Then they both walked into the lobby."

"What did this guy look like?"

"He was around the same age as Sophia. He looked like he was around average height, average build. He had short brown hair. He was dressed in jeans and a dark-blue polo shirt."

"How long were they at the motel?"

"Well, this is the strange part. They both left the motel about half an hour later."

"They never checked into a room?" I asked.

"Not that I could see. Why do you think they even met in a motel versus her home? She has it all to herself now."

"A couple of possibilities. Maybe this guy lives in or near the same neighborhood as Sophia, and he doesn't want to risk a significant other seeing him or his vehicle at her house. Or maybe Sophia felt weird about sleeping with this guy in the same bed she used to share with Marco, only it's clear nothing happened since they didn't appear to get a room."

"Either way, it seems likely this guy is the father versus Phoenix."

"So why didn't this guy go with her to the doctor's office instead of Phoenix?"

"Maybe she hasn't told him yet that she's pregnant. Perhaps that's what she did today."

"Here's something I meant to tell you earlier and I didn't," I said, and I brought Nancy up to speed on what Detective Kalani had told me regarding Sophia's alleged open marriage with Marco and how he was seemingly okay with the child not being his.

"I don't believe that for a second. Even if they did have an open marriage, no man would be okay with raising a child when it might not be his," Nancy said.

"I'm not so sure about that. I think it happens more than you might think. Different people have different levels of forgiveness, and there might not have been anything to forgive in Marco's mind."

"What would you like me to do now? Do you want me to keep tailing Sophia?"

"We need to figure out who this mystery man is, but leave that to me. In the meantime, do me a favor and focus more on Pomaika'i. See if you can find out exactly who they do business with and who their rivals are. Maybe we're coming at this from the wrong angle, and this is more about a business deal gone wrong."

"Got it."

I ended the call with Nancy just as Alana walked back downstairs.

She'd changed into shorts and a tank top. Her mood, as judged by the look on her face, hadn't improved any.

"Was that your sidekick on the phone?" she asked.

"Yes."

"How are things working out with her?"

"Better than I could have expected. She's pretty relentless."

"Has she run up any more expensive bills?"

"Not that I know of, but I wouldn't be surprised."

I told Alana what I'd learned about Sophia's rendezvous with the brown-haired man in Kahului.

"What do you think? Does she have multiple lovers or is this Phoenix fellow more of a supportive friend?" Alana asked.

"I really don't know," I said, and I walked back into the kitchen to pick up where I'd left off on making dinner.

Alana followed me into the kitchen, and she sat on one of the stools on the outside of the island.

"What got you in a foul mood? What did Detective Kalani say to you?" I asked.

"She mentioned that you sent her a text about the Marco Giordano case. Why are you helping her with that?"

"Should I not help the police?"

"Of course, you should."

"Only there's a part of you that doesn't want me to be helping a certain cop in particular."

"I've met her kind before."

"What kind is that?"

"She's using you, Poe. She'll buddy up to anyone she thinks can help her. The moment this case gets solved, if it gets solved, she'll make sure people think you had nothing to do with it."

"I'll be okay with that."

"Why?" Alana asked.

"Because you and I will know the truth, and that's all that really matters. Detective Kalani can go before all the reporters in the world and say whatever she wants. I don't care. The less people know about me, the better. I'm just a guy who co-owns a bar in

Lahaina, and I happen to be married to the sexiest woman on the island."

"That's true," Alana said, and she finally smiled.

"I almost forgot."

I opened the refrigerator and pulled out one of the bottles of the chilled Moscato. I opened it and poured Alana a glass.

"I read about this brand in a wine magazine. It's supposed to be good," I continued, and I slid the glass across the counter to Alana.

She took a sip and put the glass back down.

"It is good. Very refreshing. So what's the occasion?"

"You mean me making dinner?"

"Yes."

"We've both been dealing with nothing but bad news the last few weeks. I thought it was time we concentrated on ourselves."

"Here's to that," she said, and she raised her wine glass.

I poured some Moscato into mine and tapped our glasses together.

"Cheers," I said.

"Hani called me this afternoon and told me about her meeting with you at Eighty-Eight," Alana said, referring to the building's previous restaurant name.

"She seemed interested when I pitched her the business idea."

"She's very interested. She's already thinking of ways to help you market the place."

"I figured she would. That's one of the reasons I asked her if she wanted to be involved."

"Foxx is okay with all of this?"

"Why wouldn't he be, and I thought you didn't want to talk about him anymore?"

"The way things are going right now, I didn't think he'd want to upset his girlfriend any more by going into business with Hani."

"It's not something we discussed. Maybe we should have."

"Was it your idea or his?"

"It was my idea to buy the building," I said.

"No, I mean was it your idea or his to involve Hani?"

"Mine, but he didn't seem to have any kind of objection. He immediately said he thought she would be great for the business."

"Why do you suppose that is?"

"I think you know why. He wants her to succeed."

Alana didn't respond to that. I wasn't sure if that's because she didn't believe it or if she was just getting tired of talking about Foxx, especially after she'd sworn to never bring him up again.

"I want to ask your opinion on something," I continued.

"What about?"

"The Marco Giordano case."

I told Alana about Nancy's discovery that Sophia had an afternoon motel meeting with an unknown man, as well as Sophia's declaration that she and Marco had an open relationship.

"It does seem to make her a much more likely suspect."

"The meeting seemed kind of reckless, don't you think?" I asked.

"In what way?"

"When Detective Kalani confronted Sophia with the knowledge that she was pregnant, Sophia must have wondered how Kalani had figured it out. If I was Sophia, I would have assumed that I'd been followed to the doctor's office. If that's the case, then I would also think that I might have been followed today as well."

"So why meet with your lover?"

"Exactly."

"Two things jump out at me."

"Which are?"

"One, if she knows she didn't murder her husband, then maybe she doesn't care if Makamae finds out about her lover. Possibility number two explains why they didn't check into a room. Maybe they didn't meet for sex. Perhaps they were trying to get their stories straight."

"I'm going with option two."

Alana took another sip of her wine.

"What do you think of Makamae?" she asked.

"In what way?"

"Her skills as a detective."

"I haven't had that much interaction with her."

"You've had a few conversations, and I happen to think you're a very perceptive person."

"Flattery will get you everywhere with me," I said.

"So what do you think of her?"

"I think she's crafty."

"Crafty?"

"You're right to be leery of her. I get the impression when I'm talking to her that she's playing the angles with me, searching for my weak spots, that sort of thing."

"Why deal with her then?" Alana asked.

"That's simple. Often people who play games aren't as smart as they think they are. She'll slip up and accidentally reveal something she doesn't want to reveal. I just have to make sure that I'm paying attention."

"Has she slipped up?"

"Not yet, at least not something that I've caught."

"How do you think she even found out about you?"

"I've been giving that a great deal of thought, and I've come up with a working theory."

I paused for dramatic effect.

"Don't keep me waiting," she said.

"I think she's after you."

"In what way?"

"She comes across as very ambitious to me."

Alana laughed.

"You think?"

"Okay, that's sort of obvious, but what do ambitious people do?"

"They scheme. They try to figure out how to get ahead."

"Yes, but they do more than that. They also look around them. They take in information by seeing who has what they want. She's got her eye on you. She wants what you have."

"And what do I have?"

"The reputation. The experience. She mentioned to me the other day that she spoke to Adcock about me."

"Adcock? I'm sure she got a really objective response."

"Yeah, we both can figure out what he said, but the point is she still asked. Why should she even care, but she does."

We both took another sip of our wine.

"This is really good," Alana said.

"I bought a second bottle."

"Don't tempt me. It's a work night."

I looked at my watch.

"It's still early. Have another glass."

"If I didn't know any better, I would think you're trying to get me drunk."

I smiled.

"Why would I do that?"

"I don't know. Why would you?"

"You know what your problem is?" I asked.

"What?"

"You're too good of a detective. Nothing slips by you. No wonder Detective Kalani wants to emulate you."

"Let's stop talking about that woman. She's ruining my mood."

"Fair enough. What would you like to talk about?"

"Pour me another glass," Alana said, and she slid her empty glass toward me.

"Yes, ma'am."

I did as she asked and returned the glass to her. She took another sip.

"Maybe we should put the talking to rest and concentrate on something else," she said.

"And what would that be?"

"Take me upstairs since that was your plan all along."

"You don't want dinner first?" I asked, and then I immediately wondered why in the hell I'd asked it.

"We can eat afterward."

I put my glass down on the kitchen island.

"Lead the way," I said.

22

THE STYLIST

MY NIGHT WITH ALANA HAD GIVEN US BOTH THE BREAK WE NEEDED
from the stress of the Bill Hodges murder investigation. There were
things I'd almost told her later that night, including the details of my
conversations with Foxx and Hani. I didn't say anything, though,
since I wanted to respect her wish to be left out of the case.

She fell asleep before I did, and I spent a considerable amount of
time just looking at her as she lay beside me. I still didn't know how I
got so lucky to be with her. I kept thinking that maybe it would finally
dawn on me one day, but it hadn't. I'm sure you're accusing me of
false modesty. "You've got to have something going for you, Poe," you
might say. I'm sure I do, but it's nowhere near in the same class as
Alana.

The next morning, I woke with a confidence that defied logic. I
was somehow convinced that I was going to solve every problem
known to mankind, or peoplekind, whatever the correct phrase is
these days. I decided to get aggressive with the Marco Giordano case
and confront Phoenix, our blond-haired Adonis who liked to wear his
shirts open to his waist. Fortunately, Hani provided me with some
ammunition for my potential interview with him.

She'd finally reached her former talent manager the previous evening and received some information that I found very enlightening. The first major piece of information was that the manager was unaware of any models who'd dated Marco or had even been propositioned by him. Granted, those models might have kept that from their manager, especially if they thought it would have looked bad for them. However, Hani let me know that her manager had a way of knowing what had happened on the shoots before the models even had time to phone and give her a recap on how the day had gone. Hani said it was always possible a model might have had an affair with Marco, but she assumed there'd be a small chance of that.

The second piece of information Hani learned was that Phoenix was not the ultra-successful make-up artist and stylist he claimed to be. He'd owned a hair salon in Kaanapali that had gone belly-up a couple of years ago. The talent manager couldn't swear the exact reason why Phoenix's business had failed, but the rumor on the street was that the stylist was lousy with his money.

After closing up shop, he'd made the transition to strictly doing make-up and styling for photoshoots. The talent manager said there were not enough high-paying commercial jobs to keep Phoenix busy, and he'd resorted to renting out his talents for weddings and other special events.

I asked Hani what the going rate was for a wedding make-up artist, and it was much lower than I'd assumed it would be, even for the larger ceremonies. The rate seemed even more depressing when one factored in the number of women he would have had to provide services for since a typical wedding package apparently included the bride, all the bridesmaids, and sometimes even the mother and mother-in-law. My assumption was that Phoenix viewed the work as beneath him, but that was just a guess.

Did all of this add up to Phoenix targeting the wealthy Sophia? Maybe. If so, did he know about his brown-haired rival for Sophia's affection? I thought it was time to see for myself.

Hani had talked the talent manager into giving her Phoenix's address. Hani texted it to me, and I saw he lived about twenty minutes past Paia. That made for a long drive from Kaanapali, but it gave me time to think and figure out an angle for my potential interview with him. Phoenix sounded like a desperate guy, and those were the easiest people to manipulate.

When I arrived at the address, I was a bit surprised to see a large house in a nice neighborhood up the hill from the coast. Then I remembered I'd already seen this house from Nancy's surveillance photographs. I didn't see how a struggling make-up artist could afford a place like this, though. I parked on the gravel driveway, walked up to the front porch, and rang the doorbell. A man in his 60s opened the door a moment later. He had a pleasant smile and greeted me with a warm "Hello, there," as if he'd been expecting my arrival. I asked him if I could speak with Phoenix, and he informed me that our make-up artist lived in a small cottage in the back of the house. That made sense since Nancy had specifically said she'd observed Phoenix and Sophia walking around the house versus going through the front door.

I thanked the owner and made my way around to the back. The word "cottage" was probably a bit too nice to describe the only structure I saw. It looked like a small shed had been converted into living quarters. Tall grass surrounded the structure. A red bicycle was leaning against the wall by the wooden door. A surfboard was propped up against the wall on the opposite side of the door. There was one window, which was opened all of the way, and I could hear rock music playing inside the cottage/shed.

I knocked on the door and saw Phoenix walk to the window.

"Can I help you?" he asked.

Wouldn't it have been easier just to open the door?

"Yes, I was wondering if I could have a moment of your time."

"Who are you?"

"My name's Edgar Rutherford."

"What is this about?"

I was tempted to say that I wanted to hire him for the island's largest photoshoot ever, but that would have been cruel. Instead, I told him I wanted to speak to him about the Pomaika'i clothing line. He paused a moment and then opened the door. He didn't invite me inside, thank goodness. Instead, we spoke in front of the surfboard I mentioned earlier.

I found it interesting that Phoenix was dressed in a pair of navy-blue shorts with frayed bottoms and a dirty white tank top. The stylish silk shirt was nowhere to be found. His long blonde hair was loose and fell across his shoulders. The guy looked more like a surfer than anything else.

"What is it you want to know about Pomaika'i?"

"I understand you do all their fashion shoots," I said.

"That's right, and also their shows. They're a good client. Do you do business with them?"

"In a manner of speaking."

"How did you find me here?"

"I have my sources. I'd like to ask you a few questions about Sophia Giordano."

"Who?"

"Come on now, Mr...Do you have a last name?" I asked.

"No, just Phoenix."

"Okay, Mr. Phoenix. We both know you're well aware of who Sophia Giordano is."

"Listen, she's a friend, and I don't give out information about my friends to people I don't know."

"That's very admirable."

I looked past him through the open door into his cottage. There was a cot against the back wall and a short, wooden table at the head of the cot. The radio that was playing the rock music was on top of the table. The floor was a concrete slab, and there was a tattered green rug over part of it. Phoenix saw me looking inside and shut the door.

"I think you should leave," he said.

I pulled out my phone and clicked on the photo application. I turned the phone toward him.

"Do you recognize this man?" I asked, showing him one of the photos Nancy had sent me of the brown-haired man standing outside the motel lobby with Sophia.

"No. I've never seen him before," Phoenix said a bit too quickly.

I flipped to the next photo, which showed Sophia and the man walking into the motel lobby.

"What about this one?" I asked.

I waited for Phoenix to reply, but he didn't.

"You don't seem upset," I said.

"Why should I be?"

"I just showed you a photograph of your lover with another man."

Phoenix laughed.

"My lover? Who told you that?" he asked.

"Who is this guy? I know you know."

"I don't know nothing."

I was tempted to correct his grammar, but I let it slide since I hate people correcting mine.

"You owned a hair salon in Kaanapali, didn't you?"

"What does that have to do with anything?" he asked.

"A couple of things, actually. I'm in the process of opening a venue in Wailea that's going to cater to weddings and other events like art shows, fashion shows, you name it. I'd love to add you to the list of people we work with. I think it could be a good thing for you."

Phoenix didn't respond, not that I expected him to. I knew what he was doing. He was trying to figure out how much crap I was full of.

"The second thing is more of an observation. Stylists are a lot like bartenders in that people feel comfortable talking to them. For example, my stylist is always telling me stories about his clients, and I'm always shocked at the things his customers freely admit to him. Then I realized I was doing the exact same thing since I was telling him about my wife, our vacations, my dog, you name it. I don't know why I do it. I just do. So forgive me if I don't believe you don't know who that guy is in the photograph with Sophia. I'm sure you know his name, his address, hell, I bet you even know his shoe size, if you get my meaning."

Phoenix still said nothing.

"I also know that stylists work for tips, so here's what I'm going to do. I'm going to ask you four questions. You answer those questions, and I'll make it worth your while."

He hesitated.

Then he said, "Let me see the money."

I pulled my wallet out of my pocket and opened it so he could see the cash inside. I'd conveniently placed a one hundred dollar bill on the outside so that would be the denomination he'd see first.

"Question one," I said, without waiting for him to reply. "Are you and Sophia having an affair?"

Phoenix laughed again.

"No. She's a great lady, but we're friends. That's all we've ever been."

"Question two. Who is the guy she met at the hotel and is he the father of her unborn child?"

"That's two questions."

"Very well."

"His name's Victor Perrin, and yes, he's the father, at least that's what Sophia told me."

"Last question. What do you know about Marco's death?" I asked.

"That's a pretty broad question."

"It's still just one question."

"I don't know much about it. Sophia told me people think she did it. The cops have met with her several times."

"Maybe that's just because she was Marco's wife."

"Maybe, but Sophia also knows Juliana is convinced she killed Marco. Sophia didn't. She would never hurt Marco. She loved him."

"Yet she'd have an affair with some other guy," I pointed out.

"Hey, if that's the arrangement they had, then who are you to judge?"

"So they did have an open marriage?"

"Sorry, but you're out of questions."

I reached into my wallet and removed my bribe, which I handed to him.

"Did you like Marco?" I asked, pushing my luck with the number of questions. Nevertheless, I had a feeling he'd be willing to answer this one.

"Yeah. I liked him. He was a great guy. He believed in me. He was willing to pay when others turned their back on me."

"Who do you think killed him?"

"I don't know. If I did, I would have told the cops by now. It wasn't Sophia, though. There's no way it was her."

I thanked Phoenix for his time and walked back to the front of the house. I typed the name Victor Perrin into the notes app on my phone. I needed to learn everything I could about Mr. Perrin. It was obvious he was either married or in a serious relationship. Otherwise, there would have been no need to meet Sophia at that crummy motel. His presumed relationships with two women made him an easy target, but I seldom liked shooting fish in the proverbial barrel. There was no challenge to it, and what is life without a challenge?

The question was: Did Victor have anything to do with Marco's death? If not, where in the world did I go next?

23

A NIGHT OUT

I'M SURE YOU'RE WONDERING WHAT I THOUGHT OF PHOENIX, OR whatever his real name is, living in the guest cottage – cottage in big, fat air quotes. The truth is I wasn't the least bit surprised. People are often not what you assume them to be. You may have another question regarding Phoenix. Did Sophia know the truth about his finances? My guess is yes, but I suspect she ignored it since she was in need of a confidant she thought she could trust.

Well, we know how that turned out. Phoenix was more than happy to tell me everything he knew about her, at least enough to satisfy my handful of questions, for a few bucks. I'm sure if she ever confronted him about it down the road, he would deny everything, and he'd probably get away with those denials. He could always blame the cops for tailing her to that Kahului motel, and that would sound like a more than plausible excuse.

I stopped in Paia on my way home and grabbed a fish sandwich and a beer from a restaurant on the corner of Paia's one and only intersection: Hana Highway and Baldwin Avenue. The restaurant was usually slammed, but I'd arrived at an off time and didn't have to wait that long. I was halfway through my delicious meal when my phone vibrated. I knew who it was even though I hadn't bothered entering the person's name into my contacts list. I'd hoped her presence in my life would be a temporary one. Unfortunately, that didn't seem to be the case. I thought about letting it go to voicemail, but insanity overtook me and I hit the talk button.

"Hello, Ashley."

"Where is he?"

"Where is who?" I asked.

"Don't play dumb. You know exactly who I'm talking about."

"Well, if you're referring to my dog, Maui, then I assume he's probably on the living room floor taking a nap until I return home."

"I'm not talking about your G.D. dog. Where is Foxx, you asshole?"

My sanity returned, and I hit the end button on my phone. I picked up my sandwich again and took another large bite. My phone vibrated a second later, but I decided not to grab it so I could concentrate on chewing the delicious fish. I washed it down with a long pull of my beer. I'd decided to go old-school and I'd ordered a Bud Light. Please forgive me, all of you beer connoisseurs.

My phone eventually stopped vibrating on the wooden table, but a few seconds later, it started again. I picked it up this time.

"Hello, this is Poe. How may I help you?"

"Don't you dare hang up on me you..."

Her words hadn't trailed off, but I didn't hear what came next since I'd ended the call again. I took another bite of the sandwich and then finished my beer.

The phone vibrated again.

"Hello," I said.

"Stop hanging up on me."

"Maybe if you would act like a pleasant person and stop cursing me, then we could have a conversation."

"Can you please tell me where Foxx is?" she asked.

"I haven't spoken to him in a while. When was the last time you talked to him?"

"He left early last night and said he had some errands to run. I asked him what they were and he just walked out the door. He still hasn't come back."

"He stayed out all night?"

"Yes, and all day today. I've called him God knows how many times."

"Okay, let me see if he'll take my call."

"I know who he's with," she said.

"Who?"

"Your sister-in-law. I went by her house last night when he didn't come back. Her car wasn't there."

"Hani parks in the garage."

"I know that. I walked up to her garage and looked through the window. It wasn't there."

"I assume your theory is that they have something going on. They don't."

"No offense, but I don't believe you. I know you'd cover for him."

That was a true statement, so I didn't bother disputing it. On another note, I was a bit surprised by her use of the phrase "No offense" since I didn't think she had any issue with offending me or anyone else for that matter.

"Hani has more than moved on from Foxx, and he hasn't been interested in her for years. The only reason they talk now is because of Ava. That's it."

"He spends the night away from home and she does too? It's no coincidence."

"I don't know what to say, Ashley. I'll try to get a hold of him and make sure he's okay, but I'm sure he is."

"If you do, tell him not to bother to come home. I'm done with him."

She ended the call before I could respond, which was just as well since I didn't really have anything funny to say. Any potential jokes flew right out of my head as I tried to figure out why she apparently assumed Foxx didn't need to come back to the home he owned, not

Ashley. Also, if she was "done" with him, as she'd just claimed, then why was she so obsessed with finding him? Well, okay, I knew the answer to that.

I was sure Foxx was okay, but this did bring up an interesting question. Had Foxx decided to give Ashley the old heave-ho and he was conferring with Hani on the best way to handle the potential fallout as it related to the Bill Hodges murder investigation? I couldn't think of another possibility since I found the romantic one Ashley assumed was going on to be absurd. I didn't think Foxx would be dumb enough to leave one crazy lady and get back involved with another one. Yes, Hani had come a long way in reaching a level of stability since becoming a mother, and I would hate to see that progress set back by her getting involved with Foxx again.

I thought of calling Foxx but decided against it. Instead, I phoned Alana and asked her if she knew anything about Hani being out the night before. She said she didn't but that she would call her mother since she assumed she would have been the one to watch Ava.

I ended the call with Alana, finished my lunch, and headed outside to my car. I decided I needed another break, and I turned in the opposite direction and drove back down Hana Highway to Ho'okipa Beach Park on Maui's north shore. If you've been to Maui, then I'm guessing you've spent at least an hour sitting on the cliff and watching the windsurfers and kiteboarders. I don't have the athletic ability to ever try the sports myself, but there's something relaxing about watching their acrobatics.

I also used the time to do some research on Victor Perrin. I found a Facebook page for him and confirmed the guy was definitely married. His wife's name was Susan, and they had two children, which I easily discovered from looking through Victor's posted photographs. The little girl looked to be around eight or nine while their son was probably five or six. It's amazing how many people don't turn on the security settings on their pages. Susan was just as careless, and I did a thorough review of her page as well.

Her most recent photograph showed the Perrin family having an ocean-side lunch in Lahaina. I knew the exact restaurant, too, since I recognized the gorgeous view of Lanai in the background. I was pretty sure Alana and I had lunch at that same table. I believe I had a blackened tuna sandwich and Alana had lobster, but I digress.

Judging by Susan's big smile at the restaurant table, she had no idea that Victor was about to become a father to a third child. Susan was an attractive lady and they looked like they had a happy family, so why had Victor decided to step out on her? It was cruel and heartless and I found myself loathing the guy when I hadn't even met him yet.

I went back to the original Google search of Victor and found a listing for him at a restaurant in Kaanapali. I discovered that he was the general manager of the place, which might have been where Sophia had met him. The restaurant was a seafood joint, which wasn't surprising since we were on an island. I'd been to the place just once. The food was okay, certainly nothing spectacular that justified the enormous bill, and I hadn't bothered to ever return.

I pulled up Sophia's Facebook page and scanned through her posts and photographs. I didn't see any images of Victor. I didn't expect to see a shot of them hugging each other while the sun set in the background, but I wondered if I might come across an image of a large event for the Pomaika'i fashion line. There were plenty of those images, but I didn't see Victor anywhere. I did see many of the models hanging around Marco, Sophia, and Juliana. I also saw Phoenix in several of them as well. There was even one shot of Sophia planting a big kiss on his cheek while they both held glasses of white wine.

I found a link to the Pomaika'i Facebook and Instagram pages. I clicked on the Instagram account first. There were dozens of shots of the models wearing Marco's fashions across the island. The photography was good but nothing earth-shattering or original about the compositions. I clicked on the company's Facebook page next and saw tons of videos of their fashion shows. There were also several videos of Marco and Juliana talking about the company. There was even a three-minute video I watched that featured a sort of behind-the-scenes moment while Marco spoke to Juliana about some of his new designs, which were hand drawn on a large pad of paper.

It would take a while to go through all the videos, and I wanted to spend my time focusing on my potential meeting with Victor. I sent Nancy a text and asked her to go to the Pomaika'i Facebook page and search through the videos for anything interesting that might pop out. She wrote me back and said that she would get started at once. She then texted me back again and asked if I'd ordered that puffin pant suit for Alana, and for some strange reason, I told her that I intended to that night.

I was about to leave the beach when I got a call from Alana. Perhaps she'd had some sort of psychic revelation that I was about to order her a hideous ensemble.

"Hey there."

"I got a hold of my mother. She confirmed that Ava was with her last night. Hani came and got Ava this morning," Alana said.

"Did your mother know where Hani was?"

"With Foxx, but she doesn't know why."

I didn't respond.

"I hope they're not doing anything stupid," she continued.

I wanted to ask Alana if she was referring to a potential criminal act, like mapping out more lies to the police, or if her mind had jumped to a possible romantic fling. Instead, I kept that question to myself since I didn't want to drag Alana into the investigation.

"According to Ashley, Foxx still hasn't come home."

"Can you blame him?" Alana asked.

"No, I can't, and maybe this is finally the time when he hands Ashley an airline ticket back to Florida."

"I hope he knows what he's doing."

"I'll try to track him down. See what he says."

"How are things going with the Marco Giordano case?"

"Fine, I think. I'm starting to get my soul dirty again being around these people."

"What did you find out?"

"I'm not sure you want to know."

"I probably don't. Good luck. Makamae Kalani is counting on you. That's the only way she's going to solve that case."

I was tempted to laugh, but I knew Alana hadn't meant it as a joke.

24

VICTOR PERRIN

As I mentioned earlier, I'd woken up feeling like I could conquer the world, or at least this little island I now lived on, so I decided not to postpone my meeting with Victor. It was nowhere near the dinner hour, so I thought now would be the perfect time to catch him at his restaurant. This was certainly going to be a hostile meeting since there was no way he was going to take it lightly that I was confronting him over his affair with Sophia.

I left Ho'okipa Beach Park and made the long drive back to Kaanapali. I put Frank Sinatra back on the car stereo. His songs "Luck Be a Lady" and "I've Got You Under My Skin" made my confidence soar even higher. For probably the millionth time since arriving on Maui, I reflected on how much my life had changed. My days stuck in a gray cubicle at the architecture firm seemed like they were from some bizarre previous life that might have been more of a dream than reality. Check that, more of a nightmare than a dream.

I arrived at the restaurant and saw Victor's dark-green Jeep parked near the back of the lot. I'd seen the vehicle on one of his Facebook posts where he'd shown a family outing to the beach. The Jeep had the top down, and I saw a few beach towels in the back. There was even a metal dog bowl. A wife, two kids, and a dog and he still wanted to cheat on Mrs. Perrin? What a jackass.

I entered the restaurant and wasn't surprised to see there was no hostess at the front since the place was empty. The sign outside stated they didn't open until five. I walked to the back where I found a bar placed near the kitchen doors. There was a guy in his twenties doing inventory of the liquor. He looked up at me from his clipboard.

"Sorry, man, but we're not open yet."

"I know. I was looking for Vic," I said, hoping I'd guessed a nickname correctly so the bartender wouldn't hesitate to think I was a friend.

"He's in the back. I'll go get him for you."

"Thanks. I appreciate it."

I leaned against the bar while I waited a few minutes for Victor to walk through the kitchen doors. He eventually appeared, wearing a pair of black dress pants and a sand-colored button-down shirt. His hair was brown and cut short, and there was no mistaking the fact that he was the same man I'd seen in Nancy's photos outside the motel. Score one for Nancy and another one for Phoenix being truthful.

"Can I help you?" he asked.

"Yes. Perhaps we can grab a booth so we can talk in private."

"What's this about?"

"The Pomaika'i clothing line. I'm thinking of investing in the company, and I understand you have a close, personal relationship with the owner."

Victor stared at me for several long seconds. Then he nodded, and I followed him to a booth near the front of the restaurant. He slid onto one of the seats while I took the other on the opposite side of the booth.

"Who are you?" he asked.

"I'm going to be honest with you because I want to make sure you understand the gravity of the trouble you're in. I'm looking into the death of Marco Giordano."

"I don't know anything about that."

"I don't believe you, not for one second."

"I know nothing," he insisted. "I think you need to leave."

"Now why would you say something like that? You wouldn't have sat down with me if you didn't know exactly what I was referring to back at the bar. You are going to answer my questions because I have photographs of you with Marco's widow at a motel. Couldn't you two have picked a nicer place by the way?"

I expected him to lash out at me after that cheap shot, but he didn't.

"Whatever there was between Sophia and me, it's over. She made that very clear."

"How long did the affair last?" I asked.

"Around six months. I was nothing but a distraction for her."

"And for you?"

"The same."

"How did the two of you meet?"

"They asked us to cater one of their shows. We don't normally do that sort of thing but it was a huge event and it sounded interesting. Sophia was there. We got to talking and then she called me the next week. Things started pretty quickly after that."

"You said she ended things with you, so why did you meet at the motel this week?"

"It was a convenient location to meet. That's when she broke things off. I guess she felt the need to do it in person. She felt guilty."

"About what?"

"She told me how much she missed her husband. She said she felt bad being with me, knowing that he was gone."

"That makes no sense."

"I understood it in a strange kind of way. She didn't try to hide our relationship from Marco. I don't think she threw it in his face, either. She said they had an understanding. But now that he's gone, I don't think she's interested in seeing anyone else for a while."

"Did Sophia ever say if Marco was seeing anyone?"

"No, and I never asked. It felt weird even talking about him."

"She would speak about him while you two were together?" I asked.

"All the time."

"What did she say to you after he was murdered?"

"She was devastated. She called me and let me know about his death, but I didn't see her again until this week at the motel."

"Did you talk about his murder?"

"Yeah. She said the police still have no idea who did it."

"Does she?"

"No, and she said she didn't think the cops would ever be able to figure it out."

"She said that?"

"She said they had no leads. I think she's going to leave the island. I think she just wants to start over somewhere else."

"How can she do that when she owns the clothing line?"

"She could pay Juliana to run it if she wanted to, but I think she wants to sell it. She's already been talking to this company about buying it. Look, I don't know anything more than that."

I wasn't going to let him off that easily. We spoke for several more minutes in which I basically asked him the same questions. He gave the exact same answers. I didn't think he was an accomplished liar. Instead, I suspected he was telling the truth. Victor came across as nothing more than a scumbag, philandering husband who saw Sophia as a plaything and nothing more. He'd gone to the motel not knowing that she intended to end her affair with him. Rather, he thought he was in for a couple of hours of fun and games with the widow of a man who'd recently been butchered to death. Victor didn't care about that. I doubted he cared about anything other than himself.

As much as I disliked Victor, I didn't think he had anything to do with Marco's death, nor did I think he knew anything about who really did it. He seemed to have no intention of leaving his wife and kids, a fact easily determined by the number of times he begged me not to tell Susan what kind of man she'd really walked down the aisle with. Granted, he didn't put it that way. Instead, he'd almost broken into tears when he declared how hurt she'd be. That part, I didn't believe. I believed he didn't want to get caught because he didn't want to have to deal with the fallout of a divorce, but I doubted he really cared about how it would affect her emotions.

I left the restaurant and texted Nancy, informing her that I'd learned nothing from my meeting with Victor except for the confirmation that he was a deadbeat. Can you tell I didn't like the guy? She immediately called me and asked me specific questions. I ran through the interview with her as I drove home. She seemed rather preoccupied with determining whether or not I thought Victor had more than one affair. I told her that I didn't know but that I would answer in the affirmative if I had to put money on it.

I asked her if she'd made much progress on the social media videos. She told me she'd watched several of them but she'd had to break away when her husband, Ross, twisted his back and needed help to get to the sofa. According to Nancy, she was rubbing Bengay on his bare lower back while talking to me. I knew what Ross looked like, and the mental image of the rail-thin Nancy lubing up the large Ross was a bit too much for me to take. I faked getting a call from Alana and informed Nancy I would talk to her later.

I got home and took Maui out to the backyard since he'd been cooped up in the house most of the day. I always marveled at his ability to go from a deep sleep to a full sprint across the yard in a matter of seconds. I've pulled leg and back muscles just limping to the bathroom in the middle of the night. I watched the Morkie run from one side of the yard to the other as if he were chasing an imaginary squirrel. He then turned suddenly and ran over to me. He stopped at my feet and looked up at me as if expecting me to bestow on him a warm "Thank you" for his efforts in keeping the Rutherford household and yard safe from those who would dare to wander onto our property. I bent over, rubbed the top of his head, and gave him an overly enthusiastic "Good boy." Satisfied by my approval, he turned again and ran to the back of the yard where he began to bark at the incoming waves. I still don't know what it is about the ocean's waves that he finds so fascinating.

I popped back into the house and grabbed a bottle of water. I then changed into my swimsuit, walked back outside, and jumped into the pool. The water was cool and I found it refreshing after all of that driving in the hot sun. I was about to reflect on my day of interviews with Phoenix and Victor when I remembered I was supposed to call Foxx and see where he was. I groaned at the thought of getting involved in this drama, but I also realized his evening with Hani might have serious ramifications to the potential case against Hani, Foxx, or both of them.

I climbed out of the pool and walked to the patio table where I'd placed my phone.

"Have you gotten a hold of him?" I heard Ashley's voice say.

For a split second, I thought the woman had grated me so badly that I could actually hear her in my head. Then Maui started barking in the distance and I saw him darting toward the gate. I turned and saw Ashley walking toward me. Maui ran up to her and I was convinced he was going to wrap his mouth around her ankle. I called out to him and he stopped a few feet from her.

"Well, what did he say?" she continued.

"I haven't called him yet. I had a couple of people I needed to meet with."

"Call him now, while I'm here."

"I'm sure he's fine, Ashley. He just needs time."

"Time for what?"

"For whatever it is that's bothering him."

"I'm sure all of this makes you happy."

"All of what?" I asked.

"The problems I'm having with Foxx. You've never liked me. I get it."

"I don't know you, Ashley. When we were in college, you were the Florida girl Foxx hooked up with on occasion. Then we met briefly in Miami, and the next thing I know you're showing up at my bar. I went with it, and you and Foxx seemed happy with each other. That was good enough for me."

She said nothing, and although I was tempted to stop, I kept going.

"Then you had to go and start messing with my family. So the answer is no. I don't like you. Maybe you and Foxx will work things out. Maybe you won't. But if you do, I'd prefer that you not come down here anymore."

"Trust me, I won't. You're the last person I want to see."

"Okay, that's fine. Please go."

Maui growled as if he'd been able to understand everything Ashley and I had said to each other, and he wanted to emphasize my desire to have her leave.

"If your dog bites me, I'll kick him," she said.

"If you dare hurt that dog, I'll toss you into the pool. Then I'll drag you out of here myself."

She stared at me for a few seconds, and I supposed she was trying to figure out if I was bluffing or not. Here's a clue. I wasn't.

Ashley finally turned from me and walked out of the backyard. Maui didn't follow her. I didn't either. The woman was gone, at least for now, but I knew that wasn't the last we'd see of her.

25

OUT

AFTER ASHLEY LEFT, I JUMPED BACK INTO THE POOL AND SWAM LAPS TO get the frustration out of my body. Despite my earlier feelings of invincibility, I realized as I swam that I really hadn't accomplished much during the day except to scratch Phoenix and Victor off my list of suspects. Maybe I should say they weren't off the list, but I'd certainly moved them to the bottom. Sophia was looking more and more like the main suspect since she checked all of the classic boxes of motive, means, and opportunity.

I climbed out of the pool after my limbs started screaming for mercy and headed into the house to take a shower and change into a t-shirt and shorts. I went back downstairs and plopped onto the sofa to watch some television before Alana got home. I found *Total Recall*, the original and not the God-awful remake, on one of the movie channels. Arnold had just arrived on Mars when I sat down to watch. Side question, do you think the events really happened or was it all just a psychotic dream in his head? Maybe you haven't even seen the film and you have no idea what I'm talking about. Oh well, let's move on.

I was about to grab a drink when Alana walked through the door.

"You're not going to believe what I just saw," she said.

"What's going on?"

"I drove past Foxx's house, and it looks like all of Ashley's things are on the driveway. There's a police car there, but I didn't see Foxx anywhere."

"I'm surprised you didn't stop."

"Are you kidding? The last thing I want to do is get involved in that drama."

I told Alana how Ashley had been over to the house a little while ago and demanded to know where Foxx was.

"Maybe you should go down there," Alana suggested.

Now it was my turn to ask who was kidding who.

"I'm not going to touch that with a ten-foot pole," I said.

Alana sat down beside me on the sofa and took a quick look at the television.

"You're not watching this, are you?"

"I guess not."

"Good because there was a program I recorded last night that I wanted to see."

"Why didn't you just watch it last night?" I asked.

"Because there was another program on that I wanted to watch instead."

"What is it?"

Alana proceeded to tell me it was about MacArthur's handling of the Pacific campaign during the Second World War. I was beginning to suspect that she might have been reincarnated from a deceased soldier considering her fascination with that topic.

Having said all of that, I was really getting into the documentary when my phone vibrated.

"That's Foxx," Alana said without taking her eyes off the television.

"How do you know that?"

"It's been at least an hour since I drove by there. He's probably gotten her off his property and now he wants someone to vent to."

I picked up my phone from the coffee table and looked at the text message. It was from Foxx, and he asked if I could come down to his house.

"Was I right?" Alana asked.

"Yeah."

"Are you going down there?"

"I don't want to."

"You should go."

"All right."

"Take the dog with you."

"Why?"

"He gets this separation anxiety thing when you leave."

I stood and called to the dog. He jumped up from his sleep and trotted over to me.

"Come on, boy. Let's go see Foxx."

I put Maui's leash on him, and we walked down the street to Foxx's house. I somewhat expected to still see some of Ashley's belongings on the lawn or perhaps her standing on the front porch and banging on the door. I didn't. I did see her car in the driveway, though, and I started to turn around and head home when Foxx opened the front door.

"Where are you going?" he yelled.

I pointed to Ashley's rental car.

"Looks like you have your hands full."

"She's gone. The car is in my name. I wouldn't let her take it."

I walked up his driveway with Maui. The dog started pulling hard on his leash since he was anxious to get in the house.

"Did you bring the little beast for protection from her? I heard she paid you a visit this afternoon," he continued.

"No, but maybe that's not a bad idea to use this guy as my permanent bodyguard."

"Come on inside. I'll grab you a beer."

I took Maui inside the house and unhooked his leash. He took off running since he knew the house well, considering that he'd lived in it for a couple of years.

We walked to the back of the house. Foxx handed me a beer and then sat on the sofa.

I took a long pull and sat on the chair off to the side.

"What the hell happened? Alana said she saw a police car at your house," I said.

"Yeah. The cops were here."

"Did you have to call them to get her to leave?"

"No. She called them. Ashley told the 911 operator that she was being unfairly evicted from her house. When the cops learned it was my place, they told her she had to leave. I called her a taxi and paid the driver to take her to a hotel in Kahului where I'd booked her a room. I paid for a whole week in advance. I also gave her some cash to cover a first-class plane ticket back to Miami."

"First class? That's way more than I would have done."

"Way more than she deserves, but I'm hoping to entice her to leave."

"Do you think it's going to work?" I asked.

"I have no idea."

"What was the final straw?"

"She told me yesterday afternoon that she can't wait for Hani to go to prison for murdering Bill. She said once that happens, I'll naturally get full custody of Ava and we can all be a family."

"'We can be a family'? As in her and you being the parents?"

"Exactly."

"What did you say?"

"I was so upset I didn't say anything. I just got up and left the house."

"Where'd you go? Ashley called me earlier today and said you didn't come home last night."

"After I left here, I drove up to Harry's to check on the construction. Then I went to see Hani. I told her what Ashley had said. I also told her we needed to talk because I was going to kick Ashley out of the house and we needed to prepare for what might come. I still think Ashley might go back to the cops. She was pretty mad when she left here."

"You think?" I asked. "Ashley believes you spent the night with Hani."

"Why does she think that?"

I told Foxx how Ashley had gone to Hani's house looking for him.

"I did spend the night with her. We went to a hotel in Kihei so we could talk everything out."

"You talked? All night in a hotel?"

"Yeah. That's all that happened. This morning Hani left and went to get Ava from her mother's. I stayed at the hotel and got a late check-out. Then I came back here and told Ashley to get lost."

"Did she ask you why you wanted to end things?"

"She did, and I said that I couldn't be with someone who would try to put my daughter's mother in prison. She asked why I was okay with a murderer taking care of Ava. That's when things got really bad."

"What did you do?"

"I started taking her stuff and tossing it into the front yard. Hell, I probably should have just kept it all. I paid for everything."

"Better to let her have it."

"That's what I figured. She'll probably sell it all anyway. She doesn't have any money. She hasn't worked one second since landing on Maui."

I was tempted to tell Foxx that's because he'd enabled her. I didn't blame him for Ashley's bad behavior, but he'd let her get away with everything, at least everything up until today.

"Well, I guess you and Hani better get ready for the crap she's going to throw at you," I said.

"Yeah, I was hoping you could help with that."

"How so?" I asked.

"Maybe you can go talk to Ashley. Convince her that it would be better if she just left the island."

"How am I going to accomplish that little task?"

"Tell her there's nothing she can really tell the cops that she hasn't already. It's just her word against mine and Hani's."

"You sure you want me to say that to her?"

"I'm also willing to make a contribution to her bank account as an incentive for her to leave."

"I see multiple problems with that," I said.

"Like what?"

"It could look to the police like you're paying for her silence."

"So? Celebrities make people sign non-disclosure agreements all the time."

"You're not a celebrity, Foxx."

"Who says I'm not? I played pro football."

I decided not to debate the issue as to whether Foxx could fairly compare himself to Tom Brady or Peyton Manning, and instead I jumped to problem number two.

"Let's say you do give her a healthy amount of cash. What's to stop her from taking the money and then talking to the cops once she gets back to Miami?"

"That's where the NDA comes in," Foxx said.

"Tell you what. Let me run this by Mara and see what she says. Maybe she'll have another recommendation. If she thinks it's a good idea, then you'll need her anyway to write up the agreement for Ashley to keep her mouth shut."

"Sounds good."

Foxx took another drink from his beer.

"How are things with Alana?" he continued.

"What do you mean?"

"Is she still angry with me?"

"I think Alana's issues with you are the least of your worries."

"I don't want her to be upset. I just want things to go back to the way they were."

"Things change. You know that."

"Yeah, I get it, and I'm sorry I let Ashley get in the way of my friendship with you and Alana."

"I believe you, but it's going to take time for Alana to get over everything. I've learned not to press her. She has her own pace, just like everyone else."

The doorbell rang, and Maui took off running toward the foyer.

"That must be the locksmith," Foxx continued.

"You're having the locks changed?"

"Every one. I got Ashley's key back from her, but my gut tells me she had a duplicate made."

"Damn, you really thought this breakup through, didn't you?"

"I had to."

I picked up Maui so he wouldn't attack the locksmith. I said goodbye to Foxx, and the dog and I headed back to our house. Once I went inside, Alana immediately muted the television and demanded that I tell her everything. I had a little fun with her and said I was surprised she wanted to know since she'd technically said she was done with Foxx. Yeah, I know. It was the second, third, or maybe even the fourth time that I'd reminded her of that, but I was just having fun with her.

After I told Alana how the conversation with Foxx had gone, she said that she agreed that paying Ashley (she didn't say her name, rather she used a more colorful metaphor that began with the letter B) would be a mistake of monumental proportions. Unfortunately, there didn't seem to be a way of guaranteeing that Ashley wasn't going to cause a huge stink. My only hope was that it could be somewhat contained.

26

I KNOW WHO DID IT

THE NEXT MORNING I WOKE UP FEELING DECIDEDLY LESS CONFIDENT than the day before. I went from thinking that I could take on the world to wanting to hide under my bed sheets in the fetal position. Let it never be said, though, that Poe is not up for a challenge. I managed to convince myself to roll out of bed. Actually, I just sort of turned and let gravity take me to the floor. Fortunately, Maui was sleeping on Alana's side of the bed so I didn't land on top of him.

After Alana left for work, I went outside to swim my laps and then take my jog around the neighborhood. I'd hoped the physical exertion would stimulate my brain, or at the very least put me in a slightly better mood. It didn't. I felt hopeless and had no idea where to turn next. Like I'd done in the past, I went into my home office and wrote down a list of everything I knew. I started with the Marco Giordano case.

Juliana had hired me with the expressed intent of proving that Sophia, her sister-in-law, had killed Marco. She blamed Sophia's greed and stated that with Marco out of the way, Sophia could sell the company and cash in. Eleanor, an employee at Pomaika'i and Marco's former personal assistant, contradicted Juliana by saying that Marco loved his wife and gave her whatever she wanted. Despite being so close to Marco, she had no idea who might have killed him. Did Eleanor have a secret she was hiding that might have made her want to kill Marco? I didn't think so, but it wouldn't be the first time I'd been wrong about a person. I made a mental note to look into Eleanor more.

I'd learned that Sophia had an affair with Victor, a general manager of an overpriced seafood restaurant. Sophia had apparently told the police, as well as her lover himself, that Marco was well aware of the affair and he was okay with it all since they had an open relationship. Phoenix had told me the same thing.

Question: Considering that it seemed likely they did indeed have an open relationship, was Marco also having an affair? If so, with who? I knew, or at least thought, that he hadn't been fooling around with any of the fashion models since Hani had spoken with her former talent manager who claimed Marco had shown no interest in the young women. Had he been having an affair with Eleanor? Was that the possible secret she was hiding?

Who were my suspects? I'd already crossed Juliana off the list since she would have placed herself in a terrible position by killing her brother. She didn't own controlling interest in the company so she'd have no way of stopping Sophia from selling Pomaika'i.

I also found it unlikely that Eleanor would have done it despite my question, based on zero evidence, that she might have something to hide. She admired Marco and had no known motive to see him dead. There was also the fact that she'd gone out of her way to contact me in secret so that she could contradict the things that Juliana had told me. If Eleanor had committed the crime, it made sense that she would try to maintain a low profile and not bring attention to herself by contacting the private investigator.

I didn't think Victor had done the evil deed, either. He seemed to have no intention of leaving his wife and children for Sophia, so why would he want Marco gone? If anything, Marco's death had ended his fun and games with Sophia.

What about Phoenix, our golden-haired boy who lived in the cottage behind that guy's house? Again, what was his motive? Apparently, Marco was the only one paying him a decent rate for his styling services after his hair salon had gone under. I didn't see why he'd kill his major source of income. So that he could concentrate on doing poorly paid make-up and hair services for brides?

All of this left Sophia as the only plausible suspect. Now that Marco was gone, she could sell the company, leave Maui, and start over somewhere else with her bucketful of cash. Victor had told me that she'd made that declaration to him in their last motel meeting when she'd told him that she wanted to leave the island for a fresh start somewhere else. Still, there were major holes in the theory that Sophia was our guilty party. I didn't think it likely that she could have stabbed her husband to death, a man who was presumably much larger than her, without injuring herself in the process. The police had apparently found no blood on her. They'd not found a murder weapon. Where would she have hidden it after killing Marco?

I was tempted to bang my head on the desk while I realized, yet again, that a case I'd initially assumed as fairly simple was stumping me so badly.

I turned the page on my notebook and started writing down my thoughts regarding the Bill Hodges investigation. Bill's body had been found on a beach with a bullet wound in his chest. The weapon of choice had been a .38. I knew that Foxx owned that caliber of weapon, and he'd originally claimed the gun had been badly damaged in the fire that consumed Harry's.

Now I knew that he'd lied to me, something I didn't think he'd ever do, and he'd also lied to the cops and his lawyer. Foxx instead gave the gun to Hani for protection from Bill. Hani had kept the gun for a while and then returned it to Foxx around the same time Bill had been killed. What prompted her to do that? Was it simply because she'd heard about Bill's death and didn't want to be found with a gun, or had she been the one to pull the trigger? If she had shot Bill, then why hadn't she ditched the gun herself? Foxx told me he'd tossed it in the ocean. That was a pretty easy thing to do, and Hani certainly didn't need Foxx to do it for her. Of course, she might have been panicked and was temporarily incapable of rational thought, so she went to a person she knew would help her.

What about Foxx? Did I think he'd murdered Bill? Hani allegedly had his gun when Bill was shot dead, but the timeline was a bit fuzzy. She might have given Foxx the gun back and then Foxx had used it on Bill. But when would he have had time to do that? He would have had to have immediately taken the gun, somehow lured Bill to that beach, and then shot him. I thought this was highly implausible, and I was shocked that I'd even written it down. That was the harsh reality of this investigation, though. I no longer believed anything anyone told me.

If Foxx didn't do it and Hani didn't do it, then who was another likely suspect? I thought about something Alana had told me the night before. She said that Ryan and his friend's sentencing date was approaching. Apparently, they'd struck a deal with the prosecutor and each was going to plead guilty to assault, but she still expected them both to get six months jail time. This was way down from the time they could have received if found guilty of assault with a deadly weapon. I remembered the conversation I'd had with Ryan outside Hani's home. He'd claimed, unbelievably I might add, that he didn't know about Bill's violent tendencies. What if he'd been honest with me, though? Bill had conned him into attacking me and now Ryan had a record and was going to jail. Maybe Ryan had confronted Bill over all of the trouble he'd caused him and things had turned violent.

I decided to pay Ryan a visit. Yeah, it was a longshot, but what else was I going to do? Hani had told me that Ryan worked at a shop in the small harbor in Lahaina. Apparently, the company he worked for arranged parasailing rides, snorkeling trips, and sailing excursions.

I closed my notebook and walked into the garage to my convertible. The sky had been overcast during my morning jog, and I saw there was now a light rain as the garage door opened. I reluctantly put the top up on the BMW and backed into the driveway. The AC had been broken on the car for a while, so I had to settle for warm air blowing through the vents. It wasn't going to be a pleasant ride.

Ryan's water activities shop was fairly easy to find. The place was slow considering the bad weather had only gotten worse on the drive over. There was now a steady rain falling, and I got thoroughly drenched as I jogged from the parking lot to the shop.

I saw Ryan as soon as I walked inside. He was behind the counter, and I saw a large bulletin board directly behind him with photos and brochures of their various water sports. Ryan and I were the only ones in the shop, and his eyes grew wide as I made my way over to him. I walked up to the counter and put my hands on it. We locked eyes but neither of us said anything.

After about ten seconds had passed, he finally asked, "Can I help you?"

"I heard you reached a deal with the prosecution. Congratulations."

"Yeah, well it doesn't feel like a good thing."

"I'm sure it doesn't. You're getting off with a slap on the wrist."

He didn't respond.

"Look at it this way, someone could have gotten killed," I continued.

"Bill did."

"Not by me."

He looked away, and I wasn't sure whether to interpret that as a sign of guilt.

"What do you think happened to him?" I asked.

"He finally messed around with the wrong person."

"Obviously, but what's your guess? Who was it?"

"How would I know?"

"I bet you were pretty upset with him when you found out what he'd really done to those girls. Then he convinces you to attack me and my friend. Now you're going to jail."

"Is this your way of asking if I had something to do with his death? Well, I didn't."

"When was the last time you saw him?" I asked.

"I don't have to answer your questions."

"Your other friend, the guy outside the bar, maybe he did it."

"Sam didn't do it. He practically worshipped Bill. He would have done anything for him."

"Including bashing my head inside out."

"And he's going to pay for that, too."

Before I could respond, the bell on the door jangled behind me and a family of four walked in.

"I'll be with you in one second," Ryan told them.

"You can't change what happened to Bill and who did it."

"What are you talking about?" I asked.

Ryan leaned closer to me and lowered his voice.

"Bill was obsessed with Hani. There was no way he was going to let her go. I know for a fact he was following her around the island after they broke up. If you ask me, she killed him. You should just drop this. God knows Bill probably deserved what he got."

The family walked up beside me. The father picked up a brochure for a snorkeling trip to Molokini Crater, while the mother smiled and said hello to Ryan. I took that as my cue to leave, which was just as well since Ryan's last comment had shaken me.

I walked outside. The rain was coming down in sheets by now. I ran to my convertible and hopped inside. I was on the main road, heading back to Kaanapali, when I heard a quick siren blast behind me. I looked in the rearview mirror. It was hard to see with the rain rolling across the plastic rear window in the car. I pulled off to the side of the road, and the unmarked police sedan rolled past me and came to a stop in front of my car. The driver's window opened, and I saw a woman's arm come out and motion for me.

I got out of my car and walked up to the sedan. It was Detective Kalani.

"Get in," she said.

I walked around the front of the car, opened the door, and climbed into the passenger seat.

"You're an easy guy to spot with that convertible," she continued.

"It isn't the most inconspicuous car," I admitted.

"I hope you don't try tailing people in that thing."

"I did when I first got started."

"You're kidding?"

"I wish I was."

She turned away from me and looked out the window at the pouring rain.

"I got another anonymous call last night."

"I'm sure you did," I said.

Detective Kalani turned back to me.

"This new call said your friend, Foxx, actually gave your sister-in-law the gun."

"That's interesting."

"I agree."

"I think we find it interesting for different reasons."

"Okay. Why do you find it interesting?" she asked.

"The anonymous caller, let's call her Ashley for fun, just proved herself to be a liar. First she said the gun was stolen from my bar. Now she claims it was given to Hani by Foxx."

"That's not a lie. That's an update to her story."

I was tempted to laugh, but I somehow managed not to.

"No. An update is something you do to your computer or the furnishings in your house. A lie is when you say one thing and then say a completely different thing the next time."

"Maybe your friend told her the gun was stolen and then admitted he'd given it away freely."

"Is this why you pulled me over? You wanted to ask me about the gun?"

"Among other things."

"May I give you a piece of advice? Don't build the foundation of your case on what Ashley tells you. You'll regret it."

"Is this you looking out for me?" she asked.

"Not quite, but I'd hate to see you look bad when your case gets tossed. I'll have no problem getting on the stand and testifying to how her story has changed multiple times. I'm not sure Ashley even knows what she believes anymore. The only thing I know for sure to be true is that we have a money-hungry person who came to Maui to live off the riches of my friend. Once Foxx grew tired of her drama and asked her to leave, she decided to get revenge by trying to frame him for a crime he had nothing to do with. That's a story that makes sense. That's something a jury will believe, not this nonsense about a gun that was stolen only it wasn't. Whoops, I was wrong again. Poe's dog, Maui, shot Bill Hodges."

"You have a dog named Maui?" she asked.

"Yes, and he has ten times the credibility as Ashley. You'd be better off putting him on the stand. He's cute and has expressive eyes. The jury would want to believe him."

"Now you're being ridiculous."

"No more than you listening to a word that woman has to say. May I go, Detective, or is there something else you'd like to talk about?"

She stared at me for several seconds.

Then she said, "Just when I thought I'd figured you out..."

Her words trailed off. I didn't respond. I just opened the passenger door and climbed out.

"Drive safe, Detective. This is some serious rain."

I shut the door and walked back to my car. Did my little dramatic performance on the veracity of Ashley's claims make a difference with Detective Kalani? I just didn't know.

27

FASHION AND SURFING

I DROVE HOME AND WENT INSIDE TO DRY OFF. EVEN THOUGH I HADN'T been in the rain that long, my clothes were still soaked. I went upstairs and changed into a fresh t-shirt and shorts. I was about to text Alana about my roadside meeting with her new workplace nemesis, when my phone vibrated. It was Juliana.

She informed me that Sophia had come by the office that morning to announce that she'd completed the negotiation for the sale of the company and the deal would be going through within a couple of days. She informed the staff that she'd recommended to the new owners that they retain everyone, but she had no way of guaranteeing anything. I didn't see why they wouldn't since I thought they were buying more than an existing brand. They were also purchasing the talent behind it. In other words, why screw up something that wasn't broken? On the other hand, companies do stupid things all the time, so what did I know?

I don't think I need to tell you how upset Juliana was at Sophia's news, and I spent the next five minutes listening to her beg me to successfully conclude my investigation, which basically meant proving that Sophia had killed her husband and therefore couldn't inherit her brother's possessions, mainly the Pomaika'i fashion brand. How do you respond to something like that? I wanted to help the lady, but so far I had no proof that Sophia had done anything wrong beyond her extramarital affairs that her husband didn't seem to have a problem with, if you believed Sophia, Phoenix, and Victor.

I called Nancy after getting off the phone with Juliana. I asked her if she'd made any progress with her online searches. She told me that she'd managed to watch all of the videos that Pomaika'i had posted. They were mostly fashion shows and several short interview clips of Marco as he talked about the company and their vision for the future. The only thing that stood out to her was that there was one model who'd appeared in all of the events. I was more than impressed with Nancy's thoroughness. Apparently, she created a log where she listed the models who appeared in the videos. She obviously didn't know their names, so she created fake names for them to help her track them.

"Debbie," a cute blond with a pixie haircut, appeared in approximately seventy percent of the videos and photos that appeared on the Pomaika'i website. "Beverly," a tall redhead, was in sixty to sixty-five percent of the online searches, and "Eunice" (not sure why she picked that name) was a raven-haired beauty who was in fifty percent.

The one model who stood out, according to Nancy, was "Grace." She was tall with brown hair that fell well past her shoulders. Grace was in every Pomaika'i fashion show posted to YouTube and at least half of the modeling photographs for the company's website. I logged onto the Pomaika'i website and quickly found the woman Nancy referred to. She was beautiful, and I could see how Marco, or whoever booked the models, would want to use her. Did that mean there was something more going on? I didn't know.

I thanked Nancy for her diligent work and then gave her a new assignment, one that had nothing to do with the Marco Giordano case. To say she was intrigued would be an understatement, and she promised to get started at once. I thanked her again after stressing how imperative it was that she not get caught. I'm sure you're wondering what I asked her to do. Don't worry. I'll tell you, just not yet.

After ending the call with Nancy, I copied one of the modeling shots of Grace and emailed it to Hani. I followed that up with a phone call and asked her if she knew who the model was. I got lucky when Hani said she'd done several photoshoots with her. It turned out her real name is Luna, which sort of sounded like a stage name to me. Hani said she also knew Luna's husband. In her opinion, the likelihood of Luna having an affair with Marco was slim to none. She said it made way more sense that the Pomaika'i staff just used Luna again and again because she was probably one of the top two models on the island. Hani said she used to fly to Oahu all the time with Luna for larger jobs and that Luna had gotten an offer to model in Los Angeles but turned it down because she didn't want to leave Maui.

I'd struck out again and I still didn't know where to turn. I decided to watch some of the fashion show videos on YouTube, which was more of a decision born out of desperation than anything else. The shows were impressive and much larger than I would have anticipated for a small fashion company on a relatively small island.

Marco would appear at the beginning of the shows and thank everyone for attending. The models would then walk the runway and show off the new fashions, followed by Marco appearing again at the conclusion to a round of enthusiastic applause. It was all a straightforward affair, but the lights, sets, music, and even the quality of the video production was done at a high level. Most things on YouTube look like they're shot with a phone that had a dirty plastic bag over the lens, and the audio quality is even worse. That wasn't the case with the Pomaika'i videos. They'd clearly been shot with multiple cameras, and the directing had been competent.

I'm a bit embarrassed to admit this, but it wasn't until the third fashion video I watched that I noticed a particular guy sitting in the front row of the audience. All of my attention had been on the models on stage since I assumed that they were the ones most likely to interact with Marco. There was also the fact that they were all good-looking women, but I'm sure you already figured that.

Anyway, back to the guy in the front row. He looked familiar to me, but I had a hard time placing him. I went back to the first and second videos I'd come across and watched them again. The guy was in both of the videos. In fact, he was in the same front-row seat. I selected two more fashion show videos and watched them until I confirmed the presence of our mystery guy. Same front row and same seat. It made sense that he might be an important customer for Marco, but was that all there was to it? I froze the video on the best frame I could find of the guy and exported a still image to my desktop. I then emailed that still to Hani. I texted her and asked her if she recognized the guy as a fashion buyer or journalist who covered those types of events.

She wrote a three word response: He's a surfer.

What's his name? I wrote back.

Her reply: Don't remember. Alana would.

I knew that Alana and Hani had both surfed while they were growing up, but Hani hadn't done it in years. Alana, on the other hand, was still active. I selected the still frame of the man again and sent it to Alana. She called a few minutes later.

"You must have a memory gap when it comes to him," she said.

"I do? Who is he?"

"Nicholas Jansen, the surfer who died in the hurricane."

"Really?"

"Where did you get that image of him?" Alana asked.

"From a fashion show."

"A fashion show?"

I told her how I'd been watching online videos for the Marco Giordano case and that I'd come across Jansen in all of the shows.

"That's weird. I have no idea why he'd be at them. Maybe they paid him to help promote the brand."

"I don't think so. I didn't see him in any of the modeling shots on their website, and he's not actually on the stage for the shows. He just seems to be a spectator."

"Call your client. Maybe they can tell you why he was there."

I ended the call with Alana and then took her advice. I reached Juliana. I could tell she was hopeful by the anxious tone in her voice.

That enthusiasm seemed to vanish as soon as I asked about Nicholas Jansen. She told me that Marco and Jansen had been friends, but she had no idea where they'd met.

I did another online search after my conversation with Juliana. My initial Google search was way too broad when I typed his name into the search bar. It came up with numerous articles about his death in the hurricane, as well as articles on what he'd meant to the surfing community. I came across one link to a YouTube video that showed him giving a tour of his house near the North Shore on Oahu. Apparently, it was an excerpt from a surfing documentary that traced the sport's history, from the earliest surfing legends to the modern ones. The show culminated in the short piece on Jansen.

A question popped into my mind: If Jansen lived on Oahu, how had he met Marco and why would he have been willing to fly to Maui for these fashion shows? It wasn't a long flight, and I was sure a surfing god with tons of sponsors could easily afford the airfare. Still, why would he have been so interested in fashion that primarily catered to women and had absolutely nothing to do with surfing? It wasn't like the Pomaika'i line had board shorts, tank tops, and flip-flops.

I went back to Google and typed in Jansen's name along with the word "Maui." I discovered that he owned a second home on Maui. There was a brief article about him at a charity event in Makawao that also mentioned near the end that he'd just bought a home in Haiku.

I sent another text to Alana: How does surfing on Maui compare to Oahu?

She called me a few moments later.

"What are you doing, Poe?"

"I just found out your boy Jansen owned a house on Maui in addition to the one he owned on Oahu."

"So? What's wrong with that? I'm sure he had the money."

"I'm just wondering why you'd want to have homes on two islands."

"Lots of people do. Plus you've been to Oahu. It's completely different to Maui. Maybe he just wanted to get away from the crowds."

"I'd buy that, but why not go to Kauai or the Big Island. There are even smaller crowds there."

"Maybe he's got friends here on Maui."

"How does the surfing compare?" I asked.

"Between Maui and Oahu?"

"Yeah."

"Oahu is the king of surfing. Everyone goes to the North Shore. That's where Jansen was discovered. He was a legend there."

"All right. Thanks for answering my question."

"Sure. All this is because you saw him in some fashion videos?" Alana asked.

"Yeah. I know. Crazy."

"It's not crazy. It's just...okay, it's crazy."

I laughed.

"How are things going there? Any workplace drama?" I asked.

"You mean have I run into Makamae?"

"Among other things."

"The answer's no."

"So no drama. Good."

"Oh, there's always drama. I'm just trying to steer clear of it."

"Thanks for the info. I'll see you later."

"Bye."

I ended the call and turned back to the laptop screen. The image was still the one of Nicholas Jansen at the Makawao event.

"So Mr. Jansen, what brought you to Maui and does it have anything to do with Marco?"

28

NDA

I wish I could say the rest of the day and evening went by without incident and that by the time Alana got home, there was no more talk of surfing, fashion shows, or Detective Kalani. Actually, the lack of talk about those topics did happen. Nevertheless, the evening was not the stress-free one I'd hoped for. Instead, I got a call from someone I'd wanted to never hear from again. There's no need to mention her name since I'm sure you can guess who it was.

Before I go much further into that topic, I received another call the following morning, this one from Hani. She told me she'd spotted a white sedan following her the previous afternoon and evening and she assumed it was Ashley, despite not getting a good look at the driver.

I have always been honest with you readers. Therefore, I must admit that I was responsible for the person following Hani. If you recall, and I'm sure you do, I gave Nancy a new assignment, which was to follow Hani. I may lose favor in your eyes, and if I do, then I regret that sincerely. Nevertheless, one must never assume they always know the truth. The truth, like anything else, must be verified, multiple times on some occasions. Although I did not think Hani murdered Bill Hodges, I wasn't sure she was completely innocent. I'm sure you didn't think so, either.

I hadn't assumed Nancy would have been spotted so quickly, though, especially after following Sophia successfully for multiple days. Hani was paranoid, though, and for good reason. I'd expected her to be more careful than Sophia, but not that much more.

I told Hani that I was sure no one was trying to do her harm but that she should stay vigilant and call me if she spotted the car again. I then called Nancy and told her to abandon the assignment since she'd been made. The news devastated poor Nancy, and she actually started to cry. She told me multiple times how sorry she was that she'd let me down. Like most men, I'm completely at a loss as to what to do when a woman cries, least of all an older woman who likes to wear fruit-adorned pant suits. I told her that it wasn't a problem and that I'd be contacting her soon for her next mission. That seemed to make her feel somewhat better.

Nancy's following of Hani had also been a bust in that she'd only observed Hani going to a resort in Wailea, presumably for an upcoming wedding. There were no secret meetings, and I chided myself for even dragging Nancy into this particular case. I wasn't sure what I expected her to find out. Again, I was desperate and desperate people do stupid things.

After the call with Nancy, I left the house and drove to Mara's office, which was the result of my call the previous night from Ashley. She, Ashley not Mara, informed me that she had a proposition to make but she wanted an attorney to be present. I asked her where Mara and I should meet her and her attorney, and Ashley said she didn't have one, which I found interesting and evidence that Foxx's claim that Ashley was broke to be more likely correct than not.

I arrived to Mara's office a few minutes early, but Ashley was already there. I knew this because I saw her through the floor-to-ceiling glass window at the front of Mara's office. I entered the lobby and said hello to Ashley. She didn't return the gesture. To say she glared at me would be an understatement. If eye daggers were a real thing, she would have killed me several times over.

We sat in the lobby for close to ten minutes. Mara's assistant said Mara was finishing up a conference call that was running late. I suspected Mara might be having fun with me by making me sit beside this lunatic named Ashley. It was a tiny lobby and Ashley and I might as well have been sitting on top of each other. Trust me when I say it would not have been a thrill despite Ashley's good looks.

Mara finally opened her office door, apologized for making us wait, and invited us back. I held my hand out and said "After you," only for Ashley to insist that I go first. I didn't think it was a gesture made out of kindness, rather I suspected she was waiting to get behind me so she could plunge a ten-inch knife between my shoulder blades that I was certain was hidden in her pants. Nevertheless, I did as she suggested and walked into the office before she did. Mara and I sat on the sofa, while Ashley took the chair to the side that I normally took.

"Good morning, Ms. Coyle. Edgar mentioned that you wanted to meet with us," Mara said.

This would have been an appropriate time for Ashley to respond, but she said nothing. She looked at Mara, then turned back to me, then looked back to Mara again.

Mara glanced at me in one of her slow, subtle moves. I was tempted to shrug my shoulders since that would have seemed like an appropriate reaction. I didn't. I was also tempted to wave my hand in front of Ashley's face to see if she was in some kind of bizarre trance. I didn't do that, either.

Finally, Ashley spoke.

"It's clear I'm not wanted."

"Wanted? In this meeting?" Mara asked.

"No, on this island."

"What is it you'd like to discuss?" Mara asked in what was an obvious attempt to try to get Ashley to focus on whatever the intent of the conversation was.

Ashley ignored her question and turned to me.

"I know what Hani did."

"What did she do?" I asked.

"She murdered Bill Hodges."

"What are you basing this claim on?" Mara asked.

"I know for a fact Foxx gave her his gun. It wasn't destroyed in that fire," Ashley said.

"Let's say for the sake of argument that your story is correct. Even if Foxx had given her that gun, that doesn't mean she used it on Bill," I said.

"Who else would have done it?" Ashley asked.

"Bill was a violent man. He probably had many enemies," Mara said.

"Maybe you did it, Ashley," I said, almost cutting Mara off.

"I did it?"

"Sure. Why not? You care deeply about Hani. She is Ava's mother and you know how much Ava means to Foxx," I said.

"I couldn't care less about that woman."

There was a pause of about five seconds in the conversation. I don't think either Mara or I knew how to respond to Ashley's statement. "I couldn't care less about that woman" wasn't exactly the harshest thing to say. I'd heard much, much worse. I'm sure Mara had, too, but Ashley had said it with such venom in her voice that it felt like a knife had just been thrust toward us.

"You obviously didn't come here just to tell Edgar about your claims regarding the gun. You know he's already well aware of them. What do you really want?" Mara asked, breaking the silence.

"I want to make a deal."

"What kind of deal?" Mara asked.

"Poe has money. Lots of it. I want my fair share."

"Your fair share?" I asked, since I was convinced my ears must have been filled with wax and I hadn't heard her correctly.

"What is it you're willing to offer in return?" Mara asked.

"I'll leave the island, and I'll take what I know about Bill's murder with me."

"I'm not sure what it is you think you know. You've told the cops contradicting stories about this gun. It seems to me I'd be paying you for nothing. You've already tried your best to damage Foxx and Hani," I said.

"That's not all I know. Foxx isn't this innocent, helpless guy."

"I never said he was, but he's not a killer. Hani isn't, either," I said.

"What other information do you have?" Mara asked.

"No. You're not getting that out of me. Pay me what I want and I leave town. That's the deal I'm offering."

"How much do you want?" I asked.

"One hundred thousand."

To my credit, I didn't whistle, whoop, slap my thigh, or any of the other things people do when they hear something preposterous. Truth be told, it was the exact same number I expected her to say, which was a lucky guess on my part.

"I'm not paying you that kind of money," I said.

"Then I call the cops as soon as I leave this room."

"Then leave," I said.

Ashley hesitated a moment.

Then she said, "Okay."

She stood and walked toward the door. I waited until she was almost there before calling out to her.

"Wait."

Ashley stopped and turned back to me.

"I can't pay that much money," I continued.

"I know you have it," she said.

"I do, but it's not liquid. Most of my money is tied up in other things."

"That's not my problem."

"Are you willing to negotiate?" I asked.

"No. That's my price. Take it or leave it."

"How do I know you'll keep your word?" I asked.

Ashley pointed to Mara.

"That's why she's here. Have her write up some non-disclosure agreement, and I'll sign it."

I turned to Mara.

"What do you think?" I asked.

"I believe that's something we should discuss in private, but it's certainly worth considering."

I turned back to Ashley. This was one of those classic negotiating moments when the next person to talk was probably going to be the one to lose. I'm sure Ashley knew that, too.

"I don't know," I said. "You've already hurt Hani a lot. Foxx, too. I don't know that I can trust you."

"Pay me the one hundred grand and I'll tell that cop anything you want me to say," she said.

I hesitated another moment and counted to ten in my head. I did the full one Mississippi, two Mississippi, you get the picture.

Then I asked, "Can you give me a couple of hours to think about it? It's a ton of money, and I still want to talk to Mara about it."

"You have until tonight. If I don't get my money by then, I'm going to that detective tomorrow morning and I'm going to bury Foxx and Hani."

"Fair enough," I said.

Ashley turned and left the office. I waited until I heard the little bell on the door leading to the parking lot jangle before I turned back to Mara.

"'Pay me the one hundred grand and I'll tell that cop anything you want me to'," I repeated Ashley's comment.

"Yes. You heard that correctly. She did say that," Mara said.

I stood.

"Thanks for your time, Mara, as always."

I was halfway out of her office when she asked, "You were recording that conversation, weren't you?"

"I had a feeling she would say something incriminating like that, so yes, I was recording it."

I reached into my pocket and removed my phone. I stopped the recording and played a few seconds of the file to verify it was there.

"Good morning, Ms. Coyle. Edgar mentioned that you wanted to meet with us," I heard Mara say on the recording.

I stopped the playback.

"I assume you're sending that to Detective Kalani?" Mara asked.

"Perhaps it would be more effective if you sent it to her, more offi-cial that way. You are Hani's attorney of record. Am I correct in thinking that Ashley's willingness to lie for money destroys what little credibility she had left?"

"I'd love to send it to Detective Kalani, and you're right. Ms. Coyle is done."

"I'll email you the file as soon as I get home."

"When do you think it will dawn on her that she's been had?"

"Not until I tell her later tonight," I said.

"What makes you think she'll contact you again?"

"She's desperate for that money. She won't be able to help herself."

"I hate to say this, but a part of me wishes I were there so I could listen to her reaction. I find that woman...unlikeable."

I laughed.

"Unlikeable? Mara, I think that's the harshest thing I've ever heard you say about anyone."

"I hope I'm not letting you down."

"Impossible, Mara. Impossible."

29

BAMBOO

The meeting with Ashley and Mara had gone better than I ever could have expected it to. I didn't think Ashley was the sharpest pencil in the box, but I also didn't believe she'd make such an incriminating statement at the end.

I decided a celebration was in order, and I drove to my favorite sushi restaurant. I called Alana along the way since it was near the police station. I invited her for a late lunch or early dinner, depending on how you looked at it, but she declined due to her work schedule. I was tempted to turn around and head home since no one, including me, likes to dine alone in a restaurant. Nevertheless, it was a big day and rainbow roll, shrimp tempura roll, and spicy California roll were in order. I even washed it all down with sake, warm, of course.

It was toward the end of my meal while I was waiting for the waiter to deliver my check that I saw something that triggered an epiphany for me. It was so obvious once I looked at the Marco Giordano case that I almost hit myself upside the head and proclaimed out loud what an idiot I'd been. I paid the bill and walked out to the car where I spent about ten minutes on my phone tracking down an address. Fortunately, I was on great terms with my former real estate agent since I'd bought a multi-million dollar house with oceanfront views. She did her little computer search and pulled up the sale history of the home I was looking for. It turned out it was just a few blocks away from Phoenix's cottage, which made sense since the surfing was much better on that side of the island.

I called Nancy and asked her to meet me in Paia where I'd climb into her sedan for the drive to the house. I could have gotten this all wrong, and I didn't want the neighbors mentioning they'd seen a silver BMW Z3 convertible on their street when they potentially called the cops about the break-in that was about to occur. I also realized that a fruit-adorned pant suit could also be rather noticeable so I instructed Nancy to wear something that would blend in with the scenery.

She took my advice literally and arrived wearing green cargo pants, a green shirt, and a green wide-brimmed hat. The woman looked like she was going on a safari. Nancy thanked me for inviting her and apologized again for Hani having seen her. I told her it was nothing, mainly because it was. She asked me if I'd ever been caught tailing someone, and I informed her, with tremendous embarrassment, that I once followed a lecherous doctor around for hours while my wife (then-girlfriend) followed me with no knowledge on my part. Alana had even managed to sneak up on me while I was hiding behind a bush and taking incriminating photos of the doctor with his young, well-endowed island girlfriend while his wife was on the mainland caring for their children.

My story of complete and total failure seemed to lighten Nancy's mood, and we switched topics to the mission at hand. We arrived at the house, and I was pleasantly surprised to see that it was hidden behind a wall of trees and vegetation. Nancy drove down the gravel driveway and turned off to the left so the car would be completely blocked from the road. We climbed out of her car and I surveyed the yard. The grass was high, as I expected it to be since no one, presumably, had lived here in weeks.

"Who lives here?" Nancy asked.

"Lived. His name was Nicholas Jansen. He died during the hurricane."

Nancy looked at the house and then turned back to me.

"The house looks undamaged."

"He wasn't here when he passed. He was surfing during the storm."

"That's insane."

"That's what I thought, only now I believe he knew exactly what he was doing."

We walked up to the front door, and I removed my lock-picking kit from my pocket. It took a few minutes to get the door open.

"Where did you learn to do that?" Nancy asked.

"YouTube."

"I'm serious."

"So am I."

We walked inside and I shut the door behind me. The house was basically one giant room with thick wooden beams placed strategically throughout to support the roof. On one side of the room was a king-size bed. A kitchen with a long breakfast bar was on the opposite. The middle of the room had one of those wrap-around sofas that faced a large-screen television. The floor was made of that gorgeous Koa wood I'd seen earlier in the lobby of the hotel where Bill had worked.

"It's a beautiful house," she said.

"Perfect for a single guy, certainly not great for a family."

I walked to the back wall. Like a lot of island homes, it was made of floor-to-ceiling windows. There was a deck on the outside that ran the full length of the house. Beyond the deck was a narrow section of grass just before a large patch of bamboo and other vegetation.

"He's got a tropical rainforest view," I continued.

"Very peaceful."

"Take a look around. Let me know if anything jumps out."

"What are we looking for?" Nancy asked.

"Evidence that Marco Giordano was here, as in multiple times."

Nancy started with an inspection of the sofa area while I walked over to the bedroom section. I found a door several feet from the bed. It was constructed in the same wood as the walls, which made the pocket door almost imperceptible. I found a small indentation and slid the door to the side, revealing a closet. It took just a few seconds of searching to discover one of the pieces of proof I thought I might find. There were a few shirts and long pairs of pants that were a different style than the predominantly casual wear that made up the majority of the closet. You may find that normal since all of us have varying styles of clothing in our closets. The thing that jumped out was that the dressier clothes were of a different size than the casual wear, substantially different.

I looked at the floor of the closet and found more evidence. There was one pair of men's sandals, sized twelve, while the rest of the shoes and sandals were sized ten. That's a pretty big difference and not the result of a pair of sandals that just run a little large.

"Have you noticed there's no bathroom?" Nancy asked.

I turned from the closet and took another look around the room.

"Maybe it's out back," I said.

"Find anything in the closet?"

"Yes. Two men lived here. Actually, I should say one man visited here. He doesn't have enough clothes to have lived here."

"I'm going outside to search the bathroom."

I followed Nancy out to the back deck. She turned to the right while I took the left. There was a sharp drop-off, so I walked down a staircase of five steps to the backyard. The narrow patch of grass was high, just like the front yard. The bamboo forest looked like it was encroaching on the yard. I saw several smaller bamboo grasses growing into the section of the yard where Jansen, or a landscaper, had been cutting the traditional grass found at most homes. I walked around the rest of the backyard and saw Jansen had several avocado trees filled with the delicious green fruit.

I found a small shed about fifty yards beyond those trees. I opened the shed and saw a lawnmower, a weed-whacker, two shovels, and several empty planters. It was all typical stuff. I left the shed and walked back to the house where I found Nancy standing on the deck.

"You were right. Two men or a least two people. I found two toothbrushes and different hair products."

"Like shampoo and conditioner?"

"No. Hair gel and hair spray. I think a guy would pick one product and stick with it. Ross uses hair gel, never hair spray. We went on vacation once and he left his gel at home. We could only find hair spray at the local stores, and he was pissed the rest of the trip."

I didn't think it necessary to tell her that I thought it was ridiculous that her husband would have let a haircare product ruin his vacation, so I kept quiet.

"What makes you think Marco was the one who came here?" Nancy asked.

"The online videos. Nicholas Jansen was at every fashion show, sitting in the front row. He wasn't one of their clients, and he didn't endorse their brand."

"He was a personal fan."

"Exactly."

"What does this have to do with Marco's death?"

"Jansen died the exact same day as Marco. I find that too much of a coincidence, don't you?"

"What made you even think of this relationship connection?" she asked.

"Sushi."

"Sushi?"

"I saw a male couple having lunch beside me at a sushi restaurant. We've been searching for a possible lover of Marco, and it never occurred to me until then that it could have been someone of the same sex."

"If Jansen did kill Marco, how do you prove it?"

"I don't know. That's the problem."

Nancy and I spent another two hours there. We went over everything multiple times. I found no photographs of Marco, nor did I find any handwritten correspondence like a card, letter, or even a note. Jansen's phone was nowhere to be found, and I assumed he'd tossed it into the ocean when he'd taken his last surfing adventure.

Before we left, I took one of the larger shirts out of the closet, laid it on the bed, and snapped a photo of it with my phone. It was a fairly distinctive shade of blue, and I felt confident someone would remember having seen Marco wearing it. I texted Juliana the photo and asked her if the shirt belonged to Marco. She wrote me back and said that it did. My phone vibrated a few seconds later, and I was predictably showered with questions. Where was I? How had I gotten a hold of Marco's shirt? Was I any closer to pinning this murder on Sophia? Were the police with me?

I managed to get off the phone by telling Juliana the truth. I'd broken into someone's home and needed to get out before I was found.

Nancy and I left shortly after the phone call. The mission had been somewhat of a success but ultimately a failure since this didn't prove anything. Nancy drove us back to Paia and dropped me off at my car. I told her I'd call her once I figured out our next move.

After she drove away, I put Nat King Cole on the car stereo. I was almost to Kahului and hallway through "Get Your Kicks on Route 66" when I made a U-turn on Hana Highway, almost causing a traffic accident in the process. I drove straight back to Jansen's house. I pulled onto his gravel driveway and walked straight for the backyard.

I knew bamboo was hard to control. It grew fast and was damn near impossible to get rid of once it was planted. That had been the main reason I hadn't planted any in my yard, despite the fact that it made for a cheap and effective privacy wall.

It was clear to see the bamboo was moving toward the house. I got closer to the front of the bamboo and saw where it had been hacked down with a blade, probably a machete. That's when I remembered the shed. I hadn't seen a machete or any other tool there that could have trimmed the bamboo. I walked back and inspected the shed a second time and verified there was nothing there. That meant Jansen either had a landscaper do it or the machete had disappeared. If Jansen did have a landscaper, then why have his own mower and weed-whacker?

I walked back to the bamboo and examined it again. I noticed something different this time. The cuts were inconsistent. Some of them were smooth slices while others appeared jagged. This matched the two different types of cuts found on Marco's body, which had caused the medical examiner to think there might have been two different types of weapons.

A question popped into my mind: If I was going to murder someone in their house, would I bring my own weapon or hope to find one while I was there? I thought the answer to that question was obvious, but why use a machete and not a gun? Maybe he didn't have a gun, or maybe it was the classic and well-discussed theory that people used blades when the crime was one of deep and personal rage. Marco had betrayed Jansen somehow, and he killed Marco for it. It all fit, and then I realized there was a person who knew the answers all along. She hadn't said anything, but why?

30

THE TRUTH

I ALREADY KNEW WHERE SOPHIA LIVED, SO I HEADED THERE STRAIGHT from Jansen's house. Things were moving fast and a part of me felt like I should put the brakes on and reflect on what I'd just learned, or thought I'd learned. Nevertheless, I got caught up in the moment, as I am prone to do.

The drive to her house was a pleasant one despite the anxiety I felt. I was about to confront a widow and demand she tell me why her husband had been murdered. So why was it a pleasant drive? Well, the sun had returned to Maui, the sky was a mesmerizing shade of deep blue, and the song "Straighten Up and Fly Right" had just started on my *Very Best of Nat King Cole* playlist. I was tempted to sing along but didn't want to look like a lunatic to anyone passing me.

I turned into Sophia's neighborhood and spotted her car in her driveway. I parked on the street, took a deep breath, and walked to her front porch. I rang the doorbell, and she answered a few moments later. She was dressed in a loose, white silk shirt and khaki shorts. It was casual and sophisticated, all at the same time, if that makes any kind of sense.

"Yes. May I help you?" she asked with a warm tone in her voice.

"Hello. My name is Edgar Rutherford. In full disclosure, I was hired to look into your husband's death."

The slight smile on her face vanished, which didn't surprise me. Still, I thought it was better to be honest, even if it was a blunt honesty, than try to make up some kind of ridiculous lie. My questions were going to be intrusive, and there was no other way to get her to answer me, unless she thought I might go to the police if she refused.

If my theory was correct, and I had no reason to suspect it wasn't, then Sophia knew exactly what happened to Marco. Nevertheless, she'd decided not to tell the police. Why? Whatever the answer was, I thought it was the same reason she might be willing to answer my questions instead of giving me the boot. I also had something that she wanted. I'd just told her that I'd been hired to investigate the murder, so my guess was that she would want to know who hired me.

"Who hired you?" she asked.

See.

Before I could answer her, which I intended to do, she guessed.

"It was Juliana," she continued.

"Yes. It was."

"Why are you here now?"

"Perhaps we could have this conversation inside," I suggested.

"I'm not sure that would be a good idea."

"I've just come from Nicholas Jansen's home. Your husband wore a size twelve shoe. Is that correct?"

I didn't think there was any way Sophia didn't know Marco's shoe size. Most wives, I suspect, know every size of clothing their husbands wear, including hat size and possibly glove size. Men, on the other hand, probably have no clue beyond a vague guess of small, medium, or large. God protect the man who guesses extra-large. Do you expect me to know Alana's dress size? No way, not even if my life depended on it.

The shoe size comment worked, for Sophia stepped back and pulled the door open wider. I walked inside, and she shut the door behind me. She led me to the back of the house, and we sat down on a comfortable beige sofa. I took a quick look around the room. Either Sophia, Marco, or both, were avid readers. There was a shelf jammed with books on one side of the room. The other side opened to an impressive kitchen similar to the one I'd seen in Jansen's house.

"What made you go to his home?" Sophia asked.

"I'm embarrassed to admit this because it took me so long, but it was the fashion show videos Pomaika'i posted online. Jansen was in the front row in all of them. At first, I thought he might have been hired to model for your online catalogue, but I didn't see him in any promotional photos."

"Marco always insisted Jansen be in the front row. He even had a particular seat reserved for him. That always surprised me. He was a very recognizable man."

"Then why would Marco want him in the front row?" I asked.

"Because Marco wanted to show off. He wanted to impress him. Juliana hired you to prove that I killed Marco, didn't she?" Sophia asked, getting to the point she really cared about.

"Among other things. She also has a lack of confidence in the police. That seems to be a rather common concern, whether the police deserve it or not. Many of my clients seem to suspect, perhaps fairly, that the police will not give one case the attention it deserves since they're saddled with multiple investigations, all screaming for their attention."

"It's what I was counting on. Does Juliana know what really happened?"

"Not yet, but I'll need to give her my report."

"How much do you know?" Sophia asked.

"Some, but not all. I assume Jansen killed Marco with a machete, or something like that. What I don't know is why? My guess is that Marco ended things with him, but again, why?"

Sophia said nothing. She turned from me and looked out the window. She did do something that made everything suddenly clear. Perhaps it had been a subconscious move on her part, perhaps not, but she touched her stomach gently with one hand.

"Your pregnancy," I continued.

She turned to me.

"You know about that, too?"

"I followed you to the doctor's office."

"Where else did you follow me?"

I didn't want to mention Nancy, so I reluctantly took credit for the other discoveries.

"The motel in Kahului where you met Victor Perrin. I also met with Victor at his restaurant."

"What did he tell you?"

"He confessed to the affair. He doesn't know about the baby, in case you're worried something was said to him."

"It would destroy his family. I have no wish to do that."

"Why be involved with a married man then?" I asked.

"Simple. It's easy to end things with them. If they get upset when I break things off, it doesn't matter. I can always threaten to tell the wife and expose the entire affair."

"You've thought it all out. It's also the reason you met at the motel, isn't it? You wanted him to think he was meeting you for another rendezvous so you could guarantee his presence. The lobby location also meant he wouldn't make a scene in public."

"You make me sound like some kind of manipulative monster."

"That wasn't my intention. I was just complimenting you on your plan. Victor gave you what you wanted, and that's why you're leaving Maui. It's not to start over. You don't want him to know you're pregnant."

"That's partially true. There would have been no reason to leave Maui if Marco were still alive. I could have just told Victor that the baby was Marco's. Even if he didn't believe me, he wouldn't challenge it."

"I assume Marco was thrilled when he learned you were pregnant. That's why he ended things with Jansen."

"He was happy, but he didn't end things, not the way you suspect he did. Marco wanted things to go on exactly as they had been, only Jansen wasn't satisfied with that proposition. He wanted Marco all to himself. That was never going to happen."

"Does Juliana know Marco was gay?"

"No, and you must not tell her."

"You don't think she deserves to know the truth?" I asked.

"I don't care one bit about Juliana, but I'm not going to betray Marco, even if he's gone."

"Eleanor knows, doesn't she?"

"What makes you think that?"

"She went out of her way to let me know how much you and Marco cared for each other. I sensed she was hiding something from me."

"She and Marco were having lunch at a restaurant when Jansen walked in. It was a complete accident that they went to the same place. Jansen walked over to the table and kissed Marco on the cheek. Marco was very upset, and he almost ended things with Jansen then."

"What was Eleanor's reaction?" I asked.

"She loved Marco like a father. She was very accepting of what he was. She was also very discreet."

"Forgive me for asking this, but why stay with a man who couldn't be a complete husband to you?"

"I thought about leaving Marco, more than once, but there were so many things he did give me. We were best friends at first, we were lovers for a time, and then we became something that transcended both of those things. I don't know how to describe it. I accepted him, no matter what he did. The same was true of him with me. I wasn't willing to walk away from that."

I thought I understood what she was talking about, and I saw no reason to debate that with her. It was her life, and it had been her decision whether to stay with a man who loved others. She seemed to do the same with her affairs. Perhaps the affairs, on both her part and Marco's, had been nothing more than physical involvements with no emotions behind them. Maybe there had been an emotional component, but it could never compare to the bond they had for each other. Love is a complicated thing, which is a massive understatement. I certainly don't feel qualified to speak as if I were an expert on the subject. Better and smarter people have tried and failed before.

"Marco seemed distant from me in the weeks before his death. I thought he was going to leave me. I knew about Jansen, but I hadn't known it was as serious as it apparently was. There had been other men before, but Marco always came back to me. I think he decided to stay when he learned I was pregnant," she continued.

"What was it about Jansen?" I asked.

"His lust for life. Sorry that I can't come up with better words than that. I think Marco saw a little of himself in Jansen. Design was the adventure for Marco. Surfing was Jansen's passion. Either way, they were both at the top of their game."

"You said you started to believe Marco might leave you. Did he say he would?"

"He started staying out at night. He'd done that from time to time, but with Jansen it was much more frequent. Marco would normally tell me he was working late and would just end up sleeping in his office. I knew the truth, though, and I told him he didn't need to hide it from me."

"So when Marco ended the affair, Jansen decided you couldn't have him, either."

Sophia nodded.

"When I came home and found Marco dead, I knew exactly who had killed him."

"You didn't tell Detective Kalani because you didn't want the truth to come out about Marco?"

"Marco's family is very traditional. They wouldn't have accepted him like I did. He couldn't bear to lose them. Then I learned that Jansen had died during the hurricane. What good would come of telling the police that my husband's killer was already dead?"

I thought a lot of good could come from it. How much time had been wasted trying to solve a crime that had already been solved?

"How could Marco's family not know, especially Juliana? She spent so much time working with him," I said.

"I didn't know for years, and I thought I knew everything there was to know about him. Marco repressed who he was for a long time.

He gave no indication of it, at least none that I noticed, and I happen to think I'm a very observant person."

I thought she was wrong about herself, especially since Nancy had followed her for days and had not gotten caught. Nevertheless, I kept those thoughts to myself.

"Juliana told me you're selling the company. Is that correct?" I asked.

"The sale will go through in the next few days. I offered to sell Juliana the company if she could come up with the money. I bet she didn't tell you that."

"No, she didn't, but I heard rumors she was trying to raise the money."

"Juliana loves to play the victim. She expects everyone to just give her things. She can't seem to understand that life doesn't work like that."

I had all the answers now. An open marriage that defied logic, at least to me. A wife determined to hide the truth, something she'd been doing for years, and a sister-in-law desperate to hang on to her lifestyle. It was all there.

"Thank you for your time, Mrs. Giordano. Let me say how sorry I am for the loss of your husband. From everything I hear, he was a truly dynamic individual."

"Will you tell Detective Kalani who killed Marco?"

"Yes, but I won't tell her why. She's a smart person, though, and she'll undoubtedly figure it out. Regarding Juliana, I'll honor your request and not tell her about Marco's sexuality."

"Thank you."

"Again, my condolences for your loss. Good luck on your upcoming move, and congratulations on your pregnancy."

Sophia didn't respond. I stood and showed myself to the door.

As I walked to my car, I couldn't help but think about Marco's ability to conceal the truth of who he was to his wife, the person who claimed to know him better than anyone else in the world. Perhaps she did. Perhaps the issue is that we can never truly know another person, no matter how much time we spend with them. Maybe we don't even know ourselves. Perhaps Marco was able to hide the truth from Sophia because he'd successfully hid it from himself for many years of his life. Now he was gone, and he wasn't ever coming back. I'd learned the truth of what had happened to him during the storm, but it was still a senseless death that I wasn't sure I'd ever be able to process.

31

HAYSTACKS

I PHONED DETECTIVE KALANI AFTER MY MEETING WITH SOPHIA. I informed her of my discovery that Nicholas Jansen was Marco's killer. She asked me multiple questions, and I declined to answer them. The only thing I said beyond the killer's identity was to suggest that she search Jansen's phone records. My guess was that Marco had a second phone that was unknown to Sophia, which he used to communicate with Jansen. That may seem strange since he apparently didn't keep his true sexuality from his wife, but I suspected Marco still wished to be as discreet as possible.

I also told her to search Jansen's credit card bills. I knew most people used cards over cash these days, and I thought it likely she'd eventually discover a purchase for a machete or knife of some kind that had both a straight and serrated edge to the blade.

I met with Juliana and Mara the next morning and told them that I expected Juliana to be contacted soon with the news that Jansen was her brother's killer. Naturally, Juliana asked me how I'd determined this. I told her that I couldn't reveal that information out of respect to the wife's wishes. This enraged Juliana, as I'm sure you could have predicted. She threatened to withhold payment from me if I didn't reveal the reason behind the murder. I didn't need the money, but I also wasn't willing to throw it away, either. I told her that she'd hired me to determine the killer's identity, which I had. She hadn't asked me to provide a "why." I know that sounds like me nitpicking, and it probably was. Nevertheless, I assumed Detective Kalani would eventually discover the killer's motivation, and the truth about Marco and Jansen's romantic relationship would be revealed. Still, I wouldn't be the one to let the secret out.

This didn't satisfy Juliana, and she stormed out of Mara's office. Mara assured me that she'd collect my fee, which was also her fee since she took a healthy cut out of it. I asked Mara to forward my check to the animal clinic where I'd adopted Maui, which is what I always did with the money. Before I left, Mara informed me Juliana had been fired that morning by Sophia in an apparent retaliation for her having hired me. I couldn't blame Sophia, but a part of me actually thought she'd do nothing and just let the eventual new owner decide whether or not they wanted to keep Juliana employed with Pomaika'i.

Juliana had lost her brother and her job. Did I feel sorry for her? Of course, especially over the loss of her brother. Regarding the loss of the job, not so much. Juliana had lied to me about Sophia when she'd painted her as the manipulative wife. Perhaps she hadn't lied, though. Maybe she really believed it all.

Detective Kalani called me a few days later and requested that we meet at the same café in Lahaina where she'd first spoken to me about Marco's case. I'd anticipated the call, and I'd tried to come up with a reason not to show. However, we must all often do things which we don't want to, and I didn't think it was a smart move to get on the wrong side of the detective.

I left the house a few minutes early so I could swing by Harry's first. The place looked like it was done on the outside, but the interior still needed work. Foxx wasn't there, and the construction crew hadn't arrived yet, either. I spent some time walking around the interior on my own. The floors weren't finished. The drywall had been put up but the seams hadn't been mudded yet, if that's the right term for it. The new bar at the head of the room had been framed, but there was no top to it yet.

I closed my eyes and remembered what the bar had looked like before. This new Harry's would probably be identical, but a part of me knew, for good and for bad, that it would always be different. What did that mean in the long run? I wasn't sure. Life goes on, if we're lucky, and the only thing for certain is that nothing stays the same.

I left the bar and walked the short distance to the café since it was another beautiful day in the little paradise we call Maui. The town was buzzing with tourists and a couple of them almost knocked me over in their exuberance to get to the next shop.

Detective Kalani approached the café door at the same time as I did. She looked inside and then turned back to me.

"It's packed in there. Maybe we should walk across the street to the park."

"No problem," I said.

We waited for a break in the heavy tourist traffic and then crossed the street. We found an empty bench near the famed Banyan trees and sat down.

"So, was my theory correct or did you bring me out here to tell me how I royally blew it?" I asked.

"You were right about Jansen. What even led you to think it was him?"

"I saw him in the videos Marco's company posted online. I started looking into it more and that's when I realized he'd done it."

"That's pretty vague. There must have been something more. I assumed you searched his house."

"That would be breaking and entering, wouldn't it? I'm certainly not going to violate the law."

"How do you manage to keep a straight face when you say those things?"

"It's always been a gift."

"I checked his phone records like you suggested. It's all there in his text messages to Marco."

"So Marco did have a second phone, a burner, I presume."

"He had a second phone, yes, but it was on Jansen's account. I couldn't find either phone, so I assume Jansen got rid of them both after he murdered Marco."

"You said it's all there in the text messages."

"The affair. Jansen was pressing him to leave Sophia. Based on the texts, it looked like Marco had agreed to do that, but then he changed his mind. I'm guessing it was the news of Sophia's pregnancy. I asked Sophia about Marco's affairs. She demanded to know if you'd told me. I said that you hadn't."

"Thank you, but I doubt she'll believe you. I brought it all into the light. I'm the one she'll blame. And Juliana, did you call her?"

"No. She called me. I told her about the relationship between Marco and Jansen."

"Did she sound surprised?" I asked.

"It was hard to tell. She didn't really react at all. I'm not sure if that means she suspected already or if it was such a shock that she couldn't process it. By the way, you were right. I did find a record of the machete purchase. The blade had a straight edge near the tip and then a serrated edge closer to the handle. I showed a photograph to the medical examiner, and he said it could have easily caused the wounds on Marco's body."

"I suppose congratulations are in order. Your first murder investigation on Maui, and you solved it."

"Is this your way of asking if I gave you any credit?"

"Not at all. I don't want, or expect, any. That's not false modesty. I just prefer keeping a low profile."

She didn't reply, and I wasn't sure how to interpret that. Maybe she'd taken the credit. Maybe she hadn't. I guessed it didn't really matter.

"What's next for you?" I asked.

"I'm still working the Bill Hodges investigation, but you know that already. Is that why you gave me Jansen's name instead of your wife giving it to me?"

"What do you mean?"

"You're trying to gain favor with me. Otherwise, you would have told your wife that Jansen was the killer, and she could have solved it."

"You're accusing us of being your competitor and playing games. That's the farthest thing from the truth. Even if I had told her, she would have passed the information to you. It's your case."

"I'm not going to stop looking at your sister-in-law," she said.

"I'm not suggesting you do, but I would have thought the audio recording of Ashley Coyle admitting she'd tell you anything for money would have influenced you some."

"It had the opposite effect."

"How is that?" I asked.

"I assumed you must have been pretty desperate to go to such lengths to discredit her."

"What lengths were those? All I did was record the conversation. Based on her previous lies, it seemed like the prudent thing to do. I didn't make her call me and demand a payoff, nor was I the one to suggest that we meet at my attorney's. She was so sure that I would go for her blackmail scheme that she was the one to suggest she'd sign a legal document, claiming she'd keep her mouth shut."

"You knew she might incriminate herself, and I have no problem believing you had someone make a suggestion to her that you'd be willing to pay for her to go away."

"Who would this mystery person be? I don't know any of Ashley's friends on the island beyond Foxx and Hani, and they certainly weren't going to talk to her."

"Either way, Hani is still a suspect."

"She's a suspect because you've stopped looking anywhere else."

"What makes you think I've stopped looking?"

"Because you've convinced yourself who did it. You may not consciously think you've stopped, but you have."

"I find that offensive."

"I don't think you do."

"Now you're telling me how I feel?" she asked.

"Not at all, but I think you know I'm not attacking you. Now you're asking yourself if you've really stopped looking, and you'll never truly answer it because you don't want to."

"Why is that?"

"Because the correct answer leads to another question, and that question is frightening. If Hani didn't shoot Bill in the chest on that beach, then who did? Either way, you're one for two right now, and I suspect it's going to stay that way. Don't worry. It's not a terrible record."

"What you mean to say is that the murder weapon was tossed and now it can never be proven who pulled the trigger."

"A thought occurred to me on the way over here. Yes, Foxx's gun is gone. I realize you think it's the murder weapon, but I don't agree. Regardless of that, it's either in a landfill or at the bottom of the ocean, depending on which narrative you believe."

"I'll agree to that."

"But you don't really need the gun to clear Hani or convict her. You need the bullets."

"What do you mean?"

"Did you ever ask Foxx why he had a gun at the bar?"

"So now you're admitting he had one? You and he told me he didn't."

"Yes. I was mistaken when I said that earlier."

"You committed perjury."

"Did I? It wasn't intentional, but I don't think you'll mind when you hear what else I have to say."

"This should be interesting."

"I'll ask the question again: Why do you think Foxx had a gun at the bar?"

"I assume it was in case you got robbed," she said.

"No. That's not the correct answer. Well, I shouldn't say that. You're right in that's why he initially got the gun, but the only time it was actually used was when someone came to kill me. The reason he kept the gun from that point forward was because he feared someone would come for me again."

"What does this have to do with me needing the bullets?"

"I'd never fired a gun before, and Foxx thought I should become familiar with it. A friend of mine, a guy named Ray London, is a bit of a gun nut, which is crazy since he's this hippy artist type. He's got a huge yard, and he built a gun range of sorts on his property. It's really not that much of a range. He just has several haystacks set up, and we fire the guns into them. Ray has a nine-millimeter gun, so those slugs won't be confused with the .38 Foxx owned. I'm sure the slugs are still in those haystacks."

"I'm supposed to believe you didn't fire some random .38 into them and then just happen to make this suggestion? Please, give me more credit than that," she said.

"I understand your skepticism, and I'd be the exact same way if someone pitched me this idea. I haven't spoken to Ray about this, though. Perhaps you could head there yourself, without me, and talk to him. Judge for yourself if you think he's lying or not. In my experience with interviewing people, most are lousy liars, especially if they're lying to law enforcement. They're trained to be intimidated by the badge and that nervousness makes them give away their physical tells. If you believe him, ask him to show you the haystacks I fired Foxx's weapon into. I'm guessing it will be pretty easy to dig one out and have it compared to the bullets the medical examiner removed from Bill Hodges' body. If they match, arrest Hani or Foxx or both of them."

"If they don't match?"

"Then the next move is up to you. You can either keep pursuing Hani or you can move on and look for the real killer," I said.

"You seem pretty sure of yourself."

"As I've said before, I know Hani. She's not a killer. Still, there's nothing in this world that would surprise me. People can be unpredictable. Let me know if you decide not to pursue this with Ray. I'll do it myself."

"Why?"

"To be sure. I'm a curious person. It's hard to let this stuff go. But neither of us can win them all. Perhaps this is the case that stumps us both."

She stood and looked down at me.

"Thank you for your assistance with the Marco Giordano case."

"You're welcome," I said.

She turned and walked back toward the street.

"Are you going to Ray's house?" I called out.

She didn't stop walking nor did she act like she'd even heard me. Instead, she continued toward the road.

Nevertheless, I thought I already knew the answer to my question. I didn't think she'd be able to stay away.

32

OFFENSE

I BELIEVE THE SPORTS PHRASE THAT WAS MOST APPLICABLE FOR MY situation is, "The best defense is a good offense." There's also an old martial arts saying that goes, "The hand that strikes also blocks."

I don't remember what morning it was when I had this realization, but it had finally dawned on me that I'd been playing a reactive game with Detective Kalani. She'd been hitting me left and right, and I was doing everything I could to defend the case that Hani and Foxx were innocent. To make matters worse, I was spending my time trying to discover who murdered Bill when all I really needed to do was prove that Hani and Foxx didn't do it. I know it's hard to prove a negative, but all I had to do was make sure the detective didn't have a legal case. Yes, I knew that we had all lied about the gun, and Detective Kalani knew that too. My gut told me Foxx and Hani were innocent, though, and I had promised Alana that I would take care of her little sister. One doesn't renege on a promise to one's wife.

I don't believe that you can predict the actions of others, certainly not on a consistent basis. I'd like to pat myself on the back, though, by stating that all of my predictions came true in the offensive game I'd decided to play with Detective Kalani that had all led up to the conversation by the banyan trees.

My first step had been to discredit Ashley. Detective Kalani had guessed correctly when she'd stated that I'd influenced Ashley into thinking I was open to paying her to keep her mouth shut. If you recall, and I'm sure you do, Foxx spent the week from hell with two of Ashley's friends during the hurricane that started this tale. You may also recall that Foxx said Ashley had met the wife while playing tennis with her. Well, I'd paid a visit to the tennis club and arranged to bump into the lady while she was having lunch after a grueling three-set match, which she lost by the way. You should have seen me in my tennis outfit. I even bought a racket for the act. I had to look the part, after all.

I'd approached her table and told her that I thought I'd met her in my bar when she was there with her friend, Ashley. Her mood had darkened, and it was obvious that Ashley had spoken to her about Foxx and the end of their relationship. I'd asked her if I could sit down, which she'd agreed to, and I'd informed her how unfair I thought Foxx had been to have kicked Ashley to the curb. I'd said that I thought it was wrong that Ashley was now hurting for money, especially after Foxx had not allowed her to work while on Maui. Sure, that wasn't true, but I did my best to make it seem like I was an Ashley ally, even though I was a reluctant one. I'd also mentioned that I'd wanted to help Ashley but I just wasn't sure how, especially since I didn't want Foxx to find out. Ashley then called the next day and asked for the payoff. Prediction number one: check.

Prediction number two: Detective Kalani would be unable to stay away from my bullet-in-the-haystack story. My friend Ray was probably the most honest guy I knew. I assumed he was capable of lying if he absolutely had to, but I felt pretty confident that he'd be completely transparent when doing so. I also knew he wouldn't say no to the police when they arrived at his house and demanded to inspect his gun range, even if they didn't have a warrant.

Ray called me after Detective Kalani had paid him a visit. He sounded more flustered than I'd ever heard him, and he apologized repeatedly if he'd gotten me into trouble. I assured him that he hadn't and apologized back to him that his property had even been visited by the cops. I gave him a CliffsNotes version of the story and assured him that Foxx's gun had not been used in a crime. I said it was all a big misunderstanding, but the police were obligated to search every lead, no matter how thin it might be. He seemed to accept my story. It was mostly true, after all, and we promised to have lunch soon at the Four Seasons where he sold his artwork once a week.

My third prediction was what would occur after the results of the ballistics test. I assumed that I'd hear nothing from Detective Kalani, and she'd do her best to quietly back away from the case once the Foxx-Hani-gun angle was dead. How did I know this? No one likes to leave anything up to chance, most of all me. I'd snuck onto Ray's property to dig one of the bullets out of the haystack before mentioning anything to Detective Kalani.

Ray's yard is huge, and I didn't think he'd notice me on the far side, especially in the middle of the night with my tiny flashlight app on my phone. I'd fired dozens of rounds into the hay, so it didn't take long to find one of the bullets. This little ninja act on my part also left Ray completely clueless as to what was going on, which allowed him to honestly play the part of the innocent friend when Detective Kalani arrived at his house.

I'd given the bullet to Alana, who had it compared to the bullet that shot Bill. In case you're wondering, Alana and the guy who does the ballistics tests have been co-workers and friends for years. He certainly wasn't going to cover up a crime for her, not that she'd ever ask him to, but he was willing to keep quiet about her request. The bullets didn't match.

All of this led to the moment I was at now. I'd finished taking Maui on a long stroll. We'd both walked into the backyard. I'd made my way into the pool while the dog jumped on my blue foam raft. From time to time he enjoys me pushing him around the pool. Alana says I look like one of those gondola guys in Venice. I realize the image you're probably conjuring in your mind right about now of me pushing a ten-pound dog around the pool is probably pretty absurd. I also realize that I spoil the pooch way too much. Anyway, this was the position I was in when Alana came home and walked outside to join us.

"You know, you spoil that dog way too much," she said.

Told you.

I pushed the raft over to the side of the pool so Maui could jump out and run to Alana to greet her. She bent over and rubbed his chest since he'd done one of his dramatic rolls in front of her.

"Now who is spoiling the dog?" I asked.

"I'm just saying hello to him."

"And I was just assisting him with a short cruise around the pool."

"Of course."

"You have a wicked smile on your face."

"Wicked? What makes it wicked?"

"Perhaps it's not so much the smile as the glint in your eyes. You know something and you're dying to tell me."

"Take a guess."

"I'm assuming it has something to do with Detective Kalani."

"You would be correct to assume that."

"What happened?" I asked.

"She came to me today and told me the results of the ballistics test."

"Did she believe them?"

"I'm sure she believes that the bullet pulled out of the haystack was not fired from the same gun as the one used to murder Bill Hodges. I'm not sure if she thinks you didn't find a way to use a different gun and manipulate the whole thing."

"Did she accuse me of manipulating it?"

"No, but there was something in the tone of her voice. She doesn't trust you."

"I'm offended."

"Don't be. Detectives don't trust anyone."

"I was just kidding when I said I was offended. I wouldn't trust me."

"Especially after the things you did."

In full disclosure, I hadn't told Alana in advance about my plan to manipulate Ashley. I did tell her how the conversation with Mara and Ashley had gone after the fact, and I also needed to tell her about the bullet since I wanted her to get it tested. What was her reaction? It had been mixed, as I thought it might. I sensed a part of her felt upset that I'd been messing with a fellow officer of the law. The other part of her believed in her sister's innocence, as well as Foxx's, despite the things she'd recently been through with him. My guess is Alana took an end-justifies-the-means view since all I'd really done is prove something to be true when we already knew it to be.

"What now? There is still a murder to be solved. Who do you think she'll look at next?" I asked.

"I don't know, and I doubt she does, either. I do know this. Makamae picked up another case today, so I suspect she'll put the Bill Hodges investigation on the backburner where it may stay forever."

"As I told her in the park, she's one for two. It's not a terrible record."

"No, but it's not one I'd be happy with," Alana said.

"Oh, I got a call from Mara earlier. She said Juliana paid her bill."

"I assumed she would. Does Mara know what Juliana is going to do now that she's lost her job?"

"I asked her that, and she said Juliana is moving to New York."

"Makes sense. Way more opportunities there for someone in fashion."

"Sure. I'm guessing the only reason she was here at all was because of her brother."

"What about Sophia? Has she left Maui yet?"

"I'm not sure, but I know it's only a matter of time. You're not going to believe this, but Victor's wife kicked him out of the house."

"Victor?"

"Yeah, the guy who Sophia was having an affair with."

"So his wife found out?" Alana asked.

"Nancy told her. Well, she didn't talk to her, but she mailed the photos she took when Victor met Sophia at the motel."

"Did you know she was going to do that?"

"I had no idea, but she said she couldn't stand the idea that Victor had done that to his family. Nancy told me she thought the wife needed to know. A part of me thought he deserved it, too. Another part of me didn't appreciate Nancy doing it behind my back."

"Is that the end of your sidekick?"

"For now. She was a big help, though. Which reminds me, I never got around to ordering your puffin pant suit."

"My puffin pant suit? What in the world is that?"

"Nancy told me the website where she buys all her clothes. I found this navy-blue pant suit with tiny puffins on it. I thought you could wear it to work. What size are you again?"

"Don't you dare."

"Just think how jealous you'd make Detective Kalani."

"I'd be the laughing stock of the entire station."

"If you say so, but Nancy knows fashion. I wouldn't second-guess her opinion."

"Now you're being mean to your former protégé," Alana said.

"I'm being mean? You should have seen the invoice she sent me. We may need to take out a second mortgage just to cover it."

Maui walked over to the edge of the pool and barked once. I pushed the raft over toward him, and he jumped on.

"You don't spoil him, huh?"

"Maybe a little," I said. "Maybe a little."

33

THE BEACH

I wish I could say life had returned to normal after the ballistics test seemingly cleared Hani and Foxx, but it hadn't. There was still no official conclusion to Bill Hodges' murder. No one spoke about it, though, at least around me. You may find it unlikely that I'd been able to let it go in terms of not continuing the investigation. I had. There was something in the back of my mind that told me to stay away. So, what did I do with my time?

I spent the next couple of months getting my new event venue in Wailea finished and ready for business. I hired Hani to get the word out, and we actually had our first reservation before the construction on the back deck was even complete. A childhood friend of Hani's had decided to get married to her long-time boyfriend, a graphics designer who'd relocated to Maui years before. They asked Hani if she could pull off a large wedding with short notice, and Hani accommodated them. I didn't ask why, but I assumed the bride-to-be was expecting, which was confirmed when I saw her in her wedding dress. Hey, I'm not judging, just trying to explain why a couple would book a wedding that large with such little notice. The good news, beyond the excitement of a new life, was that Hani always added additional fees for last minute services. Those fees also extended to my venue.

Alana and her mother were invited to the wedding since they knew the bride. I was Alana's plus-one. I would have gone anyway since I wanted to attend the inaugural event of my new business. The ceremony took place on the beach in the exact spot I had stood months before and envisioned the business, which was kind of surreal to experience.

I watched the wedding from the deck that overlooked the beach and the ocean. The wedding photographer had an assistant, and she joined me for a few minutes as she shot wider photos from the high angle.

After the ceremony, everyone walked up the hill and went inside for refreshments, dinner, and finally music and dancing. Hani had done an amazing job of planning everything, as she usually did. Of course, she got a nice, fat commission check for it.

It was a great party, and I was thoroughly enjoying myself when something happened during the reception that changed the Bill Hodges investigation. After getting a beer at the bar, I walked around the building to look for Alana. I spotted her standing on the back deck. She was looking out toward the sun setting over the ocean. It took me a couple of seconds to spot her since she was standing beside her sister and mother. The three women looked like triplets from the rear as they were all the same height, had the same color and length of hair, and possessed similar builds.

They looked like they were having a pleasant conversation, so I decided to stay inside so as not to ruin the mood for my mother-in-law, whose attitude toward me was turning frosty again after a slight thawing earlier in the year. I went looking for the bride and groom to thank them again for choosing our venue and also to wish them a successful and happy life together. I never made it to them, though. I only walked four or five steps before I realized who'd murdered Bill.

I quickly finished my beer and walked out the front door. I'm a little embarrassed to admit this, but my chest felt tight. A theory of what had happened raced through my head as if a cover of a book had blown open, and I could now see the words clearly on the page. She'd done it, and she'd gotten away with it.

What did I do? Did I look the other way? Did I pretend I didn't know? Could I live with myself if I did that? Those were all impossible questions, and I wasn't sure I'd ever be able to come up with answers that wouldn't ruin things one way or the other.

I spent the next two days in a daze of sorts. Alana knew something was wrong, and she asked me several times to talk about whatever it was that was bothering me. I told her it was a stomach bug. I even went in the bathroom a handful of times when I didn't have to. Maybe that sounds ridiculous, but it's what I did.

Later in the week, I made a trip to speak with someone. When I left a few minutes later, I knew that my theory was correct. I spent another week contemplating what to do. I finally decided that I needed to confront her about what I knew.

I waited for Alana to leave for work in the morning, and then I texted the woman and asked her to meet me on the beach where Bill had been shot to death. That's all I said. Meet me on the beach. I didn't name the beach or even the road it was off since I knew there was no way she would have forgotten. I didn't accuse her in the text of doing anything. I didn't say that I knew the truth about Bill's death. I just said meet me on the beach at this particular time.

I arrived early, parked my car on the side of the road, and walked out to the beach. I took my sandals off and strolled into the water until the waves came just above my knees. The dark clouds had returned, which somehow seemed appropriate for the discussion that was about to happen, if she showed, that is. I checked the weather app on my phone and saw a large storm was rolling our way.

I turned from the water and walked back toward the road when I saw her arrive. She parked behind my convertible, climbed out of her car, and walked onto the beach.

"How did you find out?" Ms. Hu asked.

"I saw you standing in between Alana and Hani at the wedding reception. I had a hard time telling the difference, and that was with you standing still. It would probably be a hundred times harder from a moving car."

"There must have been something else."

"There was. One of Bill's friends said that Hani had murdered Bill. I asked him why, and he said that he knew Bill had been following Hani."

"He did follow her, or maybe I should say he thought he was following her."

"Is that why you kept Hani's car so long? I asked Hani where you liked to take your car. I told her I was looking for a new mechanic. Anyway, I went there and asked about you."

"You bribed them, of course."

"It didn't take much. You had your front brakes replaced. It would have taken just a few hours, but they had your car for a week. They said they called you a few times to pick it up."

"I needed more time. I wasn't ready to return Hani's car to her."

"Where did you get the gun?" I asked.

"Gray gave it to me after we were attacked in his home. Once he went to jail, I just kept it."

Gray was Ms. Hu's former boyfriend. I knew the attack she was referring to since I'd stumbled upon it while it was happening. I was badly beaten myself.

"I guess the gun is at the bottom of the ocean," I said.

Ms. Hu said nothing.

"Do Hani and Foxx know what you did?" I asked.

"I'm not sure. I thought for a while that Hani suspected me, but she never said anything."

"The police? What did you say when they spoke to you?"

"They never did. I kept waiting for them to come, but they didn't."

"What would you have said?"

"I don't know. There's a part of me that thinks I would have admitted it. Do you know why Alana and Hani's father left me?"

"No. It's always been a bit of a mystery to me. I think Alana, too."

"I'm sure that's what she told you, but Alana knows why. So does

Hani. They're not going to say anything to you about it. They're too embarrassed, and they're also respecting my wishes."

"He beat you," I guessed.

"Alana and Hani were both young, but they were old enough to know what was happening. He hit me several times. Our neighbors knew what was happening. I tried to hide the injuries, but it was impossible. No one would do anything, though. Even the police did nothing. It didn't stop until I pulled a gun on him. In the end, I got what was best for my family. He went away."

"Then history repeats itself and the same thing happens to your youngest daughter."

"I saw the same look in her eyes that I'd seen in mine. She was more embarrassed than mad at him. That's why I told you to take care of it. I knew what you'd do to Bill. I needed to drive a wedge between Hani and Bill, so either she couldn't take him back or he would be too afraid to come back."

"You really think she would have given him another chance?"

"I don't know."

"What happened? I know you didn't intend to kill him. You don't have it in you."

"I went to Hani's house to pick up a toy for Ava. Later that morning, I came to this beach to pick up some sea shells. I've been teaching Ava how to make jewelry with them."

"I've seen the necklace you made her. She loves it."

"Ava's still too young to actually make the jewelry herself, but she likes playing with the shells. I came back to the car and bent over to put the shells in a bag I had on the passenger seat. That's when someone hit me from behind. I almost passed out from the pain and then he hit me again. He was like that man who attacked us at Gray's house. I thought I was going to die. I didn't know what to do, so in desperation I reached into my purse and pulled out my gun. I didn't even really aim. I pointed it behind me and fired. I didn't know it was Bill until I turned around and saw him on the ground."

"He must have been so close to you that there was no way you could miss," I said.

"His blood was all over me and Hani's car. That's why I kept the car those extra days. I must have cleaned that car a dozen times."

"They've dropped Hani as a suspect, as far as I know," I said.

"They'll never let it go. Never."

Tears started streaming down Ms. Hu's face.

"What are you going to do now?" she asked.

"What would you like me to do?"

She didn't respond.

"Does Alana know?" I asked.

"She would never allow herself to believe such a thing." Ms. Hu paused. Then she said, "I wanted him to stay away from Hani, but I never wanted him dead."

"I believe you," I said. "I believe you."

34

HARRY'S – PART 2

I WISH I COULD SAY THAT I PUT ON A MASTER PERFORMANCE AND fooled Alana into thinking that everything was all right with me. I didn't. I did manage to remove myself from her field of view by spending the bulk of the evenings at either Foxx's house or Harry's. Guys are easy to fool. The only way Foxx would be able to tell if something was wrong with me is if he saw me bleeding from my eyes.

Harry's was due to reopen in a few weeks, and we'd decided to throw a massive party. We invited everyone we knew, well, almost everyone. I decided to leave Alana's co-workers, Detectives Kalani and Adcock, off the list. Alana surprised me, however, when she told me she'd mentioned the grand reopening to Detective Kalani. I asked her why she'd done that, and she said that she wanted to try to melt some of the ice that was forming between the two of them. She assumed that they'd be working side by side for years, and she had no desire for that time to be strained. I understood her reasoning, but I still wasn't thrilled.

The party was a hit to say the least. Almost everyone on our invite list came, and I'm pretty sure they all brought friends of their own. The only person I noticed who didn't come was Ms. Hu, which didn't surprise me. We hadn't spoken since that day on the beach. I hadn't gone out of my way to avoid her, but I would be lying to say that I wasn't glad that we hadn't seen each other.

I spent the majority of the night standing in the back corner of Harry's. I'd planned to work the room, but it turned out most people ended up coming to me, my sister-in-law included.

"Did you invite Yuto? He's up at the bar, and he just offered to buy me a drink," she said.

"So why are you back here talking to me?"

"To confirm my theory. He said you invited him."

"Then why did you just ask me if I had? Did you think he was lying?"

"No, but it was a preamble to my next question: Are you trying to fix the two of us up?"

"Absolutely not, but he does seem to be a nice guy, and he has a successful career."

"I don't need anyone's money. I'm doing okay on my own," she said.

"I would say you're doing better than okay. You're doing fantastic, and I wasn't trying to say that he can provide for you. But his stability in his career speaks to his character. The older I get, the more I realize how important it is to be with someone who is stable."

Yes, I know, that sounds awfully boring, but it doesn't change the fact that it's true.

Hani turned and looked at Yuto at the bar.

"He is nice, but I don't know that he's my type."

"Have you heard of the definition of insanity?" I asked.

She turned back to me.

"Yes. Doing the same thing over and over again and expecting different results. Are you calling me insane?"

"No way. I'm just suggesting that you give him a chance. You say he's not your type, but you may find you have more in common with him than you think."

"Well, tonight's a night for having fun, not starting something serious."

She held her cocktail glass up to me.

"Here's to Harry's," she continued.

"And to our new business in Wailea."

I clinked my beer bottle against her glass.

"Thank you again for including me."

"Thank you for accepting my invitation. I have a feeling the venue will live or die based on your work."

"In that case, perhaps we should renegotiate my commission," she said.

"What did you say a second ago? 'Tonight's a night for having fun, not starting something serious'?"

"Agreed, so we'll talk tomorrow morning."

She smiled and headed toward the bar where she joined Alana, who was busy speaking with Kiana, one of our bartenders. Hani said something to Alana and then Alana burst out laughing. Was it a comment about me trying to hook her up with Yuto? Possibly.

I took what was left of my beer and headed outside since the bar was overcrowded and getting way too hot. I walked over to my convertible and leaned on the trunk. Foxx came outside a few minutes later and walked over to me.

"Incredible, isn't it?" he asked.

"It's good to have the place back."

"The crew did a fantastic job. I can't tell the difference between the old Harry's and this one. I'm glad you were able to reprint all your photos. That really makes the place feel like home, doesn't it?"

"Harry's is special. I can't believe you had to talk me into buying it. I should have jumped at the chance."

Foxx held up his beer.

"Here's to hoping we never have to rebuild this joint again."

I clinked my beer against his.

"Let's hope not."

"You know what makes this night even better?" he asked.

"What's that?"

"Ashley isn't here."

I laughed.

"Have you heard anything from her?" I asked.

"Not directly."

"Okay. What was the secondhand gossip you heard?"

"Oh, a mutual friend said she's been posting things on Facebook about how this asshole on Maui messed her up. Apparently, that's the thing to do now when you have a relationship end. You have to tell the whole world about it. Remember when there was such a thing as privacy?"

"I wouldn't worry about it. If they're Ashley's friends, then they already know she's a bit nutty."

"A bit?"

"Well, you dated her," I said.

"Don't remind me."

Foxx turned and looked back toward Harry's. Then he turned back to me.

"I can't tell you how happy I am that everything is back to normal. Hey, why are you out here anyway? You should be inside where the party is."

"I got a little hot. I'll be back inside in a minute."

Foxx left me, and I finished my beer. I was about to go back into Harry's when Detective Kalani drove into the parking lot. We made eye contact as she swung into a parking space. I was tempted to hide under my convertible, but I didn't. Instead, I decided to wait for her to get out of her car. She turned off her ignition, opened her door, and climbed out.

"Good evening, Detective. Glad you could make it."

"Sounds like there's a hell of a party going on."

"It's just getting started."

She paused.

Then she asked, "So, what are we to make of our relationship?"

"Our relationship?"

"Are we friends or are we enemies?"

"We're certainly not enemies, but I don't think we know each other well enough to be friends."

"Tell me, Mr. Rutherford, did you ever figure out who murdered Bill Hodges?"

"I'm afraid I didn't."

"That surprises me."

"Why is that? No one gets them all right."

"No, but something tells me you still have an unblemished record."

"I had to lose one sooner or later," I said.

"I don't think you ever lose."

I laughed.

"Then you don't know me very well."

"I'm hoping to remedy that."

I wasn't sure what she meant, so I said nothing.

"I do have another question. Why did you admit that you lied about your friend's gun? I could have arrested you for perjury and obstruction of justice - your friend and sister-in-law, too."

"I took a gamble that you cared more about the truth."

"The truth is you lied."

"Yes, and I regret that, but there's also the truth about the gun. It wasn't used to murder Bill Hodges. I thought that truth would win with you in the end."

"Still a huge risk to take."

"I agree."

"Shall we go inside?" she said.

"Lead the way."

We went into Harry's. Detective Kalani walked toward the bar, while I headed toward the back office. I didn't think I could fake a smile anymore, especially after that conversation.

I sat behind the desk and stared out the window. The moon was full, and I got a great view of it through the palm leaves of the tree outside. I thought about Foxx's words: "I'm glad everything is back to normal." I knew that wasn't true, but I couldn't take Ms. Hu away from my wife and her sister, let alone her granddaughter.

Perhaps she already assumed that to be true when she agreed to meet me on the beach that morning. Maybe she didn't. I suspect she was glad to have it off her chest in a way, even if the police still didn't know. She also accomplished another task. She'd let someone else share in the burden of whether or not to tell them the truth about Bill's death. Ms. Hu had acted in self-defense when she'd pulled the trigger. Yes, I hadn't been there to witness it myself, and I only had her version of events. But I believed her in every part of my body. I didn't know if a jury would believe in her innocence, especially after all of the time that had passed since his death on that beach. I wasn't about to take the chance.

I felt like a hypocrite. I'd spent the last few years chasing bad people. I'd stood in judgment of them when I called them out for their crimes. Was I any better? Perhaps I've fallen a few notches in your eyes by concealing what happened, maybe even several notches. But I've promised to always be honest with you. I covered up the truth by keeping my mouth shut, and now I was going to have to live with that.

The office door opened, and Alana poked her head inside.

"What in the world are you doing in here?" she asked.

"Just a headache. It's so noisy out there."

"Well, get out here and buy me a drink."

"Of course."

I stood and walked over to her.

"Are you all right?" she asked.

I thought back to my wedding vows. I'd promised to love and cherish Alana, but I thought there was another word that should have been added: protect. I couldn't allow Alana to learn her mother had fired the gun that ended Bill's life, even if it had been in self-defense.

"I'll be good," I said, but I wasn't sure if that was a lie.

35

THE BLACK MUSTANG

ABOUT A MONTH PASSED FROM THE GRAND RE-OPENING OF HARRY'S. I wish I could say everything was okay, but it wasn't. I was still haunted by my knowledge of what had really happened to Bill Hodges. I did my best to push it to the back of my mind, but none of my usual tricks worked.

You may be wondering if I'd had much communication with Ms. Hu since our conversation on the beach. I hadn't. We did see each other from time to time, usually when I'd pick up or drop off Ava at Hani's house. We wouldn't talk about Bill Hodges, but I'm sure you'd already assumed that. Did that mean I'd done nothing more in the investigation? No. Something told me it wasn't over. I wanted to be prepared should the truth ever come out, and it did.

It was a Friday and I was on a late morning run when Alana phoned me. It was maybe an hour or so from her usual lunch break and I thought she was calling to invite me to a sushi lunch. I was wrong.

"Hello."

"Makamae just arrested my mother for murdering Bill Hodges."

I stopped running, but I didn't reply.

"Poe, are you there?"

"I'm here."

"You're not surprised?"

"No, I'm not."

"Is it true? She killed him?"

"Are you alone?"

"Yes, I'm alone."

"Where is your mother now?"

"They just took her to one of the interrogation rooms. I called Mara right before I called you. She's on her way over here."

"I'll call Mara now. She can't start the interrogation until I'm there."

"Poe, what the hell is going on?"

"I'll be there as soon as I can."

I ended the call with Alana and ran the rest of the way home. I didn't bother showering. I did a quick change of clothes, grabbed a file from the safe in my office, and went back outside to my car. An hour later, I found myself sitting beside Mara and Ms. Hu in one of the interrogation rooms.

Ms. Hu looked terrified, as one would expect, and she barely even acknowledged my presence. Mara wore her usual poker face, refusing to give away what she was really thinking. I thought I was able to read her now, and I could tell she was nervous. You may wonder why I thought that, and it's difficult to put it into exact words. There was just something there. Perhaps it was an extra tap of her pen on the table or one too many crossings of her ankles. She was uncomfortable and my subconscious had picked up on it.

Detective Kalani entered the interrogation room about ten minutes after I did. Her eyes went straight to me.

"Mr. Rutherford, I didn't realize you were part of Luana Hu's defense team," she said.

"Mr. Rutherford is one of my main investigators, but you already know that," Mara countered.

Kalani sat down on the opposite side of the table. She looked at the file folder in front of me.

"Okay, what do you have to show me?" she asked.

I opened the folder and slid one of the two photographs across the table to her.

"That's a shot taken of Luana Hu's back. It was taken a few weeks after Bill Hodges' death. The data on my phone will verify the date. There are several other photos I took of her, many of which show her face in profile to prove it's her in the photos. The one you have in front of you now offers the best view of the bruises," I said.

Kalani looked at the photo.

"Those are nasty bruises, but what do you think this proves?"

"Those injuries were caused by Bill Hodges attacking my client from behind," Mara said.

"Yes, your client told me about the alleged attack."

"Alleged? It happened. He tried to kill me on that beach," Ms. Hu said.

Mara gently placed her hand on Ms. Hu's forearm.

"These bruises could have been caused by a fall," Kalani said. "Accidents happen."

"Not likely, at least not in this case, but I have another photo to show you," I said.

I slid the next photo to Kalani.

"A black Mustang," Kalani said after looking at the photo of the car.

I'd taken the shot of the Mustang while it sat in the parking lot of the apartment building where the car's owner lived.

"If you run the license plates, you'll learn that the car belongs to Sam Bingham. I'm sure you recognize his name. He was one of the guys who jumped Foxx and me in that bar parking lot."

"What does this have to do with anything?" Kalani asked.

I removed my phone from my pocket and pulled up a video clip. I angled the phone so Kalani could see the screen and I pressed play.

"This is a video clip I copied from Hani Hu's home security system on one of the days I went to her house to pick up her daughter. I searched the system's archived footage without Hani's knowledge. She still doesn't know I copied this footage. This clip was recorded the morning Bill Hodges was shot to death."

We watched as the video showed Hani's car backing out of her driveway and heading down the road. A few moments later, a black Mustang drove by her house, heading in the same direction.

"That's Hani Hu's car leaving her home. It's hard to make this out, but that was Luana Hu behind the wheel. She had Hani's car that week. The Mustang that appears seconds later was being driven by Sam Bingham," I said.

"This was the week Hani was staying with you and driving your car?" Kalani asked.

"Yes. But what I didn't learn until later, was that Hani asked her mother to go to her house that morning and retrieve a toy that Hani's daughter, Ava, had been asking about. Ms. Hu never got to my house with the toy because of what happened shortly after this recording was made. When I saw this clip, I knew I'd seen that Mustang before. Then I remembered it was in the parking lot of the bar where I was attacked. Foxx and I sat in the back of the police cruiser for a while before we were brought back here. The Mustang was in the spot beside us."

"So Mr. Bingham happened to drive by Hani Hu's house. What does that have to do with Bill Hodges' death?" Kalani asked.

"Mr. Hodges knew the police had been called to her house after he'd thrown the rock through her daughter's bedroom window. He couldn't risk being seen in her neighborhood again, so he had Mr. Bingham help him keep tabs on Hani Hu," Mara said.

"Ryan Campbell, another one of Bill's friends, told me that Sam worshipped Bill and would do anything that was asked of him. Sam followed Hani's car that morning to the beach, and he phoned Bill and told him where Hani was, not realizing that it was really Hani's mother," I said.

"It's a nice theory, and it would be even nicer for your mother-in-law if it was actually true," Kalani said.

"It's true all right. The other recording on my phone proves it," I said.

"What other recording?" Kalani asked.

"The audio recording I made when I met with Sam a few weeks

ago. The one where he confesses to following Hani's car and calling
Bill once she got to the beach and walked down to the water to
collect seashells. He thought it would be the perfect opportunity
for Bill to ambush Hani. Sam witnessed Bill's attack on Luana Hu.
He saw her shoot Bill in self-defense. Then he fled the scene," I
said.

"Why didn't he report this to the police, especially since he'd
allegedly just seen his best friend get gunned down?" Kalani asked.

"Because he was afraid. He'd already been arrested for attacking
Mr. Rutherford and Mr. Foxx. If he'd called the police, he would have
had to admit that he'd been following Hani Hu, at least who he
thought was Hani. It wouldn't be hard for you to put two and two
together. There's no way he didn't know Bill Hodges meant her harm.
Mr. Bingham hadn't been sentenced yet, and he didn't want more jail
time added if the district attorney knew he'd been helping Bill with
yet another criminal offense, one that probably would have led to
Hani's murder," Mara said.

"If all of this is true, why not come forward and admit what
happened?" Kalani asked Ms. Hu.

"I was scared. I didn't know what to do. I'd fled that beach. I'd
thrown away the gun. I didn't think you'd ever believe that I'd shot
Bill in self-defense."

Kalani said nothing. There was silence in the room for several
seconds. That's when I decided to pull my last card.

"May I have a word with you in private?" I asked Detective Kalani.

She hesitated and then nodded.

Detective Kalani stood and I followed her into another interrogation room. She shut the door behind us but made no move to sit
down at the table.

"You said you shot the photos of her injured back weeks ago,"
Kalani said.

"Yes."

"That night at Harry's when we spoke about Bill Hodges' death,
you knew who his killer was."

"Yes."

"You lied to me. You obstructed justice yet again. I can arrest you right now."

I didn't reply.

"You lied to me," she repeated, "yet you expect me to believe you now?"

"No. I expect you to believe the evidence I've presented."

She said nothing.

"Let's talk about that night at Harry's," I continued. "When we spoke again inside, you told me how upset you were that you'd lost. I don't know what led you to Luana Hu. Maybe you finally figured out that Luana having her daughter's car might have put her on a collision course with Bill Hodges. Maybe it was some other piece of evidence."

"In a way, you brought me to her doorstep. I knew you'd probably figured out who killed Bill Hodges. I even said that outside of Harry's. I assumed if you didn't come to the police with the information, especially to your wife, then it had to be someone you cared deeply about. It didn't take much for Luana to confess. All I had to do was ask," Kalani said.

"So then you thought you'd won, but now you're back to thinking you've lost. There's no jury that's going to convict a sixty-year-old woman of intentionally killing Bill Hodges, especially after they see those photographs and security video and listen to what Sam Bingham has to say on the stand. And that doesn't even include Bill's prior girlfriends who will also testify to the fact that he beat them. But you haven't lost. By my score, you're two for two. You solved a murder that most people thought was never going to be solved. So what if Luana Hu doesn't go to jail for this? You've still won. You still discovered the truth and everyone who matters knows you did. There's something else, though. Something important that I'm not sure you're thinking about."

"Which is?"

"You've got an unblemished record now, but it won't last forever. Maybe a week from now, maybe ten years from now, you're going to get a case that you can't solve. You'll have hit a wall and you won't

know where to turn. That's when you'll call me, and do you know
what I'm going to do? I'm going to say yes to you because I'll think
back to this day and remember that you did the right thing. You made
sure justice was served. Bill Hodges was an evil man. He intended to
murder a woman that morning on the beach and he got what he
deserved."

Detective Kalani didn't respond, not that I'd expected her to. I'd
thrown a lot at her in a short period. I knew she needed to process it. I
thanked her for her time and I left the station. Had I overplayed my
hand? I didn't know.

I didn't see Alana on the way out. I assumed she was trying to
keep her distance and doing her best to appear impartial, even
though everyone knew that would be impossible.

I spent the next few hours sitting on a patio chair in my backyard,
staring at the ocean and trying to make sense of everything that had
happened since Bill-the-hurricane and Bill-the-boyfriend had
appeared on the scene. I was so lost in thought that I didn't hear
Alana get home.

"Hey there," she said.

I turned and looked at her just as she sat on the chair beside me.

"I suppose you're furious with me," I said.

"For what?"

"For not telling you about your mother."

"I was angry, for about two and a half seconds. Then I remembered what I'd told you about Hani. I asked you to protect her. I told
you to do what you had to do. I'm sure you knew the same request
would extend to looking out for my mother." She paused. Then she
continued: "Mara said that in all her years as an attorney, she's never
seen anything like it."

"Like what?"

"What you did with Makamae. Mara said you were remarkable."

"That's kind of her."

"She also said that you spoke to Makamae alone, but you didn't
tell Mara what was said in the other room."

"I didn't think there was any reason for her to know."

"Why is that?" she asked.

"Because I offered Detective Kalani a deal of sorts. I'm not sure she was interested, though."

"What kind of deal?"

"I told her I would be in her debt. I admit it's not a very strong bargaining chip."

"I suspect it's stronger than you think."

"Maybe. Maybe not."

"I don't think you understand me. I spoke with Makamae a little while ago. She said she's recommending to the D.A. that my mother not be charged since the evidence you provided proves it was self-defense. I'm sure your private talk with her helped too."

"I imagine she called Sam Bingham to verify his story."

"I'm sure she did. How did you get him to talk?"

"It took some persuading on my part," I said.

"I'm sure it didn't hurt that he remembered your last interaction outside that bar. How long did it take before you discovered the black Mustang?"

"A few days after your mother told me what happened. After our discussion on the beach, I followed her back to her house and took the photos of her injuries. It was an insurance policy of sorts. I tried to get her to come forward then, but she wouldn't."

"Did she know that you continued with your investigation after that day?"

"No. No one knew. I'm glad your mother is going to be okay."

"A question popped into my mind as I was driving back here."

"What was it?" I asked.

"How did I ever get so lucky to meet someone like you?"

"You've got that wrong, Alana. I'm the lucky one."

She leaned forward and kissed me.

"I'm sorry you had to go through this alone. I knew something was wrong. I just didn't know what."

"I'm sorry I kept everything from you."

"Are you going to be okay now?" she asked.

"I'll be good," I said, and this time I knew it was true.

THE END

~

Are you ready for more in the Murder on Maui Mystery series?

Poe's next mystery, **The Last Kill**, is available now!

Lights. Camera. Murder. When lies become reality, can Poe find the truth before a killer strikes again?

As Maui's best private investigator, Edgar Allan "Poe" Rutherford understands the importance of keeping a low profile. That becomes impossible when a new reality TV show comes to the island, which features an eccentric handful of divorcees looking for love. But when one of the women is poisoned to death, the show's production comes to a grinding halt.

At the same time, a few miles down the beach, a divorce attorney is stabbed multiple times while she sits on a lounge chair and watches the sun set over the Pacific Ocean. The methods of murder, as well as the victims, couldn't be more different, yet Poe has a sneaking suspicion they're somehow related.

As Poe dives deep into the backgrounds of the show's cast and crew, as well as the attorney, he learns that nothing's real in reality TV and everyone has a dark secret.

The Last Kill is the tenth standalone novel in the Murder on Maui series. If you enjoy colorful characters, a touch of humor, and plots that bend and twist like a palm tree on a windy beach, then you'll love Robert W Stephens' mysteries.

ALSO BY ROBERT W. STEPHENS

Murder on Maui Mystery Series

If you like charismatic characters, artistic whodunnits, and twists you won't see coming, then you'll love this captivating mystery series.

Aloha Means Goodbye (Poe Book 1)

Wedding Day Dead (Poe Book 2)

Blood like the Setting Sun (Poe Book 3)

Hot Sun Cold Killer (Poe Book 4)

Choice to Kill (Poe Book 5)

Sunset Dead (Poe Book 6)

Ocean of Guilt (Poe Book 7)

The Tequila Killings (Poe Book 8)

Wave of Deception (Poe Book 9)

The Last Kill (Poe Book 10)

Mountain of Lies (Poe Book 11)

Rich and Dead (Poe Book 12)

Poe's First Law (Poe Book 13)

Poe's Justice (Poe Book 14)

Poe's Rules (Poe Book 15)

Alex Penfield Supernatural Mystery Thriller Series

If you like supernatural whodunnits, gripping actions, and heroes with a troubled past, then you'll love this series.

Ruckman Road (Penfield Book 1)

Dead Rise (Penfield Book 2)

The Eternal (Penfield Book 3)

Nature of Darkness (Penfield Book 4)

The Eighth Order (Penfield Book 5)

Ruckman Road

To solve an eerie murder, one detective must break a cardinal rule: never let the case get personal...

Alex Penfield's gunshot wounds have healed, but the shock remains raw. Working the beat could be just what the detective needs to clear his head. But when a corpse washes up on the Chesapeake Bay, Penfield's first case back could send him spiraling...

As Penfield and his partner examine the dead man's fortress of a house, an army of surveillance cameras takes the mystery to another level. When the detective sees gruesome visions that the cameras fail to capture, he begins to wonder if his past has caught up with him. To solve the murder, Penfield makes a call on a psychic who may or may not be out to kill him...

His desperate attempt to catch a killer may solve the case, but will he lose his sanity in the process?

Ruckman Road is the start of a new paranormal mystery series featuring Detective Alex Penfield. If you like supernatural whodunnits, gripping action, and heroes with a troubled past, then you'll love Robert W. Stephens' twisted tale.

Standalone Dark Thrillers

Nature of Evil

Rome, 1948. Italy reels in the aftermath of World War II. Twenty women are brutally murdered, their throats slit and their faces removed with surgical precision. Then the murders stop as abruptly as they started, and the horrifying crimes and their victims are lost to history. Now over sixty years later, the killings have begun again. This time in America. It's up to homicide detectives Marcus Carter and Angela Darden to stop the crimes, but how can they catch a serial killer who leaves no traces of evidence and no apparent motive other than the unquenchable thirst for murder?

The Drayton Diaries

He can heal people with the touch of his hand, so why does a mysterious group want Jon Drayton dead? A voice from the past sends Drayton on a desperate journey to the ruins of King's Shadow, a 17th century plantation house in Virginia that was once the home of Henry King, the wealthiest and most powerful man in North America and who has now been lost to time. There, Drayton meets the beautiful archaeologist Laura Girard, who has discovered a 400-year-old manuscript in the ruins. For Drayton, this partial journal written by a slave may somehow hold the answers to his life's mysteries

ABOUT THE AUTHOR

Robert W. Stephens is the author of the Murder on Maui series, the Alex Penfield supernatural thriller series, and the standalone dark thrillers The Drayton Diaries and Nature of Evil.

You can find more about the author at robertwstephens.com.

Visit him on Facebook at facebook.com/robertwaynestephens

ACKNOWLEDGMENTS

Thanks to you readers for investing your time in reading my story. I hope you enjoyed it. Poe, Alana, Foxx, and Maui will return.

Made in the USA
Coppell, TX
10 November 2025

62864222R10164